ENTITLEMENT

ENTITLEMENT

JONATHAN BENNETT

ECW Press

Published by ECW Press
2120 Queen Street East, Suite 200, Toronto, Ontario, Canada M4E 1E2

Library and Archives Canada Cataloguing in Publication

Bennett, Jonathan, 1970-
Entitlement / Jonathan Bennett.

ISBN 978-1-77041-035-0
ALSO ISSUED AS: 978-1-55490-856-1 (PDF); 978-1-55490-340-5 (EPUB)
Originally published in hardcover in 2008 (ISBN 978-1-55022-856-4)

1. Title.

PS8553.E534E68 2011   C813'.6   C2011-902952-9

Editor: Michael Holmes / a misFit book
BackLit editor: Jennifer Knoch
Cover and text design: Ingrid Paulson
Cover image © Gestaltbar/photocase.com
Typesetting: Troy Cunningham
Printing: Webcom   5   4   3   2   1

This book is set in Adobe Caslon

The publication of *Entitlement* has been generously supported by the Canada Council for the Arts, which last year invested $20.1 million in writing and publishing throughout Canada, by the Ontario Arts Council, by the OMDC Book Fund, an initiative of the Ontario Media Development Corporation, and by the Government of Canada through the Canada Book Fund.

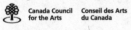

Printed and bound in Canada

For my father Vernon Bennett,
and my son Thomas Morgan.

"Since then, keen lessons that love deceives,
And wrings with wrong, have shaped to me
Your face, and the God-curst sun, and a tree,
And a pond edged with grayish leaves."

— Thomas Hardy

PART ONE

Back in the fall Andy Kronk escaped north to this cottage on Broad Lake. At the time of purchase he'd brimmed with renovation plans and enthusiasm, levelling the foundation, painting, and calling a local contractor to come by and quote on installing a new septic tank. He had been in no hurry for this last expense. The trudge to the outhouse was onerous, not unbearable. Rustic charm. He'd planned on doing it in another year. But then, in the winter, his needs abruptly changed.

When can you begin work? he'd asked the man on the phone. Good few more weeks yet, said the contractor. The ground's frozen pretty deep out by you. Lots of rock too. Be hard going if we don't wait.

To Andy, the gruff man sounded bearlike, not yet willing to emerge from hibernation. Please, said Andy, as soon as you can. Freezin' yer arse off, eh? said the contractor. Andy let the weak joke stand.

And while the long nights still assuredly fell below zero, last week he opened the side door of his cottage after lunch and in the air there was a change. The sky was light blue, the sun fragile but warm. There was no wind. He stood still enjoying the peace. Then faintly, he heard a sound. He waited. There, again. And again. He walked toward it. From the corner of his cottage, through a small hole in the eavestrough, a single drop of water slowly bulged then dripped. The temperature was above freezing. Soon the contractor could begin work.

Were he still in Toronto, weather like this would be cause for celebration. After months of truculent winter, this advance taste of spring would prompt him, along with several other lawyers, to go in search of a restaurant with a patio. There they would join the swell of rapt Torontonians heading outdoors. They would loosen their ties, roll the cuffs of their white dress shirts a turn or two, put on sunglasses, sit under gas-powered heaters, and sip at tall glasses of blond beer. They would not speak much. Instead they would drink, watch the streetcars rumble past, and, occasionally, one of them would angle a pale face directly at the sun, grin broadly, and say, Oh, right fuckin' on.

The backhoes and workmen were at it within the week — their first job of the season. Over several days they dug the primary hole and trenches. They laid pipes, installed a toilet, sink, and shower stall, replaced plumbing underneath the cottage, and debated where to put the drain field. The huge concrete tank had been ordered, Andy was told, from a reliable supplier, and would be delivered and lowered into place tomorrow, next Tuesday at the latest.

You'll have yourself a flush toilet in days there guy, the contractor had said yesterday with a slap on Andy's back.

Pushing his hands up under his armpits Andy countered with, Cold enough for you?

They were quiet for a time.

Be able to do away with that outhouse soon for good, said the man. No more putting on your Kodiaks when you need to go to the shitter, eh?

Andy smiled.

Need the name of a honey wagon?

I will, I suppose. Yes, said Andy. The man took out his wallet and gave Andy a business card.

That's my brother-in-law. Knows how to take shit alright — married my sister, didn't he?

The man revealed his generous, gap-toothed smile before walking off. Andy watched for a bit after his truck had pulled away.

At first Andy's dreams had come at night spawning horrors. He woke gasping for fresh air. Then, bolder, the dreams broke through during the day, creeping into the bathroom mirror, the lid of a pot, a knife's blade as his thumb passed over it rinsing off suds under warm running water. The images took over, vivid and loud. They ran together making complex stories. Andy believed he was inside them, experiencing a kind of authentic life so tangible that it was difficult to be unable, upon awaking, to discuss it in concrete, sane terms — especially with those who had appeared in them alongside him.

Most often he was with Colin in the dreams. When they were young, together out on the lake in a boat, then years later in New York City in an elevator, and then in a park where Colin hovered a foot off the ground, a spectre wearing a cape. The dreams were fantastical, intimate, absolutely true.

Colin, he whispered into the air. What should I tell her?

Soon it would be spring. The biographer would arrive.

Were it not for the dreams, Andy might have been able to tell the biographer that he had left the Aspinalls and Huntington House long behind. Those years were like the thrum of his own inner ear, the pulling of the ropes of blood that guaranteed him no silence, even when he was most alone. Without Colin, Andy had been alone. Huntington House was his only home, and Colin was whom he meant by the two words — full of pride and loyalty — best friend.

Drip. Drip. As a teenage boy, Colin Aspinall had long and tanned legs and a fine line of blond hair tracking a path up his flat stomach to his chest, where it fanned out in lighter, golden swirls.

Back at their boarding school, Lord Simcoe College, they'd once cut last class and headed down through the woods to the lakeshore on a similarly warm, late winter's day. At dusk they kicked at preserved crabapple husks frozen during their autumnal rot. Aiming away at the distant lighthouse blinks, they thought not much beyond the moment itself. They were young men on the shore of a large, lead-grey lake. They were confined at boarding school but that day Colin Aspinall had felt urgently alive.

Kick. Laugh. Kick. They were young and arrogant. Laugh. Kick. They were beautiful and naive. All thoughts were original and right; their lives were as vital as heat from the sun. Other people — the ones they ignored in shops or movie theatres — must have looked back at them with awe and envy. Even when he and Colin became adolescently philosophical, or grave, they remained convinced of themselves. Regardless of their moods, Colin would tell Andy whatever flashed through his impulsive mind.

Hey, he'd said motioning across the darkening lake, that light comes from America. Kick. Laugh. Kick. Colin's voice, high and roused, had the effect of dressing up his youthful words as insightful. Just over there, he continued, now pointing at the probable haze of New York State, I am *nobody*. My last name counts for nothing. Live free or die. That's what they believe.

How was the moment recovered? Did he remember or did he dream that day they'd kicked crabapples at the faraway lighthouse? January in the mid-1980s and the weather was severe about them, toques pulled down over their ears, loosened ties and fashionable Sun Ice ski jackets were zipped over their tweed sports coats. Colin had spoken then to Andy so quietly it was almost lost to the wind. At fifteen years old, on the dark winter shoreline of the lake, Colin had mouthed to Andy the words I love you.

Andy had looked down at his penny loafers, and back up. The lighthouse blinked away the moments in awkward measures. Colin had uttered the obvious, gripping bond that passed electrically and, until then, silently, between them. But tucked up inside three quavering words there was more than simple tenderness, honesty, and heartache. Why can't I be normal like you, Andy? Why can't *you* be different, like me? Andy could hear this subtle counterpoint in Colin's voice now, but not then. Years and disappointments would have to mount before he was burdened with nuance.

Andy would come to wonder why, right then and there, he hadn't just punched Colin in the face and called him a cruel name he could never take back. Or else thumped Colin hard on the shoulder, and laughed, flipping the declaration into a playful joke. Either response, though false and ignorant, would have made everything that was to come so much easier. But Andy stood reliable and firm and with a fierce reluctance to exhale unless he disturb the moment before it set hard. Out of loyalty, out of a kind of fraternity, he had said nothing.

How could he speak to the Aspinalls' biographer, of all times now? He mustn't. The Aspinalls were his only family. Yet, when the biographer contacted Andy, she had put an idea in his mind. By explaining it all, telling what he knew of the Aspinalls — Mr. and Mrs. Aspinall, Colin, his older sister Fiona, and his own years spent at Huntington House — he might finally, publicly, sever himself. Was this not what he wanted?

But what right did he have to speak out? His claim was only the memory of a friend, the sound of a word. Colin. A name that called to everything else and explained it all as far as he knew it. The five letters of another's name contained a whole story, his story.

When the three labourers and the contractor returned several days later, they were too busy with their morning coffees and donuts, and lighting cigarettes without removing their work gloves, with keeping themselves warm, to notice much of anything. Soon enough the crane lowered the pre-formed concrete tank into the hole, the heartbreaking weight of it settling and pressing downward.

Yep, yep, yelled the contractor to the other man operating the crane. Give 'er. Yep, Yep. Easy now. He raised his hand. The chains slackened.

Nice fit, said Andy, forcing himself to talk.

The rest of the day was spent hooking up, laying gravel, filling in, and spreading out top soil. By sunset, the rakes were packed up in the truck and the job was complete.

Just the inspector, who'll be by any day to check our hookup at the house, promised the contractor. He's a friend of mine so you're golden. Here's your invoice.

Alone again, Andy looked out across Broad Lake. The biographer would arrive with her questions. He pushed air out his nostrils. This was over now. Completed. And before long, spring would open out and the world would be renewed: leaves on the birch trees, large-mouth bass jumping in the lake at fishermen's twitching, shiny lures, trillium flowering over the forest floor behind his cottage. Winter, and its necessary confidences, was gone.

◆ ◆ ◆

Fiona Aspinall reached a hand up from beneath the covers. She felt her forehead. I am hot, she said aloud, weakly. I am sick. I must be sick. I have a temperature. I'm going to be sick. She wrestled herself free from the blankets, the colder air cutting right through her T-shirt. She stumbled into her ensuite. Collapsing at the toilet, the porcelain cool on her palms and wrists, she vomited. Acidic, fiery, total.

Last night she had arrived home from a party late and feeling drunk. She had not removed her makeup — as she would normally do. Rather she stripped clumsily, climbed into an oversized T-shirt, and fell into bed. As she'd laboured toward the open toilet, she'd caught a glimpse of herself: two dark eye sockets shot into a ghostly complexion. The idea of toilet bowls close enough to smell, was normally sufficient to bring on a dry retch.

I am sick, she said again, as if this were the proof she'd needed to be convinced. Fiona controlled her breathing. With the back of her hand, she wiped at the hot tears now in her eyes. She felt calm. Is this the flu? I am cold. The tiles on the bathroom floor had a heater underneath them. Radiant warmth, the estate agent had told her when she'd bought this condo last year. Were they working? I was not drunk last night. She felt relief at this. Of course she hadn't been. I had a glass of wine with dinner and only a single cocktail beforehand. Why had she thought she'd been drunk? She had been sick. She is sick.

Fiona pulled the T-shirt over her head, mopped her mouth with it and turned on the cold water. The granite countertop felt hard. She leaned in and ran warm water over the pearls that drooped around her neck. They'd flopped down into the toilet accidentally. She sloshed the water over them, rolled them about in her fingers rinsing them off. Can stomach acid hurt pearls? She filled her mouth with water, gargled, and spat. She repeated this several times then washed her face, drying it hard with the towel leaving two mascara marks and a smudge of lipstick, the towel taking on the loose semblance of a shroud. She let it fall to the floor and went back to bed.

It's Wednesday, she thought suddenly. That woman comes today. She had not bought new vacuum cleaner bags. She was out of J cloths. Her cleaning lady did not speak English. Instead, the woman left empty packages of what she needed on the counter. Fiona was left to extrapolate.

It's Fiona, she said into her bedside phone. Dad, I'm sick.

Goodness. Do you need a doctor?

I need vacuum cleaner bags. And J cloths.

I can't come over today Fiona. I'm flying to Montreal this afternoon — for the foundation board quarterly. I have yet to read all the proposals.

I'm fine.

I might have another suit made at the shop with the French name near the hotel. You liked what they did the last time, remember?

I'm going to get some sleep.

That sounds a sensible decision.

Fiona hung up pleased. She had called Huntington in the hopes her father might answer. Her father had been the one who had cared for her and Colin when, as children, they'd been ill. Colin had often had an ear infection or tonsillitis; he had pneumonia twice when he was twelve. Through it all, their father had stayed at Colin's bedside. Sick people had repelled her mother. The woman had had no nursing instincts.

Bringing her knees up to her chest, shivering a little, Fiona recalled the way her father would read books to Colin, or play checkers with him, chess if he was up to it. She pictured Colin as a boy: fragile, slight, sickly.

Her mind drifted and she fell away: she is three years old. They are in the kitchen at Huntington — before it was renovated. The stove and refrigerator are the colour of avocado. Light illuminates the window behind her father's head. She has had this dream many times.

You have a baby brother! her father is saying. Here's a photograph. Her dad's voice is soft and nurturing. He'll be home tomorrow. His name is Colin. He's only four days old now.

Daddy?

Yes, Fiona.

I want a baby sister.

I know, sweetheart. But baby brothers are just as fun.

Really?

Really.

They drink a glass of milk together. The thick taste of it is in her mouth. She uses her own big-girl cup. This is where the dream ends. She always wakes with a start, and the images linger. Fiona did not remember Colin coming home from the hospital; she had only her father's words and cold milk. To remember Colin as a baby, her imagination took over, animating a black and white photograph of a newborn's swollen head.

Why had she decided it would be a sister? She had felt pure anger when she learned it would be a brother. She always got what she wanted. You don't understand, she apparently said, I must have a baby sister. Her father and mother told her of this exchange in tender moments over the years. She felt like she remembered it, but couldn't be sure.

Fiona woke completely after an hour of dozing. She took two painkillers. Drank water, greedily. She felt well enough to get dressed. The phone rang.

Where are you? It was Kimberly Payne-White. They'd made a plan at last night's event to meet for lunch at Kimberly's house. Fiona had gone to Lord Simcoe College with Kimberly. She didn't see as much of her anymore, Kimberly having had two children: Derek, or Darren, or something, and the eldest — JP.

Why did she struggle to remember the names of her friends'

kids? She managed to commit the first to memory. But then they had more. It was the names of all the ones that came after the first Fiona could never keep straight. And the obligation to buy presents for them all as they turned one, or two, or five. She seemed perpetually late for a baptism or bris. Fiona wondered, occasionally, if the presents she bought were laughed at behind her back. It was unclear to her what is expected or appropriate. She had always known that *she* would not have children.

Kimberly, oh shit I'm so sorry. I'm really sick.

Fiona, language please! You're on speaker.

Then take me off.

I'm trying to make cookies. I need my hands.

What's the time?

Eleven. You didn't look drunk.

I wasn't drunk. I'm sick. I've got a fever.

Oh, sweetie. You want me to come over? I have Daryl, but I could bring soup?

No. Please don't. I just need more sleep.

She let the phone down slowly until she felt it click into place. Daryl, Daryl, she said over to herself several times. Children. They used to be far off — for all her friends. Then, suddenly — as if it were decided wholesale over some long weekend retreat to which she was not invited — they were all pregnant. One minute they were flying to London for weddings, to Nice for dirty weekends, to New Zealand for wine-tasting and cycling tours, the next poaching nannies from one another. Now when they met they talked about breastfeeding (Might be thrush, is she latching properly?) and C-sections (Mine is almost invisible now — he might have been a bastard, but he does nice work) and reliable nannies (Turns out mine lied — she's Indonesian not Filipino. You think that matters?).

Fiona got back into bed. She lifted up her legs and tried to imagine her stomach the size of something as big as a baby.

Now, something as big as a baby was to come out of her. No. She couldn't imagine it at all. Not from her body. Besides, she'd mothered Colin her entire life. She was an adult now and Colin was off on his own — she did not want another needy child.

Yet she'd felt those womanly urges for children. Kimberly, all of them, they looked wonderful at it. Even when they complained — and they certainly did a lot of that — they did so without real malice. She was missing out, but this stage wouldn't last. Give them all ten years. Things would change. She knew enough about being a woman to see that. Her mother's friends had been bitter and gin-drunk by their late forties. They resented the time their kids had stolen from them, the years they'd given up. Now couple that with the careers that some of her friends had chucked. Shit, Kimberly had an MFA and was a hell of a painter. Shows at galleries in Los Angeles. Now what? Crayons and Plasticine? It was all too much like compromise.

She should get up. Maybe she would go over to Kimberly's house after all. She'd call over to Mao's Zest for takeout. They'd sit out back by Kimberly's pool in the glassed sunroom and drink wine. Could she stomach wine? The first glass might be work. If she showed up with a good bottle, she could usually get Kimberly to have at least one glass. She took another painkiller and decided to make a day of it. Besides, she had to get out of here before that woman showed up and needed the cleaning supplies she'd not yet purchased.

I have a small present for Daryl, she said as Kimberly opened the front door.

Fiona, I thought you were sick.

I was, but I'm feeling better. Here, I don't know what it is. I just said I'm in a hurry so wrap a toy up for me; it'll be a surprise for all of us. I woke up and thought I should salvage the day. So

I went shopping. I have lunch for us. She made a pout. Please, she said.

Kimberly gathered up Daryl's toys and laid them on a blanket in the sunroom. Outside the weather was cold. She placed Daryl down on the blanket and he began to play with a train.

How old is he now? asked Fiona, digging into the large brown bag, handing Kimberly a spring roll and a set of chopsticks.

You were at his birthday. Can't you even pretend to try at this, Fiona? Kimberly was in good spirits. Her husband was away and her nanny, Joy, was taking the two kids for the entire weekend. She explained to Fiona that she had only to get through today with Daryl and she was free for two whole days.

Fiona poured them each a glass of white wine. Can I ask: do you all laugh behind my back at the presents I buy your kids?

Of course we don't.

Daryl was making loud, abrupt noises as he pushed his train along the edge of the blanket. They watched him for a while as they ate.

Oh, said Kimberly, I've been saving something for you. She rose to leave Fiona alone with Daryl. The boy didn't notice. He looks one, or two, or three, she thought to herself. Can't you tell by their teeth? How many they have, or if they've fallen out? She could hear Kimberly coming back down the hallway.

I ripped it out for you, she announced as she handed Fiona a piece of newspaper. On it was an advertisement for several of the coming season's theatre productions. Down the list was A Man's Castle. I was in a coffee shop, stated Kimberly, waiting for Karen Palmer — you remember her. LSC . . . Few years younger than us? Colin's class maybe? She married Paul's stepbrother — the urologist.

No. I can't place her.

Beside the point, said Kimberly. We were meeting for coffee.

She was late and I was flipping through one of those free newspapers.

Since when are newspapers free?

I'm talking about those ones that students read. They have left wing drivel in the front and, to pay for it all, ads for escort services in the back. Anyway, I saw this ad and thought I'd better clip it for you.

A university production, said Fiona. I'll bet it's going to be *special*.

You should go!

You've got to be kidding.

I was a bit.

Muma? Daryl held up a toy train engine for Kimberly to look at.

Yes, sweetie. It's a train, she said. Can you say train?

Train.

Good.

Good.

We're in the copying stage, said Kimberly to Fiona.

Good. Train.

What are you going to do with your weekend? asked Fiona.

First, I'm going to my acupuncturist. Then I'm going to meet Lisa at Gorgon and Zola's for dinner on Saturday night.

How nice.

They spent the next hour talking about friends' marriages: the good ones, the rocky ones, the guys who had turned out to be a catch, and the ones who had not.

How is it with Paul these days? Is he still at it with that travel agent? Fiona asked purely because direct questions about Kimberly's marriage made her evasive — that, and because Fiona was the only one who could get away without addressing the subject in euphemisms.

It's don't ask don't tell at the moment, said Kimberly. And

you? What about that handsome lawyer in New York? What's his name?

Christopher Llewellyn. We are still sizing each other up. I think he wants to go into politics.

American politics?

He is American. What other kind is there? His plan, as I understand it, is: my money, his brains, our looks.

Oh my god. You'd have to become an American. You'd have to have a kid. At least one: you can't be "family values" without a family.

We've hurdled that one. He thinks we should adopt an Hispanic child. Learn Spanish. Optics. Border state votes.

You're quite far along. What was your father's reaction?

Doesn't know yet, said Fiona. Not officially at least. But he'd get it.

Yes, I suppose he would. What are you going to do?

Keep thinking about it.

Isn't Colin in New York?

Just then Daryl began to cry, having tripped on the edge of the blanket and bumped his head on the door frame. Kimberly picked him up, rocked him, and cooed in his ear. Fiona watched her friend closely as she disappeared into her child, soothing his pain bit by bit.

Fiona had not thought that Colin also being in New York might have any bearing on her interest in Christopher. She wondered, briefly, if she'd subconsciously pursued this whole liaison so she could be closer to Colin? There she went again. She stood to leave.

You're good at mothering, Kimberly, she said, surprising herself somewhat.

Really? That's kind of you to say, and then Kimberly smiled and said, Fiona, he's eighteen months now.

Bye, Daryl, said Fiona turning to leave.

The idea for the book, explained Trudy Clarke, has been in the back of my mind ever since I first saw *A Man's Castle* — twenty years ago now. You remember the play?

Of course, said Humphrey.

You know it's on again soon?

It's not.

It is, she said. A local university production. Just proves my point. People are obsessed with the Aspinalls.

You're serious about pursuing this project, then? asked Humphrey.

I just can't let the Aspinall story go.

It's not much to go on, Trudy, said Humphrey.

I've got a hunch there's fresh dirt.

Humphrey scoffed. He shook his head. Stuart Aspinall would eat everyone involved for lunch. It'd be too dangerous.

Dangerous sells. She watched Humphrey carefully.

You've got nothing new here. And this is a step up for you.

What do you mean?

You don't have what it takes for a project of this scope.

I can do it.

How's Veronica? asked Humphrey.

It's not about the money.

You're a single mother. Your last book was modest, in every respect.

So what if it is about the money?

There's nothing wrong with writing for money. You lack that certain hunger to kill or be killed. This would need that. Why not something lighter, Trudy?

I can do it.

You're an historian by trade. History's made a comeback

right now. Go dig up some old local murder. He smiled.

But I want to do *this*.

She left the lunch with an unuttered, implied, *maybe*.

◆ ◆ ◆

Humphrey, said Mr. Aspinall, what a nice surprise. Let me put you on hands free. Mr. Aspinall stood up from behind his mahogany desk, and lifted his body up onto the balls of his feet, held it, and then slowly lowered himself back to the floor. His leather oxfords, newly purchased in Rome, were stiff.

Stuart, I felt I needed to call to forewarn you of a matter that concerns you. If I may.

Let me question you first, Humphrey. Perhaps just answer yes or no.

Of course.

Might you know of a filmmaker, or writer, or playwright, or some such person with artistic credentials that is peddling an idea for a new film or book or play that concerns me, or my business, or my family?

Yes. It's . . .

Please, Humphrey. I don't think it's prudent that we talk further — about this. You know how much value there is around here placed on freedom of expression. If there is some artistic effort underway, then it must endure its own birth without the meddling hands of the mother on which it intends to feed.

I just felt that it was right to alert you. Maybe I should e-mail you the outline? Just to be sure?

Unnecessary, said Mr. Aspinall. Besides, he added, I don't

e-mail. I mail, and then only when I must, he said with a half smile.

Before Mr. Aspinall was a black leather ink-blotter, two Parker pens, and a pad of yellow paper. He'd long ago decided against using a personal computer. If it needed to be written down, let the opponent do the typing.

I gather it's alright for me to cautiously proceed then, said Humphrey.

Goodbye, said Mr. Aspinall and released the call. Through his office window he watched the setting sun touch, then sink into, the horizon. He pressed the intercom and his assistant's voice rang in clear and eager:

Yes?

The Foundation Ball is over for the year, so please don't put Humphrey through again without asking me first.

Of course, I'm sorry.

Don't be, you weren't to know. On the yellow paper in front of him, Mr. Aspinall wrote the name Trudy Clarke, then buttoned his suit jacket before leaving for the day.

◆ ◆ ◆

Two days later, Trudy could not wait any longer and she called Humphrey. To her delight, he acquiesced.

Send me a sample chapter and an outline, he said. I'll start talking it up.

Trudy dove straight in, reading everything she could get her hands on. She began to phone people connected to the Aspinalls to arrange interviews. She also bought tickets for the play.

For a short while, her research went well. She met with the former head gardener of Huntington House. She tracked down a boyfriend of Fiona's from university. Both spoke candidly on the record, but had little in the way of new material. Then the problems began.

I've changed my mind. I've decided not to do the interview. It was the voice of the former CFO of Stuart Aspinall's now defunct holding company.

Why the change of heart, Bill? I thought we had an agreement.

No, what we had was a conversation. Look, it just doesn't feel right, he said. Got to go with my gut. I'm golfing this afternoon. Goodbye.

That afternoon another interviewee cancelled. This former acquaintance, too, did not have a clear reason. From that day on Trudy's calls went unreturned. Two weeks later, a registered letter arrived from a large law firm. It informed her that the Aspinall family was in no way supporting or endorsing her writing of this book. It went on to suggest that while she was free to write on whatever topic she might wish, she was to be assured counsel had been retained on this matter and would be reviewing the final product in careful detail, to ensure no inaccuracies, unintended or otherwise, were included.

It was their use of the word "product" that grated her the most. This was not a box on a supermarket shelf; it was serious non-fiction.

I've received a sort of cease-and-desist letter, she said when Humphrey came on the phone. I faxed it to you.

I have it. There were mumbles as he spoke with his assistant.

What should I do? she asked.

Well, Trudy, this is a bit unexpected. I suppose, for now, it'll be the book Stuart Aspinall tried to block. A marketing department might use that. I have some tentative interest.

That's wonderful! Who?

I can't say yet. Send me the excerpt.

I'm just about done. So I shouldn't worry about this letter?

Yes, worry. Be cautious. Tape each word of every interview. Make copies and store them elsewhere. Send the backups to me for safekeeping. We might need proof some day. And whatever you do, don't play loose with the facts. If I suspect this is beginning to go south, I'll let you know.

Trudy hung up the phone. Her hand was shaking. She lifted the letter out of the fax machine and reread it. She looked up to see her daughter, Veronica, at the door of her study.

Mommy! I can't find my other shoe.

Be patient darling. It'll drop.

What?

Never mind, I'll be with you in just a minute. Her daughter turned and strode, unevenly, away. Trudy began to rifle through her notes for the Aspinall project. The last interview she had done was with a former employee of Mr. Aspinall's current company. The man she'd interviewed had not been an insider and did not have much beyond dated office gossip. He had characterized Stuart Aspinall as a *tough customer* and a *shrewd operator.* Useless. She needed new leads.

From booze in the early years, to electronics and commercial printing, then for a while retail chain stores, now the Aspinall family empire appeared, to her at least, interested in the movement of nothing but money itself. Logic dictated to her that no one could get and stay that wealthy without stepping on people, without making enemies, without becoming a target in the sights of other ambitious people. But who were they? Why was no one talking?

A Man's Castle had been a stage sensation in Toronto twenty years earlier. Although the playwright, a then young and strident Davida Duttington, never admitted it, her characters were generally seen as a loose portrayal of the Aspinall family during the sixties. The play's setting was more or less their family estate, Huntington House.

Beyond that, the real life trail for the critics, then the academics, and now herself as the family's biographer, went cold. Thematically, the play was about old-fashioned greed. But it could also be read, as it was by those same critics and academics, as a feminist play. By telling the story of four women — the rich wife, the mistress, the spoiled daughter, and the housekeeper — the play, they argued, was making a more general comment about the plight of women in Canadian society.

For Trudy, it had been different. She'd understood the female characters to be just as concerned with greed as their male counterparts. Would it stand the test of time? She hoped so; she had tickets to the student production the following night.

Trudy had already considered interviewing Davida who was still in Toronto writing plays, but Davida had steadfastly refused to speak about the Aspinall link at the time. Trudy wondered if anything had changed for her? Was Davida still the same combative feminist? Trudy heard Davida speak at U of T back in '85 or was it '86? Trudy had looked up to Davida, admired her passion, her politics. But it was somehow quaint now. Was that unfair? Trudy had been through so much as a mother, wife, single parent, and writer. There were aspects to all the parts of herself that she loved and, at other times, equally resented. In her estimation, she'd somehow grown stronger and weaker. And because of this, everywhere Trudy turned, both pride and guilt lurked.

A Man's Castle had much fiction. In real life, there was no "other" woman. Mr. and Mrs. Aspinall were, and remained by all accounts, happily married. They also never had a long-term housekeeper. While there was always "help" at Huntington House, apparently they had come and gone — this being modern-day Canada and not Victorian England after all. While they'd had, and still did have, a spoiled daughter in Fiona Aspinall, when this play was staged Fiona had been a teenager, and, more to the point, it was set in the 1960s, when Fiona was not yet born. If only, Trudy thought suddenly, Fiona would talk.

Mom, I need you!

In a minute, Veronica. Her daughter's shoe would be buried in her bedroom under toys or books.

Trudy looked about her study. She reached for her old copy of A Man's Castle. On the back cover was Davida's photograph, endless ringlets of hair and large hoop earrings. The 1980s felt so long ago. Perhaps Davida would talk now about what she did know back then?

Trudy made two quick calls — to a friend, then to a friend of the friend — and easily obtained Davida's current phone number.

Let me interrupt you, said Davida on the other end of the line. Of course I know who you are, Trudy. I read about your last book. It sounded great. So, believe me, I don't mean to be difficult, but I don't want to be interviewed.

Off the record then, said Trudy, thinking of, but ignoring, Humphrey's advice that she tape everything.

I'm sorry, but no.

May I ask why?

He ruins people he doesn't like, said Davida. It's how he pleasures himself. Her voice was droll, her trademark stage-play humour acidic when delivered in person. Don't get involved with him, pressed Davida. Stuart Aspinall made it his pet-project to wreck my career. He succeeded for a long time. I thought I had ten years of bad luck following that play. A theatre company went bankrupt on the eve of my next one opening. Then the rights to my following two efforts were purchased for a tidy sum but the plays were never mounted — caught in red tape, production companies owned by larger companies, no one ever seemed able to give me a straight answer. The things I've subsequently suspected . . . I can't prove anything. He's so bloody dangerous. Egotistical. He's letting this play have a run out of pure vanity, but only as a student production. So it has no chance of getting press, or being professionally mounted. No, I have to stop. Forgive me. I just can't get into this.

◆ ◆ ◆

A single spotlight made an oval on centre stage and the house lights dimmed to black. The audience's chatter petered out. Someone coughed. Several voices giggled in anticipation. A man shushed them loudly. From the wings, two female actors walked onto the stage and into the spot. One was carrying a chair that she placed on the floor. She stood behind the chair. The other sat on it facing the audience. Light grew on the stage around them. They were in a bedroom. The set consisted of a large four-poster bed and a chest of drawers. The one standing began to brush the hair of the one sitting. They both looked forward, out to the audience, into a mirror.

He asked me to marry him, said the seated woman.

I thought he might.

What should I do?

What do you want to do?

He's asked three other girls I know. They all turned him down.

Why?

He doesn't like women.

What do you mean?

I mean what I mean.

So why does he court these women? Why ask you to marry him if he knows that you know this? He must suspect you will answer him with a *no*.

He does.

I don't understand.

It's how he pleasures himself.

Fiona Aspinall had a sheer black scarf wrapped around her neck and head. Her glasses did not have darkened lenses, but the frames were heavy. She did not need glasses to see. The seat next to her was open. In her pocket were two ticket stubs. She was on the aisle, two rows from the back, at the exit. It was dark and, about her, everyone's attention was on the stage. As she watched the opening scene of the play, she felt self-conscious. She was glad her mother wasn't here to see this. Even if she wasn't so ill, it was unlikely she'd have come. Heat welled up in Fiona's armpits and across her lower back. She almost got up to leave.

Second row centre, Trudy Clarke had smuggled in a tape recorder. In her lap were a program and her copy of the play. Beside her sat Veronica. And on the other side of her daughter, her ex-husband, Patrick. As the house lights had dimmed and the spotlight had made an oval on the stage, the three of them had exchanged smiles as if to say, isn't this exciting — the three of us at a play! Patrick had leaned in to Trudy and motioned for her not to forget to press record. She'd made a goofy, forgetful smile. Veronica was eating Skittles — keeping her lips pressed together tightly and forcing each one through. As Trudy had watched the two women walk onto the stage, she'd seen a man standing in the wings. He had heavy stage makeup on and his hair was powdered grey. Then the actors had begun saying their lines; she became engrossed in the play.

During intermission, Fiona did not rise from her seat. Instead, she buried her head in a program, pivoting her hips into the aisle letting the other people in her row file out. She read the program.

> *Welcome to Opening Night! Of all Canada's great plays,* A
> Man's Castle *might be my favourite. First mounted in Toronto
> in 1983, the play has enjoyed a long life on university and college
> theatre courses from Halifax to Victoria. The students are
> thrilled to have in tonight's audience, Davida Duttington, the
> playwright. What an honour. Finally, we could not have
> remounted this play without your support. Every dollar from
> ticket sales goes back directly into our theatre program. Your
> presence tonight is helping to ensure that theatre in Canada
> stays vibrant and strong for years to come. Sit back and enjoy! —
> Prof. Gerry*

Trudy and Veronica waited in the foyer with the other audience members. People were sipping coffees and cokes. Veronica complained about a stomach ache. Patrick had gone to the bathroom.

Hello! said Trudy, abruptly, as a woman turned in front of her.

Yes, said the woman.

I'm Trudy Clarke.

Oh, said Davida, I'm sorry I didn't recognize you right away.

Well, we've never met, said Trudy.

From author photographs, I mean. Who's this? asked Davida.

Veronica, say hello.

Hello, said Veronica.

This is the woman who wrote the play, said Trudy to Veronica.

Is a play a book? asked Veronica.

It can be, said Davida. But plays belong in the mouths of

actors. Veronica nodded, but looked unsure about to what she was agreeing.

I see Dad, she said and skipped away. Trudy and Davida were alone.

Is that a tape recorder? asked Davida.

It's not on, said Trudy. This isn't an interview? I still don't want to be interviewed.

Sorry to interrupt, said a man. Davida, I'd like you to meet someone. Please excuse us, he said to Trudy, as he led Davida away.

How'd that go? asked Patrick as he and Veronica approached through the crowd of audience members chatting in groups.

Not well, said Trudy. The lights in the foyer began to flicker on and off. She's not interested at all.

It's time to go back in, announced Veronica.

Fiona carefully watched the young woman playing her. It appeared she'd been miscast — the actor was a thin, second-generation Mediterranean-looking woman. The young woman had a long hard nose and high cheekbones. All the actors wore black, tight fitting clothes. It was a budget production; the audience was expected to imagine, intuit, wealth. Her character spoke the lines with no thought of class or upbringing, did nothing to affect any kind of realism.

She and Colin had written a play when they were children. It was Christmas and her father had hired men to come and install lights all over Huntington. The winter wonderland had inspired them to write a play about a girl and her brother. She had been a princess and he a prince.

The prince and the princess, she began in an assured, storyteller's voice, went gallivanting on their horses all over the kingdom.

You mean galloping, darling, said her mother from the single-row audience.

But she'd ignored the interruption, narrating away. And wherever they went, coloured lights were hung in their honour.

Colin had been sick that Christmas, but he wanted to be in the play. She'd allowed him to lie down on stage so he was more comfortable. Their mother and father had been the only audience members. At the end of the play her father scooped her up in a hug. They all had hot chocolate and sat around Colin's bed to keep him company. Even her mother sat with them. She was worried about germs usually. But this time, because it was Christmas, she was willing to drop her guard.

Trudy leaned back in her seat. Her arm was slung around Veronica who had fallen asleep not long after intermission. Patrick rested his hand over hers, smiling at her. He looked down at their daughter. They smiled, briefly, at one another, and then looked back up at the stage.

The final words were spoken. A meaningful quiet bloomed throughout the theatre. Then the audience rose to their feet in applause. The various female actors returned to the stage and, as each did, the audience clapped harder. At the end, the few men who had made brief appearances also took the stage for the curtain call. It was during this time that Fiona Aspinall ducked out.

What did *you* think? asked Patrick.

I liked it! said Veronica.

You were asleep, silly, for most of it, said Trudy.

Was not.

Was too.

Who wants hot chocolate? asked Patrick.

Tim Hortons! said Veronica.

It's too late, said Trudy.

Is not! said Veronica.

We'll get them to go. How about that? And the three of them walked out into the night, holding hands, Trudy and Patrick linked by Veronica who, periodically, lifted her feet off the ground, expecting to be swung forward and back.

◆ ◆ ◆

As the last few audience members filed out and drifted away down Toronto's streets, a long black limousine pulled up outside the theatre. Jim Nadeau watched as Mr. Stuart Aspinall got out and waited down the street beyond the backstage door. Aspinall was dressed in a grey suit with a light blue tie. His thinning hair was short. They shook hands firmly.

Davida Duttington was one of this country's brightest talents, at the time, said Mr. Aspinall. Has she done anything recently, do you know?

No, said Jim. I don't know.

Well, I don't see my family or myself in the play, continued Mr. Aspinall. Never knew what all the fuss was about. Did you enjoy it?

I wasn't watching the play. I was watching Trudy.

Of course. The consummate professional. Well, I do not want to keep you, said Mr. Aspinall. Anything to report?

Bits, said Jim. Trudy was there with her daughter and her ex-husband. I don't believe Davida has been interviewed.

Why's that?

They spoke at intermission. But not for long. Davida looked disengaged, put out.

I see. They stood in silence for a moment. It occurs to me, you might be the perfect man for another job it seems I now need doing. Actually, it involves a bit of acting. I pay well. Would you be interested in discussing this further?

I do work for the chief from time to time doing odd assignments. If he's okay with it, then I'm okay with it.

I suspect he will be, said Mr. Aspinall. Thank you.

One more thing, said Jim.

Yes?

Your daughter was in the audience. She was alone, and, to my eye, looking purposefully inconspicuous.

Indeed. Well, Officer Nadeau, you *will* be useful. Next week then.

◆ ◆ ◆

Executive suite, how may I help you?

It's me.

Yes, Mr. Aspinall.

I'll be getting calls from a fellow named Jim Nadeau. Please don't put him through, just take messages and I will get back to him, as I'm able.

Shall I start a file? What's it regarding?

No, no file. It's regarding a family matter. Don't keep any paper on this.

Of course, Mr. Aspinall.

Now tell me, how is your cat?

On Tuesday night . . . I had to put him down.

I'm sorry to hear that. Do you need some time?

No. Thank you. Very nice of you to offer. No. I want to keep busy.

I understand. I like to do that too. Pets are family, don't let anyone tell you otherwise. Well, have a good evening. I won't be in tomorrow, but I will call in for messages.

Of course.

♦ ♦ ♦

It was 1979. Trudy's friend, Shauna, had arrived unexpectedly.

I'm taking you to hear a band, Shauna had said at the apartment door.

I'm too old for this, protested Trudy, feebly. She slunk into her bedroom and pulled on a pair of black jeans. She looked about. I can't find anything clean, she called out.

Trudy, time you had some fun, and it's punk. Dirty is better. Her friend had lit a cigarette and was speaking and exhaling at the same time.

Trudy had been in graduate school at the University of Toronto doing a master's degree in history. She liked it. She liked how it allowed her to behave. Old, busy, poor, and serious. But to friends like Shauna, she was growing squarer as the months rolled on. That she knew it and fought it less and less was now cause for her friend's concern.

Standing with two T-shirts in hand, she wondered at her change in plans tonight. Before this intervention, she'd been listening to the CBC — waiting to hear Trudeau. Crowds were gathering at Maple Leaf Gardens to hear him speak. She stopped and sighed. What hope was there for her at twenty-four if, at fifteen, the only man she'd had a crush on was not a movie star, or the cute guy in math class, but the prime minister? That schoolgirl had watched the news almost nightly, eager to see a glimpse of Pierre Elliott Trudeau. She'd tried harder in French class so she could understand him fully — get to know him better. Privately, she suspected he was even funnier, even more himself in French. It was all the incentive she needed to be an A student throughout high school. Now, as an adult, her bilingualism seemed a strange by-product of a teenager's wish to be deflowered by the pm.

She'd grown out of Trudeau, but she still carried a gentle torch. And he was in town that night. To miss seeing him battle for re-election felt wrong. Toronto's hockey arena was only a short streetcar ride away and she had thought about going to join the thousands of others. But something held her back. Could she share him with all those people? And, generally, she preferred, or at least was more comfortable, reading about such events the next day. Experiencing them required a kind of courage she, increasingly, didn't possess.

When she emerged from her bedroom dressed in a white T-shirt with a jean jacket over top, her friend said, Well, I s'pose that will have to do. Can I at least do your hair?

I have some wine, said Trudy.

We'll need that too then, said Shauna.

Later, when they were on their way, the rain belting down outside as they careened across the city, Trudy reached across the back seat of the cab and squeezed her friend's hand. Thanks, she said. I needed to get out.

The band played a sustained, discordant, sonic barrage. They relied heavily on the versatility of the lyric *fuck right off and die fuckers*. Although Trudy couldn't play an electric guitar, she grew convinced that neither could the lead singer. He knew only one fingering pattern, which he played from time to time when he remembered he was strapped to an instrument.

Alone in the crowd, Shauna now lost on the way to the bar, Trudy found herself hypnotized by the drummer's performance. It was the way he concentrated. The lines on his brow furrowing, and his hair, curls wet with sweat, stuck to his head. He was not wearing a T-shirt as the stage was too hot from the low row of red and green lights blazing above him. It was May and his body was still white from the winter. He drummed with such physical presence she found herself imagining what it might be like to be with such a man (or boy, for he was, she suspected, several years younger than her). Had she ever felt such an urge to hold another human being — save Trudeau — before now? He belted his cymbals with impudence, as if he knew that without his steady beat their music would inch away from raw punk to chaotic noise.

In the weeks that followed, between her own reading on the Spanish Civil War, doing research work for a professor on nineteenth-century British military battle plans, and her teaching responsibilities, she monitored the band listings in the campus newspaper, running her finger down the columns in the hope of an announcement for their next performance. Then she saw it. The Bearded Clams. She felt light-headed.

Trudy's father had been a conductor and was a professor emeritus in the Music Faculty at the University of Toronto; her mother, an opera singer. Although she showed no aptitude herself, she had a deep listener's appreciation and would talk to her father for hours about this symphony, or that concerto. It was a kind of music itself. Given her rich musical home life, she had always, rather single-mindedly, given the avalanche of adolescent peer-pressure, steadfastly preferred violins to electric guitars, Bach to the Beatles.

Her drummer's name was Patrick.

And on the pots and pans is fucking Patrick, the fucking

loud fuck, said the lead singer, Needle, with good cheer and a put-on Manchester accent.

The Bearded Clams are playing again on Tuesday, Trudy said to Shauna on the phone. Help me branch out, she added, laughing thinly. And so they went. Patrick kept his shirt on that evening. He looked distracted. She worried that he might have something he needed to talk about. Problems at home? Drugs? She could listen to him. She could make him soup and they could talk for hours — if that's what he needed.

What a pussy crowd you are! said Needle at the end of the show. Well, we are the Bearded Clams, Oi! And we'll be playing again here next Tuesday night.

She went to this next show, and to the ones after that. Alone. She developed a routine. She'd order a beer — a drink she didn't particularly enjoy — lean up against the sidewall, and take in the show drinking in short, greedy gulps. This lasted through the spring and into the summer. All the summer shows were hot. Patrick often went shirtless.

At the beginning of the fall term she walked confidently in to teach her modern history course. With his shirt on and hair dry and light, Patrick sat on the far side of the long table. The sight of him so close all but threw her. Trudeau had lost the spring election. And now her drummer was before her, close enough to touch. She stole several glances at him as she forced her way through the class less composed than she ever was at one of the Bearded Clams' shows.

As a teacher of history, she was casually confident and able. That the material had not changed in the six years since she herself had taken it helped. The first year of her master's degree, and her first teaching assignment had passed by easily. But now Patrick was before her. She was expected to lead serious discussions. Mao. McCarthyism. The Marshall Plan.

Eight months later she marked Patrick's final paper on his

naked back. Thankfully, he was a good student. She didn't help him a stitch and he never asked for it. He didn't care about marks; they came easily to him in all courses, hers included. He wrote decent essays effortlessly, which, in her experience, was rare for a first year student. His smarts made their affair, for that's what it was in the beginning, easy to justify in her mind. He was an exception to every rule.

She'd decided against a life in academia the moment he first entered her. She roiled back inside herself with pain. Who had she been all these years? What was she waiting for? As his hips stirred, the salty taste of him all about her, life, she understood, had been happening without her participation.

Patrick, this boy with his mop of blond hair had energy for adventure that she found herself taken in by. He would show up at all hours, pumped up after practising drums or playing a show, and he'd want to go out and eat a huge meal in Chinatown, or go to the art gallery, or see a foreign film. He was hysterical one minute about a link he felt he'd found between the work of Camus and Benjamin Britten, and not two minutes later he'd be on to Henry Miller and Toulouse-Lautrec, or Borges and Wagner, or Sylvia Plath and Anaïs Nin. He was an orgy of undergraduateness.

She fell in love eagerly. At first there was a question after class. She laughed too hard at his attempt to be funny. She heard herself confess, unprompted, to having seen him play drums once, somewhere or other.

Come to my next show, he'd said, broaching the line, telling her where it was, and the time they'd be on stage.

She already knew all this. But she'd said, Maybe. I'll see.

You don't look punk, he said through pouty lips and loose curls.

You don't look like an A student, she replied, red coursing involuntarily at her cheeks.

Finding her in the crowd, he came to her after the show, hot, sweaty, reaching for her hand, saying, Trudy, I've been watching you watch me.

What? The house music pounded about them.

You. He said through the noise. You and me.

Was it not a coincidence that you ended up in my tutorial group?

But he couldn't hear her. They smiled at their helplessness. He held her still by the hand, and now he pulled her closer. She could feel the heat of him. Her ears were ringing from the music. She felt light-headed from her beer. Then the house lights came on and the music stopped. They were exposed and raw in the bright quiet.

Let's get out of here, they both said.

On the street corner, the smell of fall in the air, he grabbed her by the back of the neck and they kissed. A taxi pulled up. They looked at the driver, who looked at them. Did they want to go somewhere? Did they? He asked if she was hungry. And she was.

They sat close, legs touching all the way uptown to Yonge and St. Clair. In a booth at Fran's Restaurant, they drank coffee and ate grilled cheese sandwiches. He smoked.

What are we doing? she said.

You said in class you like classical music. We're hoping we see crazy Glenn Gould — he just about lives in here. We came in once after a show. He sat behind us. Needle asked if he liked the Clash.

What'd he say?

Nothing. Then a bit later he hummed one of their songs from start to finish. Every fucking note. It was far out. Course we were high.

You know what I mean, she said.

I'll drop the course. It's not important to me.

It should be, history is. But he raised his hand to her mouth, touching her lips, the taste of him. And, somehow with that touch, it was understood they would become lovers. He did not drop the course. It turned into more time they could spend together. But she would not become a professor like her father; it would be she who would drop out, finishing only her master's — enough of life in the past. Now she needed to live, to work, to love. Her new course of action felt logical and alive. For the first time in her life, through Patrick at the beginning, but gradually on her own, she engaged with the world. She vowed to leave other people's history to her own past. And, for a time, she did.

◆ ◆ ◆

Morning sunlight filled the restaurant; the waiters drifted from table to table, serving men in dark suits and women with firmly set hair. Jim Nadeau had ordered eggs florentine and freshly squeezed orange juice. The dishes were white and the silverware heavy. He was on to his toast, the cold butter tasting better than butter usually did, when Mr. Aspinall described the job.

I'm trying to track down the whereabouts of my son, said Mr. Aspinall. Colin is a grown man, he's been on his own for years, but no one has seen him for months. We are becoming distraught.

Jim nodded.

I knew you'd understand, said Mr. Aspinall. We've even gone so far as to hire a private investigator. He's come up with nothing. That's why I've involved the chief, and in turn, he's now involved you.

No explanation needed, said Jim.

Colin's always doing this — taking off. But never for this long. No contact with his sister, his old friends or family. We are worried he's . . . not well.

Jim sipped his pulpy juice — freshly squeezed. He nodded and creased his forehead, pressing his lips together, and biting down on the lower one at one point.

We think there is a serious problem this time, Mr. Aspinall was saying. Because, if you want the truth, Jim, Colin has a credit card that he uses regularly. And I have a friend who — but Mr. Aspinall stopped himself. Let's just say I am privy to Colin's monthly statements. Now, I recognize that this may appear to some as deceitful, spying on my son, but I know you can understand — this is simply a matter of a father's concern.

Jim nodded in three measured beats.

There have been times that this is the only way we've known for certain Colin was alive, and safe. You can see the lengths to which I've had to go. And now, nothing. No e-mails with his sister, no phone calls, no credit card charges whatsoever. Jim, I don't mind confessing, it's nerve-wracking.

I know what it's like to lose someone you care about, said Jim. He went on to say he would do whatever he could. A waiter cleared his plate.

The first order of business . . . Do you think, Mr. Aspinall continued with an extra air of caution added to his voice, with your impressive skills, you could help me with a man named Andy Kronk? He goes way back with our son Colin — they were school chums at LSC, that's Lord Simcoe College. I don't know for sure, but I suspect he may know something. Andy won't talk to me. He'll protect Colin's privacy to the last. Yes, he's loyal to Colin, completely loyal. But Andy Kronk can be trusted to tell the truth. He is a survivor. He's achieved what he has against all social expectations. I just need him to talk.

The man paused, and Jim waited for him to begin again.

Can you be trusted? Are you that kind of man, Jim?

I am, said Jim flatly.

I've come up with a plan.

Okay, said Jim.

Andy lived with us — at our home — on and off for several years. As I mentioned, he went to LSC with Colin. During that time, tragically, his father died. He was already motherless. All very sad; we took him in, naturally. Now, Trudy Clarke is thorough. I know she will discover Andy Kronk, eventually. He paused. I'd like to tip off Trudy Clarke about the importance of Andy Kronk — to the research of her book. I'd like you to help me set her up to go and speak with Andy as soon as possible.

She's going to find him anyway? confirmed Jim.

Correct.

We are speeding up the inevitable, in other words?

Exactly, said Mr. Aspinall.

The sun had moved enough to be shining right in Jim's eyes, so he edged over his chair and raised his hand for shade.

I must discover what Andy knows. As I say, he won't tell me directly but you see, *he just might tell Trudy*. As a bona fide author she'll be able to charm him, I'm sure of it. Mr. Aspinall leaned back in his chair and took a sip of his coffee before continuing. You'll meet with Trudy. We're going to tell Trudy that there is a police investigation into my company. The investigation needs some critical information from Andy Kronk about my past, and that Andy Kronk holds secret information on the Aspinalls. We will deliver Andy Kronk to her for her book, if she'll help us with our investigation. Quid pro quo.

She can get what she needs for her biography, and the investigation gets what it needs.

Precisely, said Mr. Aspinall. You'll be the principal officer on *the case*.

I want nothing left to chance, said Jim.

This will be a simple enough task for you.

You'll want a taped record?

Yes. Everything Andy tells Trudy. I will be in touch, said Mr. Aspinall standing to go.

Jim also stood. They shook hands. Each man's grip was firm but not overly so. In this way, each could only guess at how much strength the other held in reserve.

Three further meetings followed where they ironed out all the necessary details.

♦ ♦ ♦

Stuart Aspinall stepped off the cobblestone pathway and onto the dewy lawn. The hill before him faded to the lake's edge at Huntington House. He padded his way toward the cream-coloured boathouse, his leather oxfords black and shiny, hands casually in the pockets of his suit pants. It was an unseasonably warm day. At least it was when he felt the direct sun on his clean-shaven cheeks and neck. He had removed his jacket and tie, left them in the foyer of the house.

He often came down here to think before dinner. It was the half-hour a day — not every day but often enough — that he saved for himself. Reaching the boathouse, he sat on the burgundy Muskoka chair angled at the lake's centre. The lap of the water against the dock was rhythmical. Far away a loon called out. Light wind played the branches of the firs down the way.

Lately, he'd felt the unease. Felt it deepening within him. He knew its source and cause too well. It was almost as old as Colin himself. A chronic, imprecise hurt that a woman might call heartache. He chose, long ago, not to address it directly.

Rather he monitored it, weighed it, and negotiated it down, always down, into a manageable size. If it were true that the child was lost to him, and it sadly was, then he had always supposed that one did what one must, to go on. To cope, as it were. Why did the two of them engage in such emotional sport that had no clear rules and never ended? Fact: Colin is an Aspinall. That cannot be changed. So he mustn't hurt the family, or weaken the name.

Were Colin there at the shore with him, and were he able to speak to his son frankly, even truthfully, he might tell Colin of all he knew. But how would he begin? He looked out at the lake. You're from a country ignorant of success, he'd say. To think otherwise is foolish. This is principal to Canada. When success does occur, people either wilfully disregard it or do not recognize it. Colin, son, we are too large to be seen, too central to be accountable.

As its citizens pull out of single-car driveways and head to unionized jobs, as they eat a fast-food breakfast on their lap while cleverly steering with one knee, as they go about thriving on gargantuan coffees and last night's hockey win, our influence does not register. In America, those with billions are envied. In England, those with title can curry favour and trade on a last name. Why not here?

Think about it, son. We have it on both of them.

In Canada, families like ours are unburdened by the lights of publicity, free from public scrutiny and therefore private liability. Wealth doesn't matter here. So we adjust what they view and hear and read, control who they vote for, profit from what they consume. Notoriety and fame are all downside; with them comes the chance to fall. What we have is an intoxicating freedom and a free rein.

Stuart Aspinall breathed. The sky was darkening. He forced all thoughts of his son back down within. Enough.

Out on the lake a single loon surfaced: its cry was crisp and clear. Mr. Aspinall was no longer in his burgundy Muskoka chair. The door to the cream boathouse was ajar. The clank of latches and doors opening and closing rang across the lake. When he re-emerged he glanced up and down the shoreline, but saw no boats or fishermen. His steadied himself, his index finger squeezed, and the loon was picked up out of the water, its head and neck wrenched unnaturally by the force, by the buckshot, in a spray of water and down. The sour smell of gunpowder hung in the air about Stuart Aspinall. The recoil from the old twelve-gauge was fierce.

◆ ◆ ◆

Did you bend all the way down and check under your bed? Trudy asked.

At nine, Veronica had experienced another growth spurt. Trudy's ex-husband — and Veronica's father — Patrick, was a tall man. Trudy wasn't short herself. Lately, she had begun to wonder if Veronica would be *too* tall. Veronica was currently balancing on her left foot to emphasize the continued absence of her right shoe.

I did already, Veronica replied.

Her daughter's bedroom was the stuff of tornado aftermath. Dolls' heads, felt markers, sweaters, jeans, socks, bedding, Nancy Drew mysteries, and CDs were left strewn. Trudy looked and found the shoe in a corner.

It was under your wet towel, she said.

Veronica let out a dramatic huff. It was becoming the girl's signature expression: part *I'm very upset with you*, and part *I couldn't care less about what you think.*

I'd like you to clean this all up.

But Mom, Anita is already waiting, said Veronica. Veronica's hair reached down almost to the small of her back.

Okay, go. Trudy reached out and touched her daughter's cheek. Clean later though.

Thanks, Mom, said Veronica, striding from the room.

Say hi to Indira for me, Trudy called after her. The balance between soft and tough love was a difficult one to strike. Could Veronica hear her inner debate?

Trudy began to pick up markers and put on their lids. She would get a start on cleaning. What if Patrick dropped around?

Anita was a tiny, paper-thin thing whose nose ran. She and Veronica had been playmates since they were five. They went to the same school and were in the same class. They were best friends.

Indira cooked everything from scratch: beautiful meals of rice, meats, curry, and flat breads. As a result, the two girls often ate dinner at Indira's kitchen table. Later the girls would come back through the gate in the fence. Anita would appear at Trudy's study door with her homework under her arm, her nose running down over her lip. When she spoke at all, the girl with the large dark eyes spoke only in questions — a tiny world of serial wonder, confusion, and awe.

They were raising their girls together, in an unofficial and socially unrecognized partnership. Trudy had never asked Indira what happened to her marriage. What she'd seen that morning out her front window . . . Dilip packing up a U-Haul, hugging Anita and Indira, kissing them on the foreheads.

The phone was ringing.

She trotted out of Veronica's room with a marker lid in her hand. The room was cleaner.

My name's Officer Jim Nyland. I'm with the RCMP, said a voice on the line.

Goodness, yes?

I need to be brief, but I am conducting an investigation. I understand you are writing a book. I suspect there is some overlap. Could we get together?

Although she was hesitant, they set a date to meet later in the week.

◆ ◆ ◆

Trudy Clarke shook the hand of Officer Jim Nyland and sat, tucking her knees under the outdoor table. About her the world was alive to the first marvellous day of spring in Toronto. The university students in shorts were baring their youthful legs; the sight of sunglasses on the faces of pallid passersby was welcome.

I'll have a glass of white wine, she said to the young waitress.

I appreciate your meeting me, said Nyland. He ordered a coffee.

This was the first day the café's patio was open and the good weather had taken the wait staff by surprise. Trudy overheard a snippet of conversation, one saying to the other the patio condiments weren't ready. A seagull landed on the corner of the railing five feet from where Trudy sat. There was not a cloud in the sky. Her cellphone was ringing.

Veronica? I'm in a meeting. I'll call you back in half an hour. She hung up. My daughter. You have children?

A teenage girl. Well, almost a teen. Mandy is twelve.

Do I have a lot to look forward to then? she said and smiled at him. Nyland had the prerequisite police-thick forearms and neck, but he had an unkempt goatee and hair that was curly, thick, and longer than she might have expected. The waitress arrived with their drinks.

Where are you at with your book? said Nyland. How many people have you interviewed in your research so far? Nyland wore a large diver's wristwatch. He did not have a wedding band.

Not many, I'm afraid. Four, I think. People are not particularly forthcoming.

Is that typical? he asked.

People are cautious around being interviewed. At the beginning, at least. After they speak with you, then trust develops. Momentarily, she turned these words on herself, wondering if she should be speaking so easily like this. Should she have called a lawyer, or spoken with Humphrey, or checked up on this officer? How does one even do that? Check up on a police officer?

A young man on a unicycle wove his way in and out of the traffic in front of the café, yelling, *Find your balance with Jesus.* For stability, his arms were outstretched in an exaggerated cross. People around them laughed. The first burst of spring in a city like this was a thing to behold. She'd said this to her rarely seen neighbour that very morning, the mathematics professor. He had been reaching his arms up into the sky in a stretch. *Spring,* she'd said declaratively to the neighbour, *it's a thing to behold.* And the mathematics professor scratched himself across the chest and did not disagree.

How many more people, the officer continued, are on your list to speak with in connection with this book? Surely, this meeting needed some explanation if she were to continue. So few people, she thought, even knew what she was working on. How? Why did the police find out?

It's such early days in my research, she said. It's not much of a list as it stands. I'm still building it as I go. Following leads. Of course, you'd understand. Probably similar to the way you investigate. It's not uncommon for the best information to come from more distant sources. They have less to lose, no strong ties to betray or ongoing concerns to protect, or sometimes they even wish to . . . she paused, looking for the right words . . . cement their often tenuous link to the subject. Especially if the subject is a Canadian dynasty — like in this case. It's often just pure vanity that gets people to talk.

She smiled, hoping she'd said enough. She would never reveal the names of her sources to this officer — if that were what he was after. Should she call Humphrey?

I see, he said and used his thick paw of a hand to twist at the whiskers of his chin.

So, I'm still spinning my wheels, I'm afraid.

Well, he said pausing and leaning in, Trudy, I think we can help one another.

◆ ◆ ◆

Fiona took the turn too fast. As the back end of her Jaguar struggled for traction, she geared down in the turn and the engine roared. She had owned a string of beautiful cars. Her passion led her, rather publicly at twenty-five, to race open-wheeled cars for a half season. She felt she was blazing a trail for women in the sport. But she had hit a guardrail and another car, suffering a serious concussion. The press release put out by her father's company quoted her as saying, "It was a great experience. I will always love to drive. But now I need some time to reflect on what I've learned this year." The media chalked it up to a rich kid's whimsy. Ten years later, she still receives copies of her official racing poster in the mail from collectors asking her for a signature. Her hair was long then, a checkered flag fluttering in the reflection of her red Ray-Bans. Her father had forced her to quit.

The old lakeshore road leading into Huntington was a series of fade-away blind turns. She decided to slow down and take them leisurely. On one side of her was the lake, on the other were stands of cedar and maple that broke open to reveal the pitch and roll of farmers' fields bare with patches of snow. After Christmas she would return this Jaguar and get something else. Last summer she'd driven a Mercedes that was so souped up it was illegal. Maybe another Benz? There was that trip to Quebec she'd been mulling over. An old friend had a place in the Eastern Townships. Great place to drive. Or maybe she'd motor to New York? Take some back ways through New England once the spring arrived?

Hi Dad, she said as she stepped from her car. Her father was getting into the back of his limo.

I didn't know you were coming, he said, pressing his lips together in genuine disappointment. I'm on my way to Rome.

It's okay. I wanted to get out of the city, so I took a drive.

I'll be back on Saturday.

She did up her brown leather jacket. It's cold, she added, mostly to herself. How is Mom?

No change. Go up and see her. Here, give your father a kiss.

She first kissed, then embraced her father. His lips and cheek were still warm. He had broad shoulders. Her hand patted his back. His coat was fine wool. The man always had the same smell, not too strong, but it was distinct. They stood there like this for a few seconds.

Maybe I could go later, he said. Spend some time with you now you've come?

Dad, don't be silly.

I'll call the plane. We can postpone departure.

Fiona sat in the kitchen at the long table while her father made them espresso.

Looks fancy, Dad, she said with a smile.

It's what all the real coffee aficionados use. I found it last week in Rome. I'm still learning its deeper secrets. See that knob, the copper one? I don't know what it does. I even read the manual.

Read the instructions! Father, I can't believe you'd give in so easily.

Please don't tell the boys.

This was one of her father's favourite lines. The idea of him having friends that he'd refer to as "the boys" was very funny — especially to him. Although it had been years since anyone had laughed, he worked it in whenever he could. They took their coffees and sat in the drawing room. Mr. Aspinall opened one of the windows a crack.

It's stuffy, he said. He was looking out across the lawns down to the lake. Fiona, tell me, he took a sip, tell me what you are doing now.

Oh Dad, we're not going to do this, are we?

No, no. Just conversation.

After Fiona graduated from McGill with a degree in psychology, her father first put to her the idea of working for the family company. But she'd wanted to race cars. You'll work with me. You'll learn, he'd promised. Up until that time, it wasn't ever made clear to her what he'd expected her to do. To fill that gap, she'd thought she'd race. Driving gave her a thrill like nothing else. So she'd turned him down and headed for the track. He agreed to back her for one year only. After she crashed, partway through the season, he put his foot down, pulling her funding.

Colin has no interest in business, he'd said. It has to be you. You have a responsibility.

Business had never interested her either, but as he controlled her money she'd agreed to think it over. That was ten years ago. Ten years of limbo, of monthly allowance, of case-by-case pleading for trips, a condo, cars. Periodically, he raised the question of her future with the company.

I'm considering an offer, she said.

We are talking about the American lawyer, he said.

I rather suspected you'd have heard.

What are you going to do?

I don't know yet.

I think you should marry him, said her father.

You do? She lurched forward involuntarily. Her father, she would have guessed, would have done anything to keep her tethered to the family and its businesses.

I read his graduate thesis, he said. He went to Princeton.

I know, Dad.

Have you read it?

No.

You should. It's on campaign finance reform. He was smiling at her.

It was not.

No, it wasn't. I haven't read it. It doesn't exist. He didn't finish his graduate degree. He dropped out after a term and went to law school instead. I wonder what changed his mind.

I'll ask him.

Yes. Ask him. And, before you say yes or no, ask him to tell you every single other item about his entire life. His father was a West Pointer.

Dad, I know *that*.

So why didn't *he* go?

She shrugged. I'll talk to him. I'll find out everything.

You can tell a lot about a boy if you understand his relationship with his mother, but if you want to know about a man, you must understand his relationship with his father.

They were silent for a minute. The gas fireplace clicked on as the room chilled. Mr. Aspinall stood and walked over to the window to close it.

I think he wants to be president some day.

Good god girl, they all do.

If I do this, she began, it means your money is going to become American.

All money is American, Fiona. Besides, it's your money too. You've never grasped this. Aspinall is your last name as well. The money was handed to me. I will hand it to you. You will hand it to your children. I assume you will have children with this man?

She ignored this last question. You've checked into him completely then I take it, she said.

You want that life? he asked.

I can't live up here forever, Dad.

Mr. Aspinall leaned in. Christopher Llewellyn's father, General Llewellyn, is from California — originally. I understand Christopher is thinking of running for Congress there. His father wants him to. His old man has backers. Not huge money, but enough.

He hasn't told me that, she said.

This is what I'm hearing, said her father. But Christopher has good roots, on his mother's side, in Pennsylvania. Her people are still there. I spoke to a senior Democrat. They've had their eye on Christopher for several years now — because of this. Waiting for him to get older. Make connections. So for now, they are seeing how serious he is, and whom he marries will have to be, or at least become, an American. The party will lean on him to run in Pennsylvania — either for Congress, maybe governor, if you marry him. That's where you would have to move, live, fundraise.

So, she said, they would take him seriously — if he has money.

Our money, he said.

Yes, she said.

Yes.

She laughed and shook her head. This all seems absurd. We're just dating and they are already looking at electability twenty years ahead based on marriage alliances. It's feudal. This is why you put off your trip to Rome.

My girl needed me.

You've always paid attention, Dad. No one could fault you for that. She reached over and touched him on the knee. What should I do?

If you're asking me if he's a contender, if it is *conceivable* that one day you might be first lady, I'd say yes.

But why? You said it yourself, there are so many smart lawyers with money who dream of becoming president. Why him?

He wants to walk into a room one day and have a man in a uniform with four stars say, *Yes, sir!* when he gives an unpopular order. He wants to watch that man hate him to the core of his being, but be unable to do anything about it. That's why. He wants, metaphorically, to bust his father's balls.

She followed her father's limousine across the gravel of Huntington's circular driveway and out to the main road. In the air a bird soared and circled. Its wingspan stretched out as it rode the drafts. She watched it, as best she could, while driving. Eventually, it disappeared behind her. Her father's limo took the expressway turnoff heading toward the airport. She'd go back to the city via back roads. It took much longer, but she needed to think. Along the lake she'd be able to watch the ice breaking apart. The small summer houses closed up — tarps over people's little motorboats. The road was narrow with good hills.

◆ ◆ ◆

Trudy's first thought, as she'd drawn more out from Nyland and begun to understand what she was hearing, was that headlines would be bold and ugly for the Aspinalls. Then, a line from *A Man's Castle* had popped into her head. The character of the maid spoke it on the eve of the husband's affair hitting the press. It was, on the surface, an attempt to fortify the wife.

This family is as close to British royalty as Canada can ever hope to get.

With the play fresh in her mind, Trudy could see the scene, the actors onstage. Behind them, looking down from the set's wall is the portrait of the patriarch.

She was buzzing. There were risks, but police involvement meant book sales. Even though Davida had refused to talk with her, Trudy felt a sudden urge to reread the play — touch the oracle that had begun it all so many years earlier.

It was plain to her that Nyland's offer was *the* way into the Aspinalls' private world. While a biography must account for, collate, and re-examine what is already in the public domain, good ones also break news. In the past, in her other books, the more new information she'd managed to find, the better received a biography had been. Nyland's offer was her chance to make this a big book, to make the news.

According to Officer Nyland, the key for them both was a man named Andy Kronk, who was, at one time, friends with Colin Aspinall. Kronk had lived, over the course of a decade, at the Aspinalls' estate. He was someone who knew Huntington House from the inside.

Colin Aspinall had always been, if not reclusive, at least elusive. He had not been a part of the family's public face since he'd been a teenager. Why was that, she wondered? The eldest son should be a playboy. There was talk he was gay. Perhaps the family has kept him hidden? As his childhood friend, Kronk must at least know the reasons for Colin Aspinall's shyness. And from there, she supposed, the hallways and garden paths of Huntington House could lead anywhere.

There was something else. Gossip-column buzz she'd read in an old newspaper clipping. Something about Fiona Aspinall. She had had a secret man in her life: that they'd known each other for many years, through Colin. As far as Trudy had read, nothing ever came of that. Was this Andy Kronk? There had been other rumours. Fiona Aspinall was a target for speculators; she, unlike Colin, *was* a public figure and in the society pages.

In fact, Trudy had met Fiona Aspinall about five years ago at a charity dinner party. She'd found Fiona irritatingly reticent and talked only when direct questions were asked of her. Her dress had been haute couture. She'd worn a string of pearls that inexplicably drew more attention to her neck and throat than themselves, and she held herself flawlessly — as only a socialite could. In her thirties, Fiona remained unmarried. Why?

Eventually, the conversation with Officer Nyland had come around to what he wanted, why he'd asked for the meeting.

I'd like you to interview Andy Kronk, he'd said. Get everything Kronk knows about Mr. Stuart Aspinall. We suspect he won't tell the police. We need whatever information he has for our investigation. We believe he's sitting on pivotal evidence.

Why are you investigating Mr. Aspinall? she had asked, she thought, naturally enough.

I can't say.

Then how will I know what questions to ask?

I will brief you on the lines of questioning we need you to pursue. This is an undercover operation, Ms. Clarke. You are obliged to keep this conversation and all the information in it confidential until we have a solid case built. But after that time, you are free to write about it in your book.

Surely this wasn't legal. Was he playing her? But then she had pictured herself back in her study, leafing through her Aspinall file, their paltry offerings. This made her think more clearly. Without this lead, she had no book. She needed what Nyland had to offer. But how might her direct involvement in an investigation harm her journalistic efforts, much less her integrity? What if this became jammed up in court and there was a gag order placed on her book? It could last for years. Humphrey would kill her.

She had, on gut instinct alone, agreed to work with Nyland. She was going to have to get what Nyland requested, and yet remain untangled, to be able to write her book. But, she did this after she'd insisted that Officer Nyland disclose to her why the police were after Mr. Aspinall.

Fraud, he said reluctantly.

Good god, she said.

We're going to get him, he said.

What did he do?

I'm not prepared to say.

That's probably for the better, she said.

Well, he said, signalling to the waiter for the bill. I'll be in touch.

◆ ◆ ◆

In the summer of her seventeenth year, Fiona Aspinall had resisted accompanying her parents and brother to England. The plan was that Colin would join them in the UK, following a short stint in Paris to learn French. This was something Fiona had never been offered. Why should Colin get to go alone to Paris? Well, not alone, he was at a special language school by day, and was staying with family friends. But it seemed unfair to her somehow. All she got by way of summer vacation was two weeks outside London, stranded in the countryside at the Bailey-Millers' estate with her whole family.

The first few days consisted of excursions to nearby shops and a castle an hour away, horseback riding, tea here and there, at this village and that, and a visit to the local pub at which she was permitted one glass of wine. Her parents were in light moods, as Mr. and Mrs. Bailey-Miller were among their closest friends. This was a long stretch away from work for her father, and he was as relaxed as she'd ever seen him. Her mother adored Mrs. Bailey-Miller and was therefore easily talked into whatever Fiona might fancy — a new pair of shoes, a watch. So, although she was generally bored, the days were gliding by easily.

One afternoon, the sun was out and she sat in the conservatorium with the fresh smelling house plants about her and the windows thrown open to the outside air. She was reading. Although not attracted to books the way Colin was, she would, from time to time, find herself surprisingly lost in the pages of a book someone had pressed upon her. With a breeze, gentle and warm curling in through the window, she read contentedly for some time, pulled from the pages only when her mother and Colin stopped close by outside. They'd been on a walk and were in the middle of a conversation. They did not know she could hear.

It's just a suggestion, her mother was saying.

But I don't want to be so far away from you, Fiona, and Andy, said Colin.

What's Andy got to do with this?

Everything.

You'll meet other friends.

I don't want to.

But it's not normal. Boys your age should have many friends. You should be playing sports and running about. You should be interested in girls.

I do find girls interesting.

I think you know what I mean, Colin.

After that Fiona lost the thread of the conversation. Colin had, evidently, stood up, and continued walking — his mother following along behind.

The Bailey-Millers' house had beautiful gardens, hedges, and fountains. They owned two red setters. When let loose, the dogs would bound directly through the garden beds. Instead of getting upset, Mrs. Bailey-Miller would laugh. Fiona wondered how she found the destruction of her wonderfully manicured gardens so amusing.

Don't look so concerned Fiona, the woman remarked, upon seeing Fiona's expression aghast at a dog peeing on a statue. They are dogs, she continued. They don't see the world as we do. We try to trim nature into straight pathways, but they don't recognize the legitimacy of such efforts. They play, run, and urinate! Wherever it pleases them. We should be reminded that we are a part of nature too, not above it, or absent from it.

At this, her mother laughed.

Fiona liked Mrs. Bailey-Miller too. She thought Mr. Bailey-Miller handsome for an older man. She admired their house and gardens. This would be a nice place to live. She rather thought she understood England a bit better now, the point to being so crowded onto a little island. If people like the

Bailey-Millers had space, it counted for something here. Especially if they made it so beautiful. No one much noticed Huntington House — and it was about the same size, although new in comparison. But yesterday people emptied out of buses and toured the house and gardens. They had returned from their outing to the pub just as the last tourists were boarding the coach to leave. The manager of the house was standing at the driveway waving to them. They all waved back.

It's lovely to be able to show it off, said Mrs. Bailey-Miller.

Yes, the people adore it, added Mr. Bailey-Miller. They eat up its history, and the art and armoury are especially sought-after.

Don't you find it an intrusion? asked her father.

It's only Saturday afternoons. You know we own it, but the history belongs to the whole country, said Mr. Bailey-Miller. We are obliged to share it, I believe.

Can you imagine Canadians touring Huntington by the busload, Mommy? Fiona asked.

Your room would never be clean enough!

And they laughed at that.

We get Canadians here quite often, said Mrs. Bailey-Miller. Commonwealth tourists are among the most interested in the history.

You're killing me over here, said Fiona's father.

Good, I'm trying, teased Mrs. Bailey-Miller.

Fiona, Colin, their mother and father went on a walk together before dinner. Mr. Aspinall placed his arm around their mother as they strode. Colin collected small flowers in the grass along the way, and tied them together to make a chain. Fiona carried her book, reading as she dawdled behind them.

Family! her father announced. They all looked at him. About them fat puffy clouds hung in the air, robins sang, a light wind stirred the leaves and branches of a weeping beech tree down the way. Would you like to move to England?

You said we were not going to discuss this with them, her mother said between clenched teeth.

I'm asking you all. I'm asking you for your input. This will be a democratic decision. I have some business that I must do in the UK over the next few years, and if you all agree, we could move here together.

I told Mom yesterday that I didn't want to go to a boarding school here by myself, said Colin.

Why is nobody talking to me? Fiona heard herself say. I have two more years of school.

And you could do them anywhere, said Mr. Aspinall.

Please, please, said her mother firmly. Stop it. Stop this. I was just enjoying myself. It was just a fun thing. That was all. Why can't you let a whimsical idea stand for even a day? Many people enjoy daydreaming.

Daydreaming is for people who feel trapped by their own lives. Do you? Are you trapped? Are you powerless to change your circumstances? Is the only meaningful life you live a private one, deep within the folds of your mind and memory where you secretly swoon over fanciful plans and longings?

You can be hateful, said Fiona's mother, and stormed off, back toward the house.

Fiona had never seen them fight. This was a fight. She'd seen her mother bitterly cross before. But she had never seen her speak to her father like this. Not in front of her, in any case. Fiona felt worried. Her father wouldn't stand for it, would react badly, strongly at being disagreed with, even if he had already put her mother in her place. Were she to have said something so strident, so critical, she'd be punished in ways direct and indirect. Suddenly she understood that her mother would be, had always been, treated no different than her.

Colin lifted a chain of flowers over his head and turned his back on the scene, wandering over toward the weeping beech.

Colin, come back here, we're going, said her father. We are all going home tonight. I've decided.

But Colin did not stop. She watched his strides, which remained measured and purposeful until he reached the arching branches of the tree, where he lowered his head as if bowing, then disappeared underneath them. She took a half step toward him.

Fiona, said her father. Over there, and he pointed to Colin's tree, is never-ending childhood. And there, and he pointed to her mother now a diminishing dot at the hilltop near the house, is a romantic defeated. But here, and he put his hand briefly to his heart and breathed in deeply, here is purpose, dignity, and honesty. And he offered his hand for her to take. Let's continue our walk, shall we? By that time your mother will have cooled off, Colin will be back, and I can apologize to you all at once. We were having a nice holiday together. I hope I haven't spoiled it.

Together, Fiona and her father traversed the clover-covered hillside in a wide arcing radius around the grand house. A rabbit leapt out of a hole in the hedge and startled them. They laughed together, father and daughter. Their eyes and smiles were similar. Everyone said so.

◆ ◆ ◆

The light was dim in the hotel's library bar forcing a cozy, homey feel. Jim Nadeau squinted at featureless people shaking hands, kissing cheeks, coming and going over by the entrance. He'd chosen a brown leather wingback chair pushed against the wall farthest from the door. The bar was only partially full, and the waiter, who was as attentive as one might expect for a place this expensive, was forced to thread his way in and out of some ten tables and chairs to bring Jim a beer, or refresh his bowl of peanuts. Both of which he'd already done twice.

Are you still expecting someone? asked the waiter.

He's running late it appears, answered Jim. I'll stick it out a bit longer. The waiter gestured at Jim's almost-empty beer. Sure, why not, he said.

There is a phone at the bar if you need to make a call.

Jim had come early for the meeting. A heater on the wall near his feet forced warm air all around him, and he was almost drifting off to sleep when a dark shape stood before him.

My jet was delayed, said Mr. Aspinall.

I got here early, said Jim, making to stand.

Please sit. There was silence for a few moments while Stuart Aspinall settled down into his chair and looked about. I don't have long I'm afraid, he added.

The waiter appeared with Jim's third beer and smiled at Mr. Aspinall.

A Scotch with one ice cube, said Mr. Aspinall. The waiter nodded his head and left them. Mr. Aspinall wore a dark-blue suit with a solid burgundy tie. From his inside breast pocket he produced a pair of rimless bifocal glasses that he perched on the bridge of his nose. He then lifted a thin black satchel onto his lap and withdrew a manila envelope from it, placing it on the table in front of him.

The waiter arrived with the Scotch, lifted it off his tray, and placed it on a silver-plated coaster.

Will that be all, gentlemen?

Thank you, for now, yes, said Mr. Aspinall. Jim watched the waiter in retreat. He reached forward for his beer.

Well, Jim? said Mr. Aspinall.

It was a success, said Jim.

What name did you choose? asked Mr. Aspinall. I've been curious.

Oh, I went with *Nyland, Officer Jim Nyland*. I've used it before, it keeps it close to Jim Nadeau — were someone I know to see me, call out my name. . . .

Very good, said Mr. Aspinall. And, tell me, did Trudy ask why the police are investigating me?

Jim reported he had done exactly as he'd been asked, postponed giving an answer and tried to avoid giving any response at all. But she was pushy on this point, he explained, so he used the fallback position: fraud.

Nothing she said led you to suspect she questioned your motives?

He shook his head no. We stayed focused on Andy Kronk. There was a short pause in the conversation. Jim had taken in a breath as if to speak, but held it for a minute, gathering his thoughts. I don't think, he began slowly, that she is as far along in her research as you might have thought. She has only concluded three or four interviews. She admitted, more or less, that she is stalled now.

Thank you for that observation. But she was intrigued at the prospect of getting to Kronk?

Very. As discussed, I suggested we arrange a weekend in May. I'm quite sure she felt she was being handed a gift, that it was her lucky break.

Now that Andy's moved up to that lake — for god knows what reason — I hope he stays put. I can't imagine it is much fun wintering there, said Stuart Aspinall more to himself than to Jim. Well, Mr. Aspinall sighed, this went well indeed.

Mr. Aspinall glanced down at the envelope, then back up at Jim, and smiled just a little. Mr. Aspinall stood. He reached into his breast pocket once again, this time producing a billfold. He unclipped a hundred dollar bill and placed it on the table, tucking the edge of it underneath the silver coaster. He returned the billfold and bifocals to his pocket.

Thank you, Mr. Aspinall, said Jim. But Mr. Aspinall had already turned to make his way out. The man simply lifted an arm up a little, raising a finger or two in the kind of belated reply that comes from someone who has already moved on in their thoughts and is over-accustomed to being thanked. Jim reached forward and pulled the envelope toward him.

In the distance the waiter worked behind the bar and other patrons were scattered here and there in clusters. In his corner, sunken into the leather chair, the heat billowing up around him, Jim was quite alone. He opened the envelope carefully. Out slid a cheque for ten thousand dollars. It was made out to Cash. The signatory on the cheque was not Mr. Aspinall, but was, rather, someone named Yuri Oshi. The name of the bank was written in an Asian language. He'd been hoping for bills. There was a Russian jeweller that Jim and a few other cops used for awkward banking like this. He'd drop in on him that afternoon. With that decided, Jim signalled with a raised hand across the dark library bar, and the waiter responded immediately weaving his way in through the tables to bring the bill. It came to just less than sixty dollars.

◆ ◆ ◆

Garlic and rosemary, medallions of beef, searing sea bass, espresso — the kitchen was open concept and Fiona could see and smell it all. She was forced to wait a few moments while the maître d' seated an older couple who had arrived at Gorgon and Zola's just before her, and, as she did so, she separated out the smells of the place. How many times had she eaten here? There was nothing on the menu she'd not tried — it was all beautiful — but the trout was her favourite. She'd walked out of the restaurant once before upon discovering they'd pulled it from the menu. It had been a signature dish of the place ever since. Yet, begrudgingly, she agreed with Kimberly who said — just recently — that it might be drifting from the best place to go, to be seen. But the food remained superior to anything else in Toronto; this restaurant could almost be in New York. It was inexplicable to her that an American restaurateur had not poached the head chef.

I've got bad news, said Kimberly as Fiona was seated. They are out of the trout; I know it's your favourite. Tell me you don't care there is no trout this once?

Fiona smiled and shook her head gently. Kimberly was forty pounds heavier than she'd been in high school. To Fiona, she looked fresh and happy to be sitting across the table from her. This was the way it was for her friends with kids. They went out much less often — although she and Kimberly somehow made it here almost monthly.

You look beautiful, said Fiona. Kimberly lurched theatrically in her chair and threw her hand over her heart.

What? said Kimberly. How long have I known you — twenty years? You've never once, in that entire time, said I looked beautiful.

Of course I have.

Fiona Aspinall! You are lying through your teeth.

Maybe I am, Fiona conceded. Is that terrible of me?

If that sort of thing mattered to me, I'd have stopped loving you years ago.

The word love, even casually, had never been used before between the two of them. It produced an odd breach in their conversation. A waiter swooped in and offered them wine lists, and ran over the specials.

And Ms. Aspinall, Chef Nguyen wanted me to let you

know the grouper is especially good this evening. They exchanged thank yous.

Wait, began Kimberly. See that table over there? The guy with the short hair. Isn't that someone?

It's pointless the way you do this, you know, notice people. Who is he?

Oh. Stop. Okay. I met him last year, said Fiona. At a thing in New York.

Was he nice?

We didn't really talk. There was a large group being annoyingly gregarious.

I can't remember his name, said Kimberly.

Neither can I. Is he an actor?

Probably. They all look the same, those people.

When are you going back to New York, to see your future president?

Christopher. Christopher Llewellyn, and I'm not sure. Maybe next week.

The conversation turned to Kimberly's children for a time.

Can I ask you something personal? said Kimberly, leaning in as their coffees arrived at the table. Fiona nodded. If you marry Christopher Llewellyn and move to New York, will you do it because you love him? They were quiet for a moment. I hope, continued Kimberly, that I don't sound naive, but some people still use it as a reason to get married. She smiled.

That word love again, thought Fiona. Kimberly, she began, I am never going to tell you that you look beautiful ever again if . . . But she stopped herself, and simply smiled.

I'm worried about you, said Kimberly.

Good god, why?

You are treating this relationship as a business merger.

From many angles, said Fiona, it is. Look, if it makes you feel any better I will sleep with him first and promise you that if he's horrible in bed, I won't go through with it. Kimberly smiled back at her, weakly.

You haven't asked me if I ever went to the play, said Fiona shifting the topic.

What play?

A Man's Castle.

I'd forgotten. When was it?

Last week.

You didn't!

I did.

I can't believe it. You're so unpredictable. What was it like?

Horrible acting. Abysmal production. I remember our high school production of *Guys and Dolls* being more professional.

You remember generously, said Kimberly.

The play has dated, said Fiona. Still, it did take me back. I got nostalgic in parts. My father used to recite some of the lines in a mock-Shakespearean actor's voice. Deep down, he loves that a play was written about us.

It's unflattering, said Kimberly.

For Dad, that's true only if you look at what it's trying to say. That it was written at all, that it needed to be, he takes as a great compliment, I think.

Your father is an odd duck.

No, if he's a bird, my father is more . . . She paused. He's more of an osprey. Everyone thinks he is noble and striking, but they forget he is circling them, watching from on high. He's a mannered savage. A handsome threat.

The waiter brought their bill with a smile.

That's a pretty grim description, said Kimberly.

I'll get it, said Fiona. Then added, In our family, surely the title of *odd duck* goes to Colin.

Officer Nyland? What a surprise, said Trudy.

I wondered if you could spare a few minutes? he said.

Of course, come in, she said.

Veronica and Anita were at the kitchen table. Occasionally Trudy's guilt at never making anything homemade would overwhelm her and she would sit the girls down and the three of them would bake something: usually cookies or brownies out of a box that never needed much more than an egg or a cup of milk. But it was the idea that she could send Anita home with something warm from the oven.

Girls, this is Officer Nyland. Both Veronica and Anita said nothing.

Hey, manners please.

Together they chimed, Hel-lo Officer Ny-land.

Trudy motioned for Jim to move into the living room. She caught a whiff of his aftershave. Patrick had not worn the stuff. He used to think it absurd to inflict more pain to the raw skin of his cheeks and neck.

Can we keep making them, Mommy? asked Veronica.

You can place them on the cookie sheet, but don't touch the oven until I get back. Okay?

Okay, they both answered and then giggled.

Sit, please. Only last year she'd bought herself a new suede sofa and oak end tables from a friend who owned an expensive shop. She'd got them at such a bargain it still made her proud. She loved the look of her new stuff. It would be new to her for years to come. She was like that, slow to incorporate change into her life. Slow to process the relative handsomeness of a police officer. Even slower to admit how much she missed Patrick.

For his part, Jim noted that the brown girl had a terrible cold, and was making cookies with hands that must have touched her runny nose. The other one looked startlingly like Trudy.

Can I get you a drink? she asked.

No, thank you. On the job. Maybe some other time though. After this is all over? he said.

Well, right to it then, she said. What have you got for me? She looked over his dimples and strong-looking forearms.

Jim reviewed Trudy's instructions. She was to call Andy Kronk. She was to go to his cottage up on Broad Lake. Stay at a B&B nearby, the name and address of which he'd given her on a piece of paper. She was to ask Andy whatever questions she might want, and to please use her best professional judgment, but eventually, what the police needed, he told her, was as much information on Mr. Stuart Aspinall as possible. Anything might be useful. Andy would know a great deal about Colin of course. It's possible the son is involved in the fraud as well. So everything on Colin is good information too.

I go more by instinct than anything else, but I get your point, she said.

Please tape the entire interview, so it can hold up in court.

I think it may take a couple of days. To get everything for both of us, she said.

Stay as long as you need. Get him as comfortable as you can. We will cover any expenses you might incur.

I won't take money from the police, she said. I'm comfortable in helping with your case, given what I'm getting out of it, but I'm writing a book. It's the optics.

I completely understand, he said. Let me know how it goes when you phone Andy. Assuming well, then you can confirm with me the date you are to leave.

Trudy let the door latch into place slowly. In the kitchen the girls were giggling in a continual stream. How did they stay so carefree? When, or more to the point, why, did that ever have to change?

Mommy, can we go and play at Anita's now?

Those look beautiful, girls! said Trudy as she entered the kitchen. Yes, you may go, but come back in half an hour. The cookies will be out in a few moments and cool enough to eat by then. I'll give you some to take back for your mother, Anita.

No sooner had she said this, Anita's face collapsed into a flood of tears. With Anita over so often, Trudy had a stash of Kleenex close at hand and she swooped in — as Patrick used to say with a laugh — with a mitt full of them as if Anita's head were a fly ball.

Darling, what on earth is wrong?

Anita did not speak.

She's sad, Mom, said Veronica.

Why is Anita sad?

Hearing this, Anita looked at Veronica with such confusion Trudy wondered if Anita had no idea why she was crying but was about to learn the horrible reason from her best friend.

Her dad is moving to Calgary.

Oh, darling, really? Well, that is sad isn't it! There was a pause. You'll miss him a lot, I'm sure.

Mom, she has to go with him. And with this Trudy's own daughter erupted into a great gush of tears that, in turn, only prompted Anita to cry harder herself.

Through her desperate attempt to convince the two of them to stop crying, she smelled something. The cookies. Burning. Shit.

No oven mitt. Should she use a wet J cloth? No. Open the oven door — let cold air in. Billows of smoke set the alarm off in a high-pitched wail, drowning out the two girls who were still crying but, due to the great noise of the alarm, seemed to be no longer making noise. She was fanning, frantically, at the smoke detector. Standing on a chair, Trudy ripped the alarm's plastic casing from the ceiling, picked at the battery to unsnap it. The noise ceased. The girls stopped too. She looked in the oven and pulled out charred hockey pucks where light fluffy cookie dough had gone in.

Daddy! said Veronica.

Trudy looked up to see her ex-husband, Patrick, standing at the kitchen door. Veronica leapt from her chair, giggling once more, as Patrick swept her up in a hug.

Let myself in, he said. Everything all right here?

There was a policeman here, Daddy. And Anita is leaving forever. The cookies are burned and the fire alarm went off. And Mom said a bad word. Patrick looked at Trudy with a smirk.

We're great here, she said, clearing away the smoke with wide dramatic sweeps of her arm. Everything is just great.

◆ ◆ ◆

Fiona and Christopher spent Friday night alone. They'd eaten at an Italian place in the Village, then had drinks next door at a bar. They needed to talk. Their childhoods, high school years, first serious relationships. Regrets. Successes. And plans for the future. They spent the longest time on this. They spoke in parallel lines. Never intersecting their visions of the future, rather laying them down side-by-side and admiring how closely they matched.

The senior partner at my firm is having a party tomorrow night, said Christopher.

I'm not sure. The minute we walk in the door . . .

People *are* already talking, he said.

How could they be?

Nothing is accidental in New York. That we were introduced, that was set up.

The senator was playing Cupid?

The senator was playing politics.

I know, I know. It's just that if we are seen together, there might be no stopping this. Are we ready? Do we know our lines?

They stayed at the party for an hour. That was all anyone there needed. As Fiona walked into the foyer, Christopher reached out and, casually, took hold of her hand. He smiled at the room generally. All the heads turned. There was not a Democrat in New York who was unaware of Christopher Llewellyn's political ambitions, or his potential.

Christopher, said his boss's wife, who do you have here?

My name is Fiona Aspinall, said Fiona before Christopher was able to introduce her.

She met them all. The name Aspinall made no impression on them, not immediately. But as she was pivoted from one group to another, she felt as if she were the moon, pulling behind her a tide of covert chatter. For a time Christopher left her side. She talked with the wife of a judge and learned all the gossip about the Court of Appeals for the Second Circuit. On the table beside her was a Tiffany lamp.

I hear your father is a Canadian tycoon, said the judge's wife after a time.

Oh, you must be mistaken, she said with a smile. We don't have tycoons in Canada; they make too much mess. They both laughed.

Yes, sweetie, said the woman, you'll need a sense of humour where you're going.

I'm not sure where that is just yet.

As one woman who never got there, to another who might, of course you do.

Back at Christopher's apartment they ordered Thai food. While they were waiting, Fiona drank a gin and tonic. His place was big for one person, and big for Manhattan, she thought. But its size didn't impress her. More that his rugs matched, were nicely angled, and had recent vacuum lines on them. And not clean so much as classy. The original artwork on the walls was neither conservative nor impossible to decipher. He had books, and framed photos of himself with groups of friends going back to college and high school. The faces that peered out at her looked as if they liked Christopher's company a great deal. He was in the centre of them all, surrounded by good cheer and warmth.

"You have taste," she said as the doorbell rang. They ate noodles and laughed, shared spring rolls dunked in sweet chili sauce. There was another gin and tonic, music. He lit several candles.

"I should go," she said finally, and stood. Now at eye level with a window, she looked out to the night sky. A glowing thin band of amber hung between the nearby buildings. He rose too, and moved closer, not touching her, but almost.

"Why don't you stay?" he asked. Fiona looked away momentarily, pressing together her lips. "The night . . ." he added without finishing his thought.

She *could* stay. It would mean taking off her clothes. It would mean this would be even more difficult to retreat from, if she needed to. No. She stopped herself from spiralling inward with questions too difficult to answer. Kimberly had been right. She had to open herself to this man if this was going to work. She knew all about him without knowing him at all. So it was something simple, even alluringly simplistic that, in the end, transformed her nervy inclination to stay into a firm decision.

Come with me, he said. She followed him into a glassed solarium.

Christopher flicked switches that turned on underwater lights and started up the hot tub's motors. He then busied himself by getting them each another drink, and lighting more candles. The moon was a wedge in the New York sky; she was surprised she could see it at all. She guessed that if someone wanted to, they could be seen, watched, from one of those buildings. Maybe they were. And, privately, she acknowledged this as a moment of change. From now on, her most personal moments would be public. She would cope. This, more or less, was how she'd lived her life up until now anyway. A life with Christopher would merely heighten the focus.

"I'll be back in a minute. Get in," he said.

She slid out of her clothes and into the water. Steam rose about her in the hot tub. She felt free in the total warmth of it. There was a faint smell of chlorine and cedar decking. Christopher returned and stepped in, displacing a wave of water over the edge. His body was thin and taut — from busyness rather than recent exercise. They laughed spontaneously. He moved to her side. Her head found a resting place in the crook of his neck. The candles he'd lit were flickering now in the steam and she looked at the fine whiskers on his throat, his eyebrows, and the light-grey wisps about his temples. She touched them all. Across the decking a film of water shimmered.

She woke next to him. Through the closed window, even up this high, she heard traffic, New York life. Today was Sunday, and across the city people were shopping, or getting dressed for church, or sitting in small groups talking as they watched their kids play in parks and on sidewalks. She supposed, fleetingly, other people were likely engaged in any number of activities important to them, or not. Who were these Americans? Why did they believe — rich and poor — they deserved it all? But, mostly, she was aware of an unfamiliar expression on her face. She was grinning. Her hand ran down and across the skin of her body and she felt the morning sun, the happy warmth of it, on her shoulders, thighs, and chest.

PART TWO

Andy Kronk watched as Trudy Clarke placed the tape recorder on his coffee table. She looked up at him smiling.

I'm going to make a note for my records, she said. It might be months before I transcribe it. Trudy said this apologetically, as if he must endure some tedious administrative procedure, but the task took all of ten seconds.

This interview — she began to speak right at the recorder — is number seven for the Aspinall Project. Mr. Andy Kronk is a long-standing family friend. Code this transcript for chapters two and three, and the conclusion. Then Trudy looked up once more, giving him another smile of reassurance.

Oh, I'll be fine, he said.

Of course you will, she said. It'll be a cinch.

I'm a lawyer. I'm used to taping myself. Notes for dictation. That sort of thing. I'm not practising law at the moment, he added without being sure why.

We have lots of time, she said. I can stay as long as need be. We'll get to it all.

On the shelf behind Trudy were his stacks of books, magazines, and articles printed off the Internet — all about antique furniture. The various styles and periods. Famous makers. How to refinish and repair. How to spot a fake from an original. How to craft a fake to look just like an original. When Andy had left the practice last year he'd sold his condo and stocks, eaten the steep lease penalty on the Audi. He was too young to be worth more than a promise of a wealthy future, but his lifestyle illustrated this promise. The bank financed it. He got out with enough for this simple cottage on a remote lake and a ten-year-old Toyota pickup.

Andy had been dating a colleague, Sondra. The long hours at work found them together more often than not. Both had histories of half-hearted relationships. They had commiserated together from time to time over a quick dim sum lunch, or pressure-relieving Heinekens at the chrome and frosted-glass bar in the basement of their office tower in downtown Toronto. He had found Sondra smart, if harsh-featured, and egregiously driven by work. She was attractive without being completely appealing. When, eventually, drunker than he realized, he proposed they sleep together, she said nothing more than, *Sure, why not.* The sex turned out to be better than he'd anticipated. That one time, fuelled by mutual laziness and mutual cynicism, grew toward habit.

Do you think I'm cheap? she asked him on a Tuesday morning at his place.

Do you care what I think?

I didn't used to, she said. I might be starting to. Can you handle that?

Can you?

Gradually, he found there were parts of Sondra that were as soft as regular women. She smelled good, as well. After sex, she did not talk too much. She was content to just be next to him, still, and offer the odd, wistfully contemplative insight in response to his own contemplatively wistful observation.

Are you interested in coming to my family's cottage for a weekend? she asked as they waited for lattes — they had taken to having morning coffee together whenever they could fit it in. Sure, he said. Why not. This was becoming *their* line. One that cast doubt and the cool safety of irony on anything coming from the heart.

Nothing they had previously said or done hinted that they'd moved to some new level, or were ready to spend a weekend together away, let alone meeting family. He vaguely assumed he was being used as a pawn in one familial game or another, and didn't much care. *Sure, why not.*

Later that week, right in a meeting with a potential client, Sondra slid him a doodle of a canoe with two pairs of legs sticking up out of its gunwales. She winked.

What's going on here? he said to her afterward.

Humour, she answered. Other men find me funny you know. Don't you ever laugh?

Where are these other men now?

Are you suggesting they were just humouring me?

Sondra's family cottage was on a large, well-appointed lake that supported a prestigious weekender community. Sondra's father, Leyland, a retired lawyer himself, had recently taken a watercolour painting course at a local community college.

It's just something I'd always wanted to do, he told Andy. Wife thought I was nuts. I said, man's got to keep busy. Beer?

Leyland went on to talk about getting the paints, buying supplies, going on picnics to paint a covered bridge in Prince Edward County, a railway viaduct in Northumberland, and a lift lock in the Trent-Severn waterway. He'd seen half of Ontario. Never knew how much of it was out there. All because, he said with great aplomb, I opened my eyes.

Hearing him tell it, the man had found god, or if not that, then at least something richer than the law. Sitting on the deck nursing beers, motorboats pulling water skiers as they swished past with an affluent wave, he confided further in Andy.

I wasted my time practising law. Hated it. I'm good with my hands. I've got a bit of a knack for this painting. I might even put together a showing next year with some of the others from my class. But, it's all too late. I've realized too damn late that I should have dedicated myself to painting beautiful things. Not structuring real estate deals for developers.

But you have time to do it now, Andy said simply. You can afford to do it.

I'm not well, he said.

Sondra had mentioned.

Haven't been since the first operation. Takes its toll, Andy. You think it's all going to pass. That things will get back to normal. They don't. Normal is a man's vision of the future. Once the future itself is compromised, then normal isn't possible any longer.

What are you boys talking about down there? Sondra and her mother were up on the verandah. Need anything? They waved and smiled.

Andy was relieved to hear Sondra's voice calling to them. It broke the moment.

Sondra's driven, said Leyland.

She's a success all right, said Andy.

She's been a success since she was able to walk and talk, said Leyland. Went to the same law school that I did. When she graduated, boy. I'll never forget that day. Yep, she's following her old man all the way.

During the car ride back to the city, Andy wondered if he'd been too quick to see the older man's talk as sad. Over a summer at university, he had worked at an antique store. Spent hours engrossed in the history of furniture. He'd already decided on law school, but for several weeks he'd fantasized about changing course. He would deal in antiques. Yes, he would learn it all, become an expert, and buy and sell all around the world. Live a simple life with nothing to look after but himself, his store, and his customers' esoteric collections.

Why was he with Sondra, just passively letting this attraction between them metastasize? Was this the future he had dreamed of in boarding school, the covers pulled up under his chin? Then, he'd wanted only to play hockey. When did the law become his dream? Had he properly questioned this? Had he cheated himself out of happiness? Should he be in the antiques trade? Had he taken a wrong turn?

He called in sick to work on the Monday. And again the following Thursday. Then he announced he was taking a week of vacation — for personal reasons. During this time, he committed to doing the unthinkable: quitting the firm and completely extricating himself from his life.

You took my father seriously? said Sondra once he was done explaining himself. They were at the bar in the lobby of their building. A senior partner was within earshot drinking with a client. They spoke in harsh whispers so she couldn't hear.

Your father's full of regrets, he said.

He's dying, Andy. He loved the law. Everyone knows that. It was his one great passion. He doesn't regret his life. He just doesn't want to die, that's all. The man's scared.

Don't you ever think this is a superficial existence? asked Andy more to himself than to Sondra.

Do what you want, she said, but don't do it because my sick father told you to. Are you having a breakdown?

I just don't feel sure that this is what I'm supposed to be doing.

Last year I went through this period where all I could think of was having a baby. A friend told me that my body's biology was *busting out of my intellectual corset*. I loved that line. Anyway, you know what I did? I had sex, unprotected sex, with two separate guys on nine different occasions over three months. Nothing. Period was right on time each month. So I figured, must not have been meant to be.

Was that your attempt at empathy?

No, sorry Andy. You are right. Throw everything away. *Sure, why not.* I don't give a fuck what you're feeling. She became aware that their boss might be able to hear her, so she leaned in and whispered again. Andy, you're a sweet guy. You're an ordinary lawyer. I very much enjoyed sleeping with you. But, as my father used to say, it's eat or be eaten. She stood and placed her hand on his shoulder. I'd have made a bitch-of-a-Filipino-nanny-hiring mother anyway. She gave him a sharp squeeze. Take care, she said.

He thought her voice warbled a touch at the end. Had she been trying to have a child with him too? The sex they'd had happened so recklessly. And it had set a tone they'd continued on with. He'd assumed she was on the pill. You don't ask a woman who thinks of everything if she's on birth control.

Sondra? She was already gone.

He sat for an hour longer at the bar by himself.

It took several months to fully extricate himself, but by the fall he'd bought the cottage and had begun to teach himself the fundamentals of the antique business from reference books. The winter had been long and nights blended into one long sleep. He lost weight. He began to design furniture, drawings, sketches. He listened to the radio for company and went into town for groceries once every few days, or to get gas for his truck.

Then the letter from Trudy arrived.

His whole life had tracked him down in her letter. There was no new beginning.

Let's start, Trudy said; the tape was recording. Tell me about the time before you first met the Aspinalls? I'm looking for what it was like — the context in which you came into their . . . He watched as she struggled, as if trying to choose the best of three worthy phrases; circle of influence was what she finally chose.

He was immediately relieved that Trudy was not going to pretend, the way some did, that the Aspinalls were just another comfortably well-off family.

Her hands were smooth. Did a manicurist do her nails and cuticles? Either that or she was fastidious about her appearance. But she didn't look the type. He guessed she was the sort who would spoil herself occasionally. Duck away to a spa. Guilty and pleasurable.

When it came to his own hygiene, he had let himself go up here. Before she arrived he drove into town for a haircut, and did several loads at the Laundromat. He scrubbed the kitchen floor, found mould under the sink.

Start with your story, she was saying. Tell me all about Andy. What was Andy Kronk like way back when — before he met the Aspinalls?

Andy's eyes drifted over her shoulder to outside. The sun was climbing higher in the sky and the light ricocheted in all directions off the lake. There was a single red canoe with a man kneeling in the stern, paddling a run of even, firm J-strokes. A woman sat tucked in the bow. She had binoculars. She was bird-watching. Andy had seen them doing this together almost every day for the past month. He had come to understand they were studying the local osprey.

Perhaps, Trudy said breaking the silence, you'd like to talk about something more recent. Getting started can be hard. Tell me about yourself; you're moving into antiques?

When I moved to the cottage this past fall, he began, I figured I could turn the shed out back into a workshop. You know, begin to refinish pieces, until I had enough. Then, my plan was, is still I guess, to open a store in one of the nearby towns. Antiques do well up here: lots of retirees, old Toronto money, taking day trips. I thought I'd settle down — lead a quieter life.

And is it? Quieter?

In a way, Andy said. The morning sun bounced off the lake and into the trees outside the kitchen window. He remembered the recent winter winds. How they had whipped about the cottage, finding entries in a hundred compliant cracks and joints. Weather's nicer now, he continued, but the place just about froze me to death in February. It's going to need a lot more work than I'd been counting on.

And your workshop? It's coming along?

I don't know if I can make enough money up here to live on. I've been thinking lately I might have to go back to practising law, part-time. He gave her a weak smile. It was the first time he'd admitted this to anyone. He hated the sound of it aloud.

Andy experienced a wave of guilt. He'd been alone for so many months he'd begun to behave irrationally. When Trudy arrived this morning, he'd watched from his bedroom window as she'd stepped from her car and walked toward his cottage, a small tote bag slung over her left shoulder and a clutch purse in her right hand. Then she'd stopped. Keys in hand, she turned. Pointed them at her vehicle. Its lights flashed. Horn briefly sounded. Who, did she suppose, was going to steal her car up here? Was she brave to visit him alone, or foolhardy? She didn't know him. Simply that he was a friend of the Aspinalls. Was that, in itself, substantiation of character?

With Trudy's car locked and alarmed, walking toward his door, she'd looked purposeful and well groomed. The coffee Andy'd had was churning in his stomach. He should have eaten. She was almost at the door. Her skin was tight on her face and it made her look younger than someone who had hair so greying. She had small, rectangular glasses. Knocking. He stole a few more seconds, peering at her through the slit between the curtains in the bedroom that looked out onto the front grass. She checked her watch, waiting.

In the kitchen she'd stood with her back to him, looking outside at the lake while he brewed tea. They chatted about her trip; did she find the turnoff at the highway, him feigning relief that his directions — ones he knew were precise — were at all adequate.

Would you prefer Earl Grey or English Breakfast? Do you think you'll be comfortable at the B&B? If there is anything more I can do to make you feel comfortable . . . just ask.

She defended ably against his graciousness. What a lovely lake. How jealous I am! This, she pronounced, is the ideal life.

Mr. Aspinall used to say that no politer conversation could be held than that between two Canadians on first meeting. Canadians, he was known to remark either during a formal dinner speech or a witty Canadian Club luncheon, were *antagonistically* polite. And the audience, Canadian, would laugh politely, and then pause, only to laugh self-consciously a second time. They are perfectionists, continued Mr. Aspinall with the intent of wounding the already wounded, at putting the needs of another before their own. If Canadians have a common trait, it's an ability to make nice — no matter the cost.

Yet, Mr. Aspinall was as Canadian as one could be. Was he not, therefore, also gently insulting himself? Andy had long ago understood the paradox at work, that being Mr. Aspinall was both quintessentially Canadian, all the while being stations above his birthplace. He had taken on the trappings of a British accent — he went to school there for a brief time. It was this across-the-pond ease that afforded him enough detachment to get away with these observations. It was the Aspinall name, a name as Canadian as cold, that gave him the authority to make them in the first place.

Andy poured Trudy and himself a cup of tea. As he did, the background noise of CBC radio produced Trudy's voice. She was being interviewed about her previously published biography. They stopped, involuntarily, and listened.

Is this live? asked Andy with a smile.

Evidently, it was a radio interview she had given months ago, an "encore" presentation. Trudy was, naturally enough, embarrassed and apologized for this kind of gratuitous success. Canadians do not, Mr. Aspinall liked to say, prefer a winner. They don't even like a fellow if he's in the top three. Now fourth, contended Mr. Aspinall, fourth showed aptitude, left open the possibility that a better result might have been achieved were the top three competitors not so unrelenting. When Mr. Aspinall used a word like unrelenting in this context, he meant American — as any Canadian knew full well. Fourth, he would continue, was the ideal position for a Canadian to finish: a good outcome, but not crudely so, and at fourth and just one off the podium, Canadians positioned themselves for a prize more coveted by them than any shiny gold, silver, or bronze medal — a chance to display publicly just how polite and impossibly good-natured they were after having come so close.

Trudy commented that her voice sounded oddly thin on the radio. Andy leapt at this, apologized for the age of his machine, that it came with the place and that it was beyond the limit of laziness that he shouldn't have purchased a new one by now. But her voice continued to articulate her previous book. She was eloquent and charming, well read, and dextrously apologetic for its popularity.

· Andy recalled that Mr. Aspinall referred to people like Trudy as "professional Canadians." If they are not cleverly ridiculing me in magazine columns or plays, then they are holding galas honouring me so they can raise the money to finance them. Either way, he'd scoff, families like ours are needed; we are the perpetual hosts on which they feed.

Trudy asked him to turn the volume down. It was making her feel awkward, self-conscious. Of course, of course, he apologized, and promptly turned it right off. In the silence that followed, as if on cue, a loon called out across the lake.

They sat in silence, sighing once in a while, the musical exhales acting as words, which said — very clearly between two Canadians — such things as: that it is nice to be up here and out of the city, and sorry to be intruding, and, in response, I hope you'll enjoy your stay, and sorry the B&B accommodations are so meagre.

About Canadians, his own kind too after all, Andy had learned a great deal from Mr. Aspinall. In this case, with the sighing back and forth, that even when Canadians were not speaking in hand-wringing double negatives, they were, at least, being polite — if not outright pre-emptively apologizing for some, as yet to occur, affront. An affront that itself would never occur due to their nationality.

Mr. Aspinall's imposing voice was all around him. Talking to him as if he were in the room, as if he and Andy had only recently stopped having private conversations. He knew well enough that Trudy would ask him about Mr. Aspinall at length. But what should he be guarding against?

I guess it all starts with hockey.

Okay, good, she said.

I'd played an away game in Mississauga. Hockey was my life, my dad's life too. He was proud of me.

Did he push you? Was he one of those demanding hockey parents you read about?

Yes. I guess he did, I guess so.

How old were you at this point?

Fourteen.

Do you resent him for the way he pressed you into the sport?

Somehow after Trudy's initial coaxing and pleasantries over tea, Andy, tentatively, had found a way to begin. Trudy began to nod, to smile at him and his answers. It made him feel as if *his* past — and not just as it related to the Aspinall's — had some value to her book, even though he knew full well it did not.

As Andy spoke, he found himself drawn to Trudy, to her eager questions and easy charm. She really listened. No one ever asked him to talk about his boyhood. In the absence of sisters, brothers, or, for a long while, a parent, having an in-depth conversation about childhood was rare. These flashes of memory were from a long time ago.

As a teenager, Colin had pumped him with questions, eager to hear him talk about life at his old high school in Scarborough. He had never found another friend equal to Colin. When he lost Colin to New York City, to having simply grown up and apart the way men do, he lost the appetite to connect with others as deeply as he had done with Colin.

And all Trudy was doing was baiting him, following her instincts, and chasing down a story. Was this different from a lawyer with a witness on the stand? Tease the truth out, one knot at a time. It's not complicated. Everyone's vulnerabilities are a tangle of family secrets and childhood traumas. Then, Mr. Aspinall's voice sounded inside him as clearly as if the man were standing only feet away: ancient wounds leave the likeliest scars. It made no difference that, intellectually, he knew what she was doing, and how, and why. He was defenceless; he was willing. With each word came an inner rush, release, and roar. This was his story. And up until now, no one had ever asked to hear it.

I think it's a woman.

You sure?

No, wait. Yes, she's a woman. She locked her suv. You know, like, remotely. The lights flashed.

She set the alarm?

Yes, I assume so.

Up here?

Habit. Probably. Should I start paddling?

Let's just drift for a bit. Jot this stuff down. Time of arrival.

You think this visit might be important?

She's got a briefcase, hasn't she?

The septic tank inspector?

God. They've done that already. You've got to let that go. We missed it. The guy could have come before eight or after six. This is something new. Paddle us in closer, and then we'll do a wide loop over to the spot.

You hungry? I'm hungry. How come you don't eat in the mornings?

Just don't.

Women are strange.

Not to women they're not. Look, it's nothing. I can't face food before lunch, that's all. I could go for a coffee though.

Oh, look. Neat. There's the osprey.

◆ ◆ ◆

I'd grown taller and heavier than most of my teammates, said Andy. But I stayed fit during the summer, playing road hockey and getting ice time when I could. Also began at the gym, lifting weights. I stayed fast on the ice and being big for my age, I stood out. Could hit harder than most. I was a goal scorer too.

Trudy began to write on a small yellow notepad, as if the tape-recording wasn't enough. This, too, seeing her writing down his words made them truer and permanent, and somehow fed him strength to push on.

We were in Mississauga for a tournament, which we won easily. I'd played well. After the game I saw my dad talking to my coach along with other parents. That's when the LSC kids walked into the arena.

She lifted, politely, a finger asking him to pause. Did you know anything about the school? she asked. Anything about the Aspinalls then, before you saw the Lord Simcoe College students walk in to the arena?

No. Nothing. It was the first time I'd ever heard of Lord Simcoe College. I grew up in Scarborough. These kids were unimaginable to me. Where I came from, we didn't know any private-school kids. So when this group of about maybe thirty LSCers entered the arena, it was completely foreign to me. It felt like we were on a movie set.

Why were they there, hockey?

The LSC first team was due to play next. They bussed the students all there as supporters, to cheer the team on. I remember wondering: what kind of school is able to make its students come out to a friendly hockey game against another high school, just to cheer? It was abnormal.

Trudy stood up and stretched, walking over to his book-shelf. She picked up a large, rectangular book on Upper Canadian pine furniture restoration.

But you found them alluring too, she said, putting down the book and turning to face him.

I couldn't take my eyes off them. Their haircuts were perfect — the latest from magazines or celebrities. I think I was amazed that kids like this existed in Canada at all. I thought to look that perfect you had to be American.

That's funny, she said without laughing.

I swear to you, I was so naive. It never occurred to me that there were rich people in Canada because I'd never been to where they lived.

Tell me, what were they like? This was, what, 1985? All Polo and argyle? What were your first impressions?

I would have called them preppies. That was the word then. But they were not like the ones at my school in Scarborough. The smarter clique who dressed in fake, pink alligator shirts — they'd seen too many teen movies. Their families weren't much different than anyone else's.

They dressed that way as a teenage affectation, you mean? It was how they perceived moneyed kids would?

Exactly.

But the LSC students . . .

Looked completely different. Some wore ties. The school crests on their blazer pockets. To me, they were exotic and the height of cool.

Why are you smiling? Trudy sat back down.

At how young I was, the things I wanted. I was impressionable at that age.

Isn't everyone at fifteen?

Sure, but understand: it was impossible for me to imagine back then that anyone who wore a tie would not have been thrown into a locker and pounded as the worst kind of misfit. Yet here was a gang of these guys, confident, cool, and talking to girls.

So tell me what the girls were like?

The sweet of watermelon lip gloss, the tangy sour of kisses planted on the hot outer side of panties, the feel of breasts through Roots sweaters, the recalcitrant bra snaps, shaved thighs, clavicles, the heaving rise and fall of rib cages — this was all later, at a fall party deep in a southwestern Ontario field of wheat; on a summer's evening in the Aspinalls' pool house, while Colin's parents holidayed, oblivious, in Martinique; cottage docks at night under the aurora borealis. He would discover in precious half-inches the motivating signs and plays of their forming bodies, and they his. But on first glance in that arena, it was simpler.

They were gorgeous, Andy said. Suede or leather jackets over their school uniforms and they all had this long, thick blond or brown hair, perfectly made up, white, straight teeth. To my inexperienced and poor eyes, the whole group of them, the guys and girls, they made up a chorus of latter-day teen idols. I remember staring as they moved in a huddle through the arena to occupy an entire section of the stand. When the LSC team came on the ice, they stood up on the seats in the stands, and, instead of chanting, they sang. Hymns. You know, ones like, "Guide Me Oh Thou Great Jehovah" and "Onward Christian Soldiers."

Keep in mind where I was from. Scarborough. These kids were from Rosedale and Forest Hill. Some of them were boarders from England, or America, or Hong Kong. This wasn't normal high-school student behaviour. They floated above everyone and everything else in their own solar system, orbiting each other — little pedigree moons and comets held by a force that common everyday people, like myself, couldn't be part of.

What happened then?

Well, later my father was standing in front of me with a tall, fit-looking, older man. Dad says something like, Andy, this is Dr. Tilford. He's the coach of the team that's about to play. He's a teacher at a private school. He liked what he saw of your game. That's how I remember it, anyway. Then I think Dr. Tilford took over speaking. Of course I wasn't to have known this at the time, but his impossibly low voice — and Andy paused, dropped his chin to his chest and threw his voice down as many octaves as he could manage before going on — you should have heard it.

Goodness.

Yes, we all made fun of it. His booming voice was going to be in the background of my life for the next four years.

What was he like?

Dr. Tilford? Even in February he had his trademark golden tan. His hair was white and thinning, but he wore it a little too long — and he always combed it straight back. He liked me, but no more than his other players. He was fair, I think.

Did he like Colin?

I don't think he would have ever spoken to Colin. Colin hated sports. Dr. Tilford coached hockey, and taught phys. ed. Then Andy's mind snagged a fragment of memory. It came too quickly and the feeling of it left almost as quickly. It was the summertime following his first year at LSC.

Why? asked Colin. Why do you have to go? Stay here with me. They were together at Huntington House. Colin was lying on his bed. Andy was stretched out beneath him on the floor, resting his head on his propped up arm.

I have hockey practice, he said.

Hockey is for . . .

Say it, he said. But Colin did not finish his thought.

Don't ever tell me what to do.

I have to go to hockey today, he said. Tilford will kill me.

Tilford likes little boys, said Colin.

He does not. Why do you say that?

Trust me, said Colin. My dad told me to stay away from him, that he's got a history from other schools. Dad says he'll get what he deserves one day. I'll just call the headmaster's secretary and say you are sick. She'll get a note to Tilford.

Andy had fallen silent, his thoughts were unuttered. Outside, a loon had called across the lake. The sound startled Andy. He looked out at the lake, the scene lit by a frail sun where, only a few months ago, there had been thick ice stretching away from the shore. The ice retreated in only a few weeks — the treads of the snowmobiles, his snowshoe tracks, changing states and erasing into the lake.

Andy watched as Trudy looked down at her notes. What was she thinking?

Were you excited? she asked. I mean, a coach from a fancy private school. Isn't that the kind of attention every budding hockey player hopes for?

I'd had scouts interested before that. My father dealt with them. He wanted me to wait another year before making any commitments. He wanted me to be able to take my pick. Hang back son, he'd say. Wait for the right opportunity. Let's not jump too early.

But that's not what happened, obviously.

Dr. Tilford offered to have me train at LSC over the summer. They had their own rink and ran coaching clinics for their teams. They needed good players to mix with their teams, train with them, compete, and push them. Sparring partners. Wouldn't I like to have as much free ice time as I wanted, for a whole summer? This was essentially the offer Dr. Tilford put on the table.

What did your father think of that?

Oh, my father couldn't believe our luck. It wasn't close to our house, but he didn't care. On the way home in the car he told me how it happened. He was standing there with a group of parents when Dr. Tilford had approached them, asking if any of them knew who this Kronk star was. Kronk star. My father had loved that — he said it again and again for months. *Hey, Kronk star, pass the milk*, you know.

You made him proud.

I guess. Of course, he'd quickly owned up to being my dad and they began to talk. The deal, I later gathered had been struck well before I was even introduced.

Outside the window, Andy's eye caught a glint of sun reflecting off the birdwatchers' equipment. They'd taken to setting up camp on the other side of the lake and camouflaging themselves in a lean-to so as not to be seen by the ospreys. They had some impressive equipment — all green or brown clothes, high powered binoculars. He almost envied the dedication they had to their hobby. Perhaps they were professionals, working for the ministry of the environment? Were things different right now, he'd have called out to them, invited them over for lunch someday.

All the way home, driving along the 401, my father spoke of how a summer of endless ICE TIME would improve my game. *All for free, for free Andy!* my dad kept saying, *with world-class coaches too.* But my head was elsewhere.

You didn't want these things?

All I could think about were neckties and suede jackets, school songs, perfect haircuts. I desperately wanted to be a part of it. I knew we were not rich, in fact I knew we were occasionally almost poor, but I decided something that night in the car on the way home. I was going to play hockey so well, they were going to let me go there. This LSC would be *the* opportunity. I mumbled something to feel out my father on the idea, maybe they'd let me play for them? Maybe I could go to that school after the summer?

How'd he react?

He said that I didn't understand how these things worked. Besides, he said, they're not a competitive hockey school. He didn't want to dampen either my enthusiasm or his own good mood. He wanted me to play . . . well, not that we'd ever uttered it aloud — it was bad luck to look something so godly in the face — but he and I both knew that he had long ago decided that I was going to take a run at the NHL.

That sounds like a lot of pressure on a young man.

Me and every other kid in the Golden Horseshoe. My father was a practical man. Everything he saw in my game, stick handling, size, speed, checking, were aspects other coaches and scouts saw too. His dream felt plausible. So, it wasn't undue pressure. Nothing would stand in his way of providing me with that chance. He felt it was his duty, I think, the role of a good father. That Kronk star. It was his motivation to work hard, where he spent every extra cent of overtime wages he made. Hockey was all we talked about.

But you saw a glimpse of another life. LSC might be a chance for you to become your own man, on your own terms?

Andy was in the car again, the lights of Toronto flying by on the 401. The night had been cold and the windows of his father's Pontiac Grand LeMans were fogged up on the inside. He drank an Orange Crush, taking long gulps to quench his thirst after the game. His father smoked Export As, grinding the stub into the ashtray, or flicking it out a crack of rolled-down window. The exits flew by in a blur, Yonge Street, Bayview Avenue, the Don Valley Parkway.

I wanted, Andy said to Trudy — simply, honestly — for hockey to take me somewhere else altogether.

He'd spent many hours travelling Ontario in that car. Brantford, Hamilton, Peterborough, London, Owen Sound, Windsor. Tournaments, tryouts, playoffs. But it was that night that came back so clearly. He'd grown moody and dissatisfied with his life in Scarborough. He'd often fantasized about becoming rich. He knew that he needed to somehow move up in the world, to get out, or he'd become like his father, grease to his core.

Outside the window that night there were better cars, houses with double, even triple garages. Beautiful girls too. He had wanted it all. With the speed and lights of the moment, and the high of the game still strong, he made a promise to himself. There would be no more portable classrooms and skipping math class to roll joints cut with so much tobacco they hardly made a lick of difference. No more suffering scornful looks at the hands of headbanger chicks with big hair dating older losers at the local community college because they drove rusted Trans Ams, or easy younger ones in the grade below who'd give him and his two friends hand jobs behind the convenience store after hockey practice for five bucks apiece, or, if they were short, a stolen packet of Players regular. No more Saturday afternoons catching the TTC downtown to shoplift AC/DC T-shirts or Iron Maiden stickers from head shops up and down Yonge Street. No more fake IDs boldly stating they were 27 years old and from Newark, New Jersey, or paying a neighbour to go to the Brewers' Retail for a two-four of Labatt's Blue. No more friends' brothers with greasy long hair who would sit baked in a basement at something someone had promised would be a party, no more listening to them and their three stoner friends play Neil Young or Rush on guitar over and over again.

There had been a girl from those days. She'd come to his hockey practices and met him behind the arena. She was more than a year younger than he had been — thirteen maybe? How did he talk her into what she'd done with them? And he laughed at her with his teammates both before and afterward. During whatever she was game for that week, he was silent, hopeful, and full of shit-hot lust. Shameful even then, yes, but he'd gone along with it, wanting it, wanting her, being revolted by himself and his desires, and then, only moments later, revolted by her for agreeing to fulfill them. Where was she now? Did she escape too? What was her name? He hoped, suddenly, that wherever she was now, that she couldn't remember his. In LSC, he had glimpsed another existence, a higher calling.

Tears came upon him in a sudden wave, up his stomach and throat, hot and full with a raw ache. He got to his feet and headed for the bathroom with his forearm pushing up into his mouth. He shut the bathroom door. He dropped to his newly installed toilet bowl. The face of that girl trying to look as if she enjoyed the mouthing of his dick, his father at the dinner table quizzing him on the weekend's game, his bedroom with pictures of Wendel Clark and the Calgary rookie Joe Nieuwendyk, the ripe smell of his jersey as he pulled it over his head. He came on her sweater once accidentally. His friends laughed when he told them, patted him on the back.

His friendship with Colin had buoyed him above all this. What could keep him afloat now? Andy splashed water on his face and collected himself, pressing the towel into his eyes. He felt tired, but calm. He returned to find Trudy sitting in the chair in which he'd been sitting.

You were telling me about that night, the drive home. Your secret plan to go to LSC? Her voice was even and without discomfort or accusation. He was thankful.

We pulled onto Warden Avenue. My mind was made up. I was going to wear one of those white button-down shirts, and a tie, and one of those girls with perfect eyes and smiles would be my girlfriend. I was going to go to LSC. This was my new trophy to chase. I knew everything stood in my way, sure, but sitting there listening to my dad talk about the game I'd played that night, I figured, so what? I could already play hockey better than everyone on the LSC senior team. What could possibly matter more? This Dr. Tilford would soon see that. He'd talk my father into it. I thought nothing could hold me back.

Trudy stopped the tape with a smile and scratched some notes on her pad. He looked, furtively, but couldn't quite see what she was writing. They seemed to be points outlining general topics he'd covered. To find them quickly later, he guessed. He was saying things that she'd need to find again.

Andy looked at her as she wrote. The way she scrunched up her nose and small lines fanned out from her eyes. She used silence to her advantage. Even now, by pausing the conversation and writing, she held the control through silence. The ability not to talk came from a place of calm confidence, he supposed.

When *he* was nervous, he talked more. It had let him down in court, now that he thought about it. Yet, she just posed a question and waited. A whole minute if need be while he thought, then squirmed, then lurched at an answer, talking his way in and out and around what he wanted to say, or should have said. How did she say nothing, when something, anything would fill the void?

He watched her writing notes, sighing little bursts of air, pushing strands of hair behind her ears. She looked up at him every now and then, the corner of her mouth flickering in a semi-conscious smile, politely thanking him for his patience.

Andy stood and walked to the window, letting Trudy write on in private. He looked up at the osprey's nest perched high on an electrical pole that rose into the sky down the shoreline. Every morning the osprey left its young, swooping and soaring, riding the air currents in search of fish or mice. He remembered the vole he'd seen yesterday. Its curious blindness to life giving it an air of profundity as it went on its way. But no, it was simply a blind rodent. Mr. Aspinall loathed anthropomorphic impulses.

Dogs dressed as humans. Talking parrots. Andy had always agreed. Humans project so much meaning where none exists. It's needy, in a way.

Since moving to Broad Lake, Andy found himself prone to contemplating, at great length, abstract ideas. The vole had inspired several hours of thought on the nature of meaning itself, and, eventually, whether or not meaning even matters. He thought for so long on the word *matter* that it eventually collapsed on itself, losing all meaning and becoming a ludicrous jumble of letters. Prior subjects he had been stuck on included the subjectivity of morality — after he'd seen a dead deer on the side of the road — and the stupidity in the way humans impose narratives on history; that is, there is no *story* while an event is occurring, only afterward. There had been others.

Inevitably, all these hours led to a ruminating on death. Not always his own, but sometimes. How long did a life last? There were the years the person lived of course. But beyond, after the last sibling, friend, or acquaintance who knew a person died represented a second death. For then there were only secondary sources left — letters, film, artifacts — from which a person's character may be interpreted or deduced. And beyond that? Letters can be destroyed, film disintegrates, and personal articles and items are willed, or sold, and then re-sold until their provenance is untraceable. What then of the person? Did they ever exist? Is a name on a parish-archived marriage certificate, or an entry in a half-century old phone book stored in a public library, or a queer face peering out from the middle row of the Salvation Army Band photograph like the one he'd seen at a local antique shop, still *really* a person?

On Andy's drive to and from town there were three old churches. He'd seen couples pulled over at the side of the road wandering through the graveyards. He did it too, though alone. At first, the baby's headstones affected him the most. What, he wondered, had they died of: polio, influenza, tetanus, birth? Then he began to search out the longest-lived, the dates with the greatest spread. One woman lived eighty-six years, having died in 1899. Her name was Henrietta Dawling.

That night he'd not been able to sleep. He began to read a book on Gothic revival furniture, but his mind continued to wander to the graveyard, the dates, and names. Out of curiosity he looked up the surname Dawling in the local phone book. No entry. He returned to his book of dark furniture disappointed.

The next day, after he bought groceries and gas, he stopped by the local library. Making up a story about himself having Dawlings on his mother's side of the family, he enlisted the librarian in helping him to track down information on the woman. They came up with nothing. They looked in registries and newspapers, on town lists and church records. He went home wondering what was the point of living for eighty-six years without there being a single record of oneself one hundred years later? This won't, he reasoned, be true of the Aspinalls. They will be able to be scrutinized for generations. Was this fair? Why them? Why did heredity only deal some such a kind hand? Every family, he thought in a blaze of egalitarianism, should have a biography written about them, no matter how unimportant they are.

Early spring had been a time fraught with difficult decisions. Trudy had sent the letter in which she provided an outline of her project. It was simply addressed to "Dear interviewee." Andy had not responded. He wasn't sure how to react. Then later she called. Had he received the letter? Would he be willing to do an interview? Andy told her he'd think about it. Meanwhile, he searched for Mrs. Dawling.

He knew Trudy Clarke's name, had heard of her. He knew that she was a real, bona fide writer, but he went back to the local library — this time knowing he'd find what he was looking for. Trudy's publication list seemed impressive to his untrained eye. In her authorized biography of A. P. Hawn she had all but resurrected the former politician's reputation. Yet, her unauthorized biography of Justice Ted Clifford, Andy read in an old *Globe and Mail* article, was widely regarded to have precipitated the runaway train that his career — and ultimately life — became. There were bad reviews too. "Lightweight," charged one. "She's a regurgitist." "A populist summary that adds little to an already tired story." But beyond these public facts Andy read almost nothing of her — the person.

Then he wondered why nobody had mentioned to him that the Aspinalls were to be her next topic? He still had connections in Toronto. He'd exchanged cheery e-mails with old LSC classmates as recently as last year. Surely one of them would have heard something and dropped him a note?

Trudy had followed up again with another phone call that piqued his interest. It was how she had cast the Aspinalls, as *a national treasure*, as *Canadian royalty*. She almost suggested that he had a kind of obligation to history, or to the country, to set the record straight. She'd been persuasive, but that wasn't the reason he'd agreed to the interview. He wanted to speak for Colin, to protect his friend's chosen secrecy within the family. This book might prey on and cheapen his life as a side chapter. Feed on his differences. Andy wanted, needed, to mouth the words for his friend.

Are you hungry? he said suddenly, stepping back from the window and his view of the osprey's nest.

Andy began to prepare lunch. He put water on to boil — potato salad was his specialty. He ran his finger over the lettuce leaves that he thought looked nicest, cleaning their spines, washing dirt away. Then, crack, crack, he ripped the romaine into pieces. She turned the CBC back on.

The first bit had gone well, he thought. She'd appeared

interested in what he was saying. But he hadn't even begun the story. He hadn't yet reached Colin. Andy's fingers turned cold under the water and he blew air out between his lips as he worked.

As Trudy ate, she talked about herself, but only a little — perhaps, he considered, creating a semblance of fairness? She told a story about her parents. It *was* lightly funny, but was tinged with poignancy. Had she ever written anything about her own family, he asked. She hadn't, she said. Not yet, maybe one day. And she smiled. Andy thought then of Henrietta Dawling. He also thought of the vole.

I never knew my mother, said Andy. There is nothing to tell I'm afraid.

But I still think about her from time to time. I think that she must be out there somewhere, living a life. Likely, she goes to work each day. She eats. Shops. Watches some of the same television programs I do.

Andy had thought from time to time that given the homogeneity of the culture, they must share common experiences, and, further, because of their common biology, they must, additionally, share common likes, dislikes. He also wondered on occasion — his birthday usually — if she thought about him, or his father? He didn't even know her name.

There *is* a photograph of her. He confessed this to Trudy, so as not to come across as secretive. His mother was sitting on a step with one hand gesturing, the other on her knee.

Andy had thought, more than once, that she was caught in the act of speaking. What should your mother's voice sound like?

He didn't know that the photograph existed until his father had died. He'd found it while going through the man's papers. It was tucked into an envelope, along with a letter she'd written several months after she'd left. It was a simple letter. Naive even. It was written to thank his father for his generosity.

They had not been in love; the pregnancy, Andy, had been an accident. He explained to Trudy that he had, more or less, gathered this from his father over the years.

He didn't ever tell you about her?

I asked about her a few times. He told me what he could remember about her looks. I have her eyes. He once said she liked strawberry jam sandwiches. Lots of butter. Lots of jam.

Do you know what happened?

She'd lived with him while she carried me, but went away soon after my birth.

That's hard to believe. As a mother, I mean, I know that would be hard to do, said Trudy.

The letter itself was postmarked from Montreal, he said. I've wondered, but I have no proof, that she might have been French, a Catholic? In any case, I do know that her leaving once I had arrived had all been pre-arranged, and settled upon. He'd agreed to keep and raise me. My existence was to be kept secret.

Who from?

Her family, I assume.

And your father didn't elaborate?

I've wondered, was she too young, already married, from a different social class or religion?

Trudy smiled, then stood and said, Do you mind if we take a break? I have to make a call. I'll stretch my legs; head down to the lake for a few minutes.

Andy went into his bedroom and closed the door. He pulled a box down from the top of the wardrobe. The envelope had a blue lining. The letter, six lines long, was written on a piece of plain white paper. It was addressed to his father at the house in Scarborough where he'd grown up. It was signed only *Take care*. There was no name. He put it all back.

Trudy walked down to the lake. Andy watched her through the front window of the cottage. Cradling the phone to her ear, she kicked off her shoes and sat on the end of the dock dangling her feet in the water. Had she, Andy wondered, judged his mother for walking out? *That would be hard to do*, she had said. What had she meant? What kind of heartless or selfish soul could leave her newborn? Had the mother in her leapt up and editorialized, quashing the biographer at work? Andy knew that all professions have oaths, said and unsaid. If a doctor's, for example, were *First, do no harm*, then a biographer's must be *Do not enter, and thereby alter, the story*. What's an antique dealer's? he wondered.

As Trudy wandered back toward him, Fiona Aspinall came to mind in a flicker. He felt light-headed. Perhaps he should go for a swim. The bracing water might do him good? Droplets of lake water glistened on Trudy's legs as she approached.

Can I borrow a towel? she asked. He pointed at the bathroom. When Trudy returned to the room, she stopped, towelling down her legs and feet. Do you remember him as a good father? she asked, turning on the recorder.

He wanted what was best.

Which was hockey?

In his mind, hockey was the only thing he knew of that could elevate a boy beyond his lot. Turned out he was right.

What do you mean by that?

When I was younger, I'd sometimes spend Saturday afternoons down at the factory where he worked if he was on shift. I'd watch him build motors. He'd talk hockey to me, dissecting my previous game. Moves or mistakes I'd made. It was intense scrutiny. That was what helped me improve and playing hockey *was* my ticket out — just not the way he'd figured.

The profound grease of the place, its cold concrete floors, white fluorescent lights at a barely perceptible flicker. As a treat his father would send him to the store with a two dollar bill. Two chocolate milks, please. The taste of it still, the wet, milky cardboard of it, right there at his lip. Then a rush of curses by another man from across the factory at a bolt's stripped thread, or swear words at what a wife had packed in a lunch pail. Behind the toilet door hung a calendar — by that time already out of date — with bare-breasted women draped across Maseratis and Lamborghinis.

In a baseball cap and denim shorts, Miss June mounted a Ferrari Dino 308 GT4. Leaning forward, her hands between her thighs, her breasts pushed together, she was laughing. How clearly she returned to him all these years later. Andy had come to believe back then that she *was* laughing — that at the moment the photograph was taken something genuinely funny was said.

Andy showed Colin the photograph of Miss June toward the end of the first spring at LSC.

Why can't we go to *your* house? Colin had said. We always go to Huntington. I'm sick of it.

There's nothing to do at my place, Andy had protested. Still, Colin persisted in small ways, needling him. So, Andy compromised. He took Colin to meet his father at work — it seemed somehow cooler.

After catching two trains and a bus, they arrived unannounced at the factory. Andy's father was working on a broken motor.

Well, hey there! said his dad, looking up.

Dad, this is Colin Aspinall.

Good to meet you. Shouldn't you boys be in classes?

We had an exam this morning. We have free periods this afternoon.

Well, I'm glad you came to see me. Let me get this finished, he said clanging the wrench in his hand gently against the fuel tank. If you can wait a half hour, I'll take you men to McDonald's.

Bright plastic tables and throngs of people chewing and talking at the same time. Did he think they were kids? Worse, his father could not see it. He failed to recognize that Colin was not just another teenager. Colin lived with unimpeded access to everything. A mechanic could not treat Colin to anything. It wasn't possible. The idea of it crippled Andy with embarrassment. His father did not know his place. He did not understand how the world worked — beyond hockey and engines. Andy saw plainly, right then and there, that there was an unspoken ranking ordering people. After a year at LSC, his eyes had been opened. But why did those down the ladder, men like his father, remain ignorant?

I was a horrible teenager, he said. Andy told Trudy the story of their excursion to his father's work. She began to take notes as soon as he mentioned Colin's name.

Why did he want to see your house? she asked.

Embarrassing me wasn't Colin's aim. He'd simply never met a mechanic before. It made me, the idea of me, stranger, and somehow foreign, or alluring maybe? That day cemented our friendship, I think.

You *were* embarrassed though.

Excruciatingly so. My father was an ordinary guy. So different from Mr. Aspinall who, for example, had a driver. And as for McDonald's? I can't imagine Mr. Aspinall ever having once eaten fast food. The only kind of restaurant that Colin and his father went to had sommeliers and menus without prices. Factories. McDonald's. They were not places Colin and his father frequented. He paused. We had an acquaintance at LSC who was black. He was the son of a Ugandan diplomat. That was unremarkable to Colin. It was me who was transfixed by this guy's foreignness, his ebony skin. In contrast, it was my father, my home life that was a foreign country to Colin.

To pass the time that day, Andy had shown Colin around

the storeroom, its rows of engine parts, oily or new, small cardboard boxes brimming with nuts and bolts, fan belts. They wandered into the lunchroom with its one kettle and melamine table, greasy pink and yellow carbon paper receipts scattered about, and the tattered bamboo curtain that hung from a couple of bent hooks.

He introduced Colin to the other workers. The foreman shook Colin's hand and looked at Andy confused, at Colin's weak grip or perhaps at Colin's thinly disguised surprise at having to shake this man's hand at all. But, having decided in an instant that this would never be allowed to happen again, Andy took Colin's side, fast adopting his airs. Once he too was armoured with ironical detachment, Andy began to enjoy himself just as much.

That day was the first time I began to see the world as Colin did.

Andy pulled Colin into the bathroom, closed the door, and riffled through the calendar. There was June. Her breasts, pressed. Still laughing. He'd never shown her to anyone before.

Here, Colin had said, and tore June free from the staples. Take her.

Andy stuffed the evidence of Colin's act of vandalism into his pocket. What Colin didn't realize, but Andy knew instinctively, was that she wasn't just his. June, in some unspoken democratic way, belonged to all the men who worked there. She was collective property.

Trudy's shoes were still off. She had pulled her knees up onto the chair and was sitting cross-legged, resting her clipboard on her lap. Beside the tape recorder that was between them on the coffee table, she had, over the course of the morning, placed her earrings and watch.

I want to ask you about how your friendship with Colin began, but we skipped over how you ended up getting into LSC?

That summer of free ice time with Dr. Tilford did the trick. I was younger, but I was much better than most of the LSC senior team players. Hockey was just another sport for them to play. Of course, for me, for my father, it had been our life. I'd studied every great player. Read coaching books. Countless summer hours in the driveway practising wrist shots up against the garage door, road hockey chasing errant tennis balls down the street. My father called me the Golden Retriever. All the while dreaming I was at Maple Leaf Gardens. I'd walk home from school stickhandling a pop can along the gutter; each driveway an empty net. I scored on every NHL goalie. To the LSC boys, hockey was important fun at best. To me it was religion.

Dr. Tilford took a liking to me right away. He had me up against his biggest guys and best lines. The older LSC boys liked me too. This helped more than I knew. I later learned it was one of them who first put the idea to Dr. Tilford that I should attend LSC, that the team could use me.

So a meeting was called with my father. They gave us a tour of the campus. I remember the light streaming into the empty double gym. There was a tall guy shooting hoops. Tilford called him over.

This is Doug Hillurt. He's the head prefect, said Dr. Tilford. You'll want to be on his good side. He runs the place. We all shook hands but I already knew him from hockey — he was the captain of the team.

Dr. Tilford exaggerates, Doug said with a broad, ambassadorial smile. Welcome to LSC officially, Andy. Dr. Tilford took my father by the arm and steered him away briefly, leaving me with Doug. He had on expensive sneakers, and his slightly long hair, blond and wavy, was wet with sweat. You nervous? Doug asked.

A bit, I said.

Let me tell you something. Once you're an LSCer, you're

always one. While you're here, you'll get double out of this place what you put in. The dice are loaded for us; success is a sure thing for guys like you and me.

Dr. Tilford took us to the swimming pool and the shooting range. Personal computers were just becoming more widely available, but they already had a whole room full of them and students were taught how to program them. Latin and French, philosophy and art were all expected to be mastered. This was a university preparatory school. Its alumni included a Supreme Court judge, billionaires, the top bioethicist in the country, and several Olympians. Their stories were in the admissions materials, their pictures hung in oil in the hallways. The place was ivy and old brick, ties and grey flannel pants. Vast amounts of glory seemed certain to all who went here.

Was your father impressed?

Oh, my father wouldn't have trusted them at all. He was a unionist, and suspicious of the motives of people with more money than himself. He felt he was owed more for his labour. Always. He once told me that he often skipped off an hour early when he needed to get a haircut. Grows on their dime, I'll get it cut on their dime, was the way he saw it. He was often coming home with stuff, bits of engine parts, and the like. He'd do work on the side and get paid cash, use the company's materials whenever he could. *The brass collects air miles, gets free meals — well, scooping extra parts, taking all my sick days, these are my fringe benefits. Fair is fair.* That's the way he viewed the world.

But he let you go.

Every man has his price. My dad's was a chance at hockey stardom for his son. They told him they'd work on getting me a hockey scholarship to a big U.S. university. My dad knew this as another route to the NHL. So yes, at the end of the tour, papers were signed. The headmaster was there too, and there were handshakes all around. I remember my father turning to the headmaster, looking him in the eye and saying simply, *look after my son*. There was a quality to the timbre of his voice that I recognized as defeat.

Why would that have been? I'm not sure I understand. He did want this, or he didn't?

I was all he had. He knew that this would change our life together.

What did changing schools mean to you?

Andy thought about this before beginning. LSC students, he ventured, had an acute, almost innate awareness of status. Mr. Aspinall would say that your average *hockey and Hortons Canadian* does not recognize their place in a class structure. They assume most folks are like them and have not developed a greedy appetite for media gossip or hero worship of the rich the way the Americans and English do. Families of enormous wealth like the Aspinalls, therefore, largely keep to themselves, are left alone, and are as invisible as the next citizen. Attending LSC opened my eyes to this.

Isn't that a good quality? asked Trudy.

I guess there's something vulgar about the way most Western cultures pathologize wealth, treat those with it as de facto celebrities. But I think what Mr. Aspinall was getting at was the reverse side of this — Canadians value politeness over accountability.

Had he said too much? Andy pictured himself reading a passage in her book, Mr. Aspinall's ideas in black and white before him. Would the anecdote be traceable to him? And Mr. Aspinall had never said *hockey and Hortons*. That was his line. Was he getting too loose with the facts? He gathered himself — surely the man had made similar comments often enough in the company of others? Yes, he remained on home ice and might be playing hard but it was still a fair game.

She'd been scribbling notes. The tape recorder was on, but

she wrote anyway. In talking about Mr. Aspinall her interest increased. And for Andy, Mr. Aspinall was easy to quote almost verbatim. He had heard the man speak on these matters often, repeating the same themes over and over.

Canada is a small town, Andy, said Mr. Aspinall. The afternoon had been turning stormy and they were out on the boat, Huntington House rising up from the shoreline across the lake. Mr. Aspinall had decided that he would take Fiona, Colin, and Andy for a sail. Fiona and Colin were up at the bow, their legs dangling over the side, talking intently — as they so often did. Andy was sitting next to Mr. Aspinall. The wind had picked up, so they'd taken the sails down and were motoring home. Mr. Aspinall was giving him another talk.

There are those of us who live in this town, but earn our living and leave our money elsewhere — right around the world. We like the town because it's familiar and easy. But we don't respect it. The people here are covertly mean. They are letting in immigrants because they espouse the belief that people are all the same and should be treated that way. A sound principle, Andy. But of course, the people who are immigrating to Canada are coming from countries that are poorer than Canada. They are coming here to get ahead, to start a new and better life for themselves and their children, right?

Andy nodded. Off to his right, the white caps left the top of the lake whisked; the chop thudded against the hull.

When they come here to get ahead, continued Mr. Aspinall, what do you think that means for Canadians?

Again, Andy shrugged. He wanted to be up at the front with Fiona and Colin. He wanted to know what they were talking about. But he couldn't leave now.

It means they will change this country. He turned the steering wheel and the boat veered. Why do we know this? We know it because our ancestors once were immigrants. They got ahead by changing it.

Isn't it better today? asked Andy.

That depends on who you ask. My family bought that shore-line from the Crown at the turn of the last century. Do you know whose it was before that?

No one's? Andy said.

It was Ojibwa, Mr. Aspinall said, becoming abruptly quiet, leaving the word alone in the air — as if honouring a dissipating echo.

Sure, he finally said, it'll take these newcomers several generations. But eventually, if history teaches us anything, inevitably they too will be achievers because they are not lazy. Just like us, they too are good people, and are hungry for success. They know poverty. They have dreams. Just as everything the Aboriginals built and knew would be changed by immigration, so too will it be for us. Serves us right in a way. So, Andy, you see we are inviting our own long-term demise through complacency disguised as misplaced benevolence.

Andy nodded, but did not agree with Mr. Aspinall, if he fully understood him, that was. He still thought it was important that Canada had new immigrants. He'd learned about it at school in Scarborough, where he'd had Italian, Ukrainian, and Polish friends whose families had once been new to this country. Besides, his old teacher had insisted that immigrants built Canada.

Doesn't Canada need immigrants for our labour force? he asked.

Your head is already being filled with propaganda, Andy. Don't mistake strongly held opinion for good ideas; it's better to be right than righteous. You must resist thinking like everyone else. Shared beliefs are for other people. Mr. Aspinall smiled. Look, he said, let's view it another way. It doesn't matter that

Canada is encouraging immigration if we think the country is broken. Do we? Or do we like it?

Andy said nothing.

Which is it? pressed Mr. Aspinall.

I think we like it.

I think Canadians do too. So why are they changing it?

Because they want people from other countries to have the same opportunities we do.

Which people and from which other countries?

All people. Everyone's equal.

So everyone should come to Canada?

Well, they can't all fit, said Andy, reasonably.

So just some should come.

I guess so.

Which ones?

Andy thought about this for a moment, and then said, the ones who have the skills Canada needs.

So we are ranking people using self-interested, utilitarian principles. Doesn't sound universal or fair to me. Okay, so we rank them, then let some — the lucky, the smart, the tenacious, and the most useful — immigrate. Now they arrive. Great. We needed them. Are they able to use these skills when they get here? asked Mr. Aspinall.

Andy looked over the side of the boat, as if help might be located in the lead-grey water below. He knew full well they weren't. He'd heard all about how foreign doctors drove taxis and engineers cleaned office towers. His old teachers had taught him this too. Andy shook his head.

What is it called, Mr. Aspinall queried, rubbing the whiskers under his chin, if you say something to someone, but know it isn't true?

It's like a lie, said Andy.

It's more than *like* a lie, *it is* a lie. Canadians are liars, said

Mr. Aspinall. Their government are liars, and they are liars. These are the facts, Andy. They do not want to employ foreign professionals, rather, they want their menial tasks done by highly educated, polite, preferably nice-smelling foreigners. It's a kind of indentured servitude. And it's not just legal, it's a much loved state policy that Canadians from coast to coast vote for in election after election. I, for one, am deeply ashamed by this.

So there should be no immigration? asked Andy.

There is nothing wrong with immigration. Nothing at all. But the way Canada does it, well, it's criminal. We are punishing a whole generation of refugees and immigrants for having dreams and taking huge personal risks. There will be long-term, devastating social consequences. They will not forget. Fortunes will turn. They will enact revenge. This land, land we once stole, others will one day steal.

What should be done about it? asked Andy.

More people than me need to see our system as problematic, hypocritical, indefensible. . . . You are being handed a debt, Andy. So, I hope you're up to the challenge of repaying it.

Mr. Aspinall stopped and looked off in the distance. I wonder if this country will ever be big enough to admit it made mistakes, he added. Our tolerant values are just that, ours; they are not universally admired, accepted, or even tolerated. It's pure arrogance that we expect gratitude.

The boat drew in close to the dock at Huntington House. Grab the line there Andy will you? Mr. Aspinall said. Andy handed it to him. You're a listener. I hope you grow into a thinker.

If only Colin would be more like you.

◆ ◆ ◆

The first night, Andy climbed onto his top bunk in the LSC dorm and pulled the blankets up over his head. The lights were put out. Immediately all the boys began to talk, and tease one another. Someone farted. It was all they could do to stifle their snickers so the prefect in the next room wouldn't hear.

Deciding to attend LSC happened quickly, Andy said, looking up at Trudy. Andy stood and stretched his arms high. Then he became aware he'd done this with no warning — it being his home after all — and that, to his guest, it was a large and abrupt gesture. He felt comfortable in her presence. He fell back down into his chair adopting an apologetic smile. He tried to regain a more serious, philosophical tone.

So much of what informs teenagers is the sense that every experience is brand new. The unexpected becomes the only way of measuring reality for them. I think it's why teenagers are always complaining that things are boring, when to an adult they're not boring at all, they're relaxing, or calm, or mercifully quiet. Do you know what I mean?

When I first met Colin, most of what happened to us was happening for the first time. But because we had yet to appreciate the world around us, at least as it might be happening separate from us, it felt as if we were the centre of the entire world and that no one else could possibly understand what it was like to be going through what we were. The highs were very high and the lows tremendously low.

The way I see it now, whenever a person does, or is presented with, something big for the first time in life, it carries a gravitas. Forget teenagers for a second. Say, someone in your family gets cancer, or you are the first among your tight group of friends who is getting divorced. Each is a first incident and I think is remembered to a greater degree than those similar ones that follow — not because it's more important, but because it's the first.

The traumas and tumult of our teenage years are so, because this is the period when we do so much for the first time. Just about every week contains a first. First love, first job, first one to lose it or first to get to first base. It's a time of first successes, first failures, first attempts to define ourselves in a world we so desperately want to understand. Naturally, we don't yet know that there is nothing to understand.

Youth is wasted on the young, Trudy said, smiling.

Colin loved Oscar Wilde, he said.

Even though he was doing his best, he felt she recorded his ideas out of politeness, as if others had had them long before him, as if they would be edited out later. He'd thought deeply on teenage years, at least he always felt he had. Perhaps his ideas were well known? Did she secretly pity or — worse — belittle him? Maybe he was becoming, as Mr. Aspinall used to say, a bore.

I think, he said, hoping to turn the conversation around, we are generally hard on teenagers, don't you? We demean their first steps as inconsequential because we know that the first heartbreak will amount to nothing, that it was based on the exchange of a glance at a football game or at a fast food restaurant, that it needn't be given great weight. But the feelings are real, and, you know, teenagers have no context to work with — no other long list of similar occurrences against which to measure this one — so the pain that is felt is tempered by nothing, and can be overwhelming and profound.

She nodded and smiled. She was no longer writing. The tape was recording. She appeared to be listening.

Was Colin in the same dorm room as you at LSC? she asked.

No, in my dorm we were all new to LSC, in grade nine. Andy recalled three double bunks, six desks, and six wardrobes. He'd been too large for the bed, hanging about six inches over the end. By the end of the year, it was a clear foot.

He had known of Colin, seen him about the halls and in some of his classes. The house Colin boarded in, said Andy, was kind of special in that it was co-ed — with separate floors for boys and girls — and was, it was understood, for those students whose parents were alumni, or were large donors.

It had been unspoken, but there was a kind of pre-existing hierarchy. Friendships were forged in those early years. They'd spent most of their time with those they lived with. LSC knew this. So did parents who sent their children there. Who their children boarded with, and befriended most closely in the early years, was controlled — implicitly at least.

Andy pictured Colin, as he'd been when they'd first spoken at the LSC Halloween dance — Colin's delicate frame, still-boyish features. He sported a dark purple cape, ghostly white powder masked his face. His blond hair had been slicked back and he'd put on black eyeliner. His lips were blackened too.

Colin dressed up for special occasions, said Andy, as if they were all carnivals needing him to be the main attraction. He'd create a persona to hide behind so he could face the world. It all came from a place of fear. At least, that's how I've grown to understand it.

The LSC dances were different from the ones Andy was used to at school in Scarborough. There, the different cliques would congregate separately. Depending on the song, they would either take to the floor in jubilation as if they were the chosen tribe, or, alternatively, would gesture in overt displeasure at the DJ's poor choice. The music filled the rotten gym to capacity, each song having the effect of a shock high tide, beaching some kids like flotsam, drawing others, hypnotically, out into the deep, waving and drowning.

Yet at LSC everyone liked the same kind of music. Tightly knit groups existed, but they were more subtle, less obvious. And it had its share of eccentrics, like Colin.

LSC was not a normal school, said Andy. There existed a general understanding of the degree to which being permitted everything can mess you up. Colin, who was widely regarded as having most, was given an odd respect and much latitude. He was never beaten up for his idiosyncrasies. At the school I went to in Scarborough, he would have been; Colin wouldn't have lasted a day there. At LSC, there was an underlying acknowledgement of, or appreciation for, Colin Aspinall. He would rightfully be a wealthy and influential person in due course. He would be in their social or business orbit for their entire lives. Perhaps they might never need him as a friend per se, but they knew already — even as teenagers — that they should not be on his wrong side. Better to keep options open. So, while they may not have fully accepted him then — with his costumes and other queer habits — they might one day need him to remember them as, at least, benign.

We knew, Andy continued, LSC was not just a high school; it was the foundation for a life-long network. It turned out to be an overplayed hand — after graduation we went our separate ways, took careers in different fields, and more or less never saw each other again. At least, that's how it was for me. But that wasn't the point. The actual friendships weren't important. It was a process that we were learning. How to develop alliances, earn trust of those further up the social scale than yourself, build a reliable gang of followers, recognize a person with money at a glance, what loyalty means — how to earn it, how to use it. That's what LSC taught. It's the private code of those who enjoy absolute privilege.

Colin swooped into the gym during the opening bars of Gowan's "Strange Animal," his cape billowing behind him. The whole school had turned for a moment and gasped. Colin's intended effect. By staging periodic spectacles, Colin was allowed his other eccentricities. He was gaudy and outrageous;

their very own dandy. Colin was another reflective surface for them to see themselves in. In his actions, they could see themselves as disproportionately unconstrained, baroque, and sophisticated.

In the gym, Halloween jack-o'-lanterns were aglow, sheets draped over basketballs with ghostly faces drawn in black marker hung from the rafters, black streamers covered the entranceway. Toward the rear wall, a table with punch the colour of bile was labelled *bile*. But it was not a dance where costumes were required. One of the girls was holding a party the next evening where they were all expected to come dressed up. But Colin wasn't the only one wearing a costume.

Three other boys, new boys — Andy included — had been told that it *was* a dress-up event. That they *must* dress up. Andy arrived as Batman. It was the only costume he could rent and it was his hope it would be boring enough to let him go completely unnoticed.

◆ ◆ ◆

When he walked into the gym he saw immediately that it was a kind of hazing. He'd laughed hard at being set up. The boy who'd told him to do it — a guy on his hockey team — was a well-known practical joker. Andy took it good-naturedly, having the quick-wittedness to ask a few of the seniors if they'd seen Robin?

Just as quickly the focus shifted from costumes as more of them began to dance. Andy joined in. Later, Andy found himself at the table waiting to be served some of the bile. Colin Aspinall was standing beside him.

I think Batman was really a vampire, said Colin holding his own cape to one side.

I didn't think you were a new boy? Andy asked genuinely.

No, said Colin. I'm old. Very old.

Andy noticed the feminine-looking makeup on Colin's face. He hadn't understood why this guy was dressed up.

You know, continued Colin, my sister thinks you're a great dancer. She's sent me over here to see if you'll dance with her.

Who is your sister? Andy asked.

Colin pointed. Andy already knew her face. Everyone knew Fiona Aspinall. She was impossibly attractive, and she could be, he'd also been told, a ruthless bitch. No one gets in her pants, one teammate of his had already said.

Really, said Andy, playing it cool. Sure, I'll dance with her. But tell her I don't dance once I've turned back into Bruce Wayne.

Colin laughed.

I think you're a good dancer too, said Colin, and the boy bowed and pranced across the gym toward the far corner where his sister was holding court.

◆ ◆ ◆

When Trudy had first learned that Dilip, along with Anita, were to move to Calgary, she'd spent night after night avoiding the topic with Veronica, lest she upset her. Helping to push their move from her mind was her intensified research into the Aspinalls. By that time, she'd spoken with Andy Kronk twice on the phone. He'd been willing to do the interview. This had meant the need for much preparation. She must re-read all her notes, particularly on Colin Aspinall. But the pending upset of Anita's departure became harder to ignore. She must go next door and speak to Indira. She had to find out what was going on, and why.

I am leaving as well, said Indira, touching her palm to her face. She had beautiful eyes. The outsides were white, the centres deeply dark. I'm off to England next month, to live with my mother and sister in Reading. You know it? Near London. Indira took the teapot off the counter, and placed it on the kitchen table in front of Trudy who was sitting.

I don't understand, said Trudy. Why?

My mother is sick. I must go and help my sister take care of her. I'm afraid I'm in the soup.

Anita says Dilip is moving to Calgary?

Yes, he is. He's got a new job. At the university. He's a scientist, you know.

Of course I know.

Oh, said Indira and stopped setting the cups for tea. Yes, you do.

What's this got to do with you going to London?

Nothing. Just coincidence. Funny timing. Dilip came to me to tell me that he must move to Calgary. I am about to tell him that I must move to London. Strange how these moments occur.

How long will you be gone?

How long does it take her to die?

Trudy felt her heart rhythm shift high and light. Had she imagined their camaraderie as single mothers? She poured herself a cup of tea from the pot in front of her.

Do you take milk? asked Indira.

I do, she said. Yes. As Indira went to her fridge, Trudy watched her move. She was of slight build and glided, completely at ease in her kitchen. She wore blue jeans and a red sweater top, no shoes or socks. Her hair was mid-length and tied back. On one wrist she wore a gold bracelet. Her skin was light brown and smooth.

Dilip . . . Indira began to speak, but stopped.

Yes?

He will take Anita. He will have money and a nice house in Calgary. He will have a job. I am going to live in a crowded flat with my mother, and deaf sister, and my sister's two children, and her lecherous husband too. There will be no room there for Anita. It's better for her in Calgary with Dilip. I am trying to do what is best, for all concerned.

Trudy had finished her tea hurriedly and left. As she unhooked the latch on the gate between the two houses she sighed involuntarily. Poor Indira. Why must situations that work perfectly well be broken? She'd never give up Veronica — even for a while. Never. She'd rather die. The phone rang as she entered her house.

Hello, Trudy, it's Officer Nyland.

Hi, she had said, trying to shift gears out of the private realm. She looked for a pen, for paper.

I sent Kronk the introductory letter but no reply. So I called him, she said. We've spoken twice now: briefly the first time, the second at some length.

How receptive was he?

Initially? Not at all. He'd received the letter, but wasn't convinced. I sensed he was distracted. He agreed to think about it. I called again two days later. I explained my project to him, and who I was. I did what I usually do and stressed how important his role was to a complete understanding of the subject. I also told him, in this case, that I felt he had a moral duty: to Canada's history, to the family's legacy, the Aspinall family being such a cultural institution.

And?

He agreed — a few days in May worked for him. Hope it's

not too buggy up there. She felt, after talking with Indira, that she needed a change of scene.

As she had put the phone back into the cradle, she had returned to thinking about Indira and Anita. Veronica would be upset. A great deal at first, but it would lessen. She'd be forced to make new friends at school. Perhaps it would not be all bad? How long could their friendship remain so exclusive and intimate? Friendships so often soured, or evaporated. But this was rationalization. The feeling she was having was old-fashioned sadness. Her daughter was poised to lose her best friend. Life was unfair. It was about to deal Veronica a big blow, and there was nothing her mother could do to shield her from it. Then she had wondered how Patrick would feel about this? Could a father possibly care as much?

◆ ◆ ◆

Andy put a frozen lasagna in the oven. While waiting, they talked more about his days at LSC. I remember waking to Colin's whispers. Get up, Andy, he would be saying. It was two or three in the morning. Once, he was wearing a long, red dress and a woman's wig. He'd been drinking.

What happened then?

The other boys in the dorm slept soundly on. He said, *Follow me*. Next thing I knew, the gravel was crunching under our feet. It was impossibly loud. Surely every teacher, every housemaster for miles, would sit suddenly bolt upright in his bed.

And did they? she asked.

No one came. Ahead of me, Colin was marching off. He had running shoes on —

Which did not go with his dress. Trudy smiled.

No, he said. Not at all. And his wig slid about, so he clamped his hand up on the top of his head to hold it in place.

Andy tried to remember if Colin wore makeup that evening. His mind had so many images of Colin in lipstick, with eye shadow on, that he couldn't be sure. All he had for certain was Colin's light gait, his thin arm up on his head, the thrill of sneaking out, the anxiety of getting caught. Colin was holding a brown paper bag in which, he assumed, was booze.

He'd been thrilled to be asked to come along. They did not know one another well and he hadn't yet made a solid friend. Everyone was kind, but he was new. They were watching him. But here was Colin, who'd started to sit next to him in classes and now was sneaking him out on late night trips.

I remember whispering, *Please Colin, we're going to get gated!*

They entered the main school building through a window in the art department. Colin had unlocked it that day in preparation. They climbed the back stairs, a passageway that in four or five hours' time would be teeming with boys and girls racing between classes, nudging each other, laughing. At night though, only the glow of the exit signs was visible, giving off a patch of red light at the top of each landing. Andy looked up at Trudy who was scribbling on her notepad.

On the top floor was the teachers' lounge. Colin marched right in, he followed behind.

Sitting on lounge chairs and drinking out of similar bags to Colin, were about a half-dozen students, all of whom were older than Colin and myself. Fiona was there, sitting on the lap of Doug Hillurt.

Someone said, *What's he doing here?*

He's with me, said Colin.

And who are you wearing tonight, Colin? asked Doug.

Colin took out a cigarette. The others were smoking too. Andy must have looked shocked at this.

It's the safest place to light up, Fiona explained. The teachers puff away in here all day so it already smells. We do it all the time.

Andy sat next to Colin on a couch by the window. He was told to look out for old Mr. Hawthorne who sometimes walked his dog down the main path to the school in the middle of the night. It would be unlikely that he'd look up, but if he did he might see them. They kept the room dark. As he watched for a movement, the older kids drank and laughed.

Fiona and Doug Hillurt began to make out. Doug's hands rubbed up and down her sides in a dramatic fashion. Andy watched when he safely could. Fiona had just spoken to him for the first time since they'd briefly danced together at the Halloween party. She'd adopted a confidential tone. She must have already checked him out — decided he was to be trusted. Had she spoken to Doug? Had he been vouched for as a good hockey player? Or had Colin whispered to her that he was okay? Doug's hands groped away. The two of them like this reminded him of the parking lot of his high school in Scarborough. There, the girls in his class would make out with older guys in the backs of their cars. He'd catch glimpses of them, stunned and covertly struggling, enduring some guy's pleasure. Did Fiona like Doug? Enough that she wanted to be seen like this with him? He couldn't tell. Her face was hidden.

I don't know how many times that term Colin shook me awake and we crept up to the lounge, said Andy. I never did drink or smoke — hockey. But I was considered a good lookout. I spotted old Hawthorne walking his dog several times.

Colin never got teased about wearing dresses, really?

Maybe lightheartedly. But he was untouchable. Although

he didn't need it, Fiona provided a kind of protection too. She was the most important girl at the school and Doug Hillurt was not to be crossed. In that world, this power was as formidable as a whole army.

It was a quiet, warm evening and the surface of the lake was glass. Trudy suggested a walk down to the dock. Andy let her go alone. He watched her casually as she made a call on her cellphone. Pieces of her conversation floated up to him as he stood in the kitchen, readying dinner by getting out plates, putting butter in a dish, making sure the cutlery was clean. Trudy was talking to her daughter, he realized. Her tone was different, higher and sweeter. She stood on his dock with one hand on her hip, the other holding the phone to her ear and, from time to time, dipped her bare foot in the water, her toe pointed as if a ballerina. *Honey, if Indira says you can go, then . . .* and *Just make sure you clean up . . . you can't refuse to eat . . . your dad will come and pick you both up tomorrow to go to the movies . . .* were the snippets he heard.

◆ ◆ ◆

It's getting dark.

Ah, we can still squeeze another half-hour out of her.

Who?

What?

Who's *she?*

What do you mean?

You said squeeze another half-hour out of *her.* Why must everything resistant to men's plans be engendered female?

You read way too much into stuff.

I don't. When the car wouldn't start last week and you had your head somewhere in the engine and you hollered at me to rev the engine, do you remember what you said?

I was trying to fix the car. We were going to be late!

You said, *Okay, give 'er.*

Do you ever stop talking about this stuff?

Which is short for *give it to her*, is it not?

Maybe we should head back. I think you're hungry or something.

What's that supposed to mean?

You're getting hysterical. Is it that time of the month?

Now you're just trying to bait me. I won't play your games.

Okay, I was. But all that's just the way I talk. I'm a pretty nice guy. My wife thinks so. I got two kids. Take them to soccer and hockey. Sure, I barbecue ribs, or go fishing once a year where I run a walleye lengthwise with a blade, but it don't mean I'm some insensitive pig.

You could do better.

I like who I am.

You could have said, *I think there is another half-hour of light left.* You didn't need to talk about *squeezing her.*

I think you're being culturally insensitive.

What?

I'm from rural Ontario and these expressions are what make us colourful.

Now I've heard everything.

You're jealous.

Let's go. It's been a long day.

Wait. Is that her on the dock?

She's talking on a cellphone.

See if you can pick it up.

I'm already on it.

Well? What's she saying?

Shhh.

Are you recording it?

Yes. She's saying . . . Hang on . . . Oh she's talking to . . . It must be her daughter . . . it's a girl's voice. She wants to stay up late. The daughter's name is Veronica. The friend's name is . . .

That's not important. What's *her* name?

She's hung up.

What was her name?

Mommy?

Clearly that is a successful career woman and you can't see her beyond the context of a mother. Frankly I'm shocked and saddened by . . .

Can we *please* call it a day?

◆ ◆ ◆

My memory of the first year might not be as clear as it once was, he said when they resumed. And it's all mixed up with the time of my own father's death.

By spring term, hockey being over, he was given a break after the season. There was to be summer training of course — but for April, May, and June, he was on his own and had more time to himself. As this was his first year, he wasn't sure what he should do with it. So he studied, trying to prepare for exams. The work was much harder than he'd been used to at his high school in Scarborough. But already he was looking forward to summer. Colin was going off to Europe on a summer school program to improve his French; then he would be in England with his parents and sister for another week or two — to visit with friends of his family.

The news of my father's death was delivered to me in math class. I'd been sitting next to Colin. He'd been whispering the answers to me when the headmaster arrived at the door. I was asked to step outside. I thought I was in trouble for cheating.

Did Colin go out with you?

No. And I'd never had dealings with the headmaster — not since first being shown around the school the summer before. The man had a godlike presence in our lives. He made daily addresses to the school during lunch hour, rising from his seat at the head of the faculty table; a short cough was all it took to silence a room of five hundred students. *It has come to my attention* . . . he would begin and we would all lean forward to hear who had done what, and just which penalty would be given — hoping it would not adversely affect our next sports game or weekend leave. On this occasion though, he looked different, like an ordinary man.

Your father is sick, Andy, he said and proceeded to tell me that he would be driving me himself to the Scarborough hospital. Did I need anything before we left? It was important that we leave immediately. The news that awaited us was not going to be good, he'd said.

The highway traffic drifted by us and I looked out the window at the newly green springtime of Toronto. The headmaster had the radio on and buoyant music filled the car. That my father should be in hospital having had a massive heart attack, and that *this* would bring me so close to the headmaster that I could have gotten out of a math class . . . it felt like some strange favour. Of course, I didn't appreciate how serious it was, that my father was about to die.

Do you mind, Andy asked, if I pour myself a drink?

Not at all, said Trudy.

Like one?

Not for me. Well, do you have wine?

I do. White okay?

Half a glass. Lovely, she said.

As Andy fixed the drinks he could once again see the lino-leum floor in the hospital's waiting room. The headmaster left him for about a half an hour and returned with quarter chicken dinners from Swiss Chalet. They ate in the waiting room, run-ning out of napkins. A small boy pushed a toy car across the floor and made a buzzing sound. Andy had watched the boy, how lost in his play he was, until he too imagined a world that could be controlled through his own will power. But when he tried to picture himself in it, he couldn't.

Then a doctor sat down with him. I understand you like hockey? the man said, unhooking a stethoscope from around his neck. What do you play?

Defence, said Andy.

Do you know what a myocardial infarction is?

No, said Andy.

He threw up chicken in the toilet about ten minutes after he'd heard the news that it meant a heart attack, that his father had not survived it. They had spent most of the night there, the headmaster and he. Andy was tired and longed for his bed at school. He wondered if he'd have to retake the math test.

Who is your best friend at LSC, Andy? asked the headmaster.

Colin.

Colin Aspinall?

Yes.

I bet you two get up to some trouble behind my back!

Not really, sir.

The headmaster spoke with the doctors and nurses and made several calls. Then the headmaster took him back to school. At 5 a.m. he was shown into a room in the infirmary. Sleep here, get up when you are ready, the nurse told him. Tomorrow is Friday, and then it's the start of spring break, she'd said, clearly hoping to cheer him up. But he was exhausted, and smiled only a little as he climbed into bed. In the background of his dreams he was distantly aware of movement outside the building, boys and girls heading off to breakfast, and then hustling back to their rooms between classes.

He wandered back to his dorm mid-afternoon. Should he get dressed and go to class? It wasn't at all obvious what he should do. Being the final few classes before vacation, movies would be shown and serious work would be avoided as the school wound down its efforts and eagerly looked forward to spring vacation.

A knock on the door and the headmaster entered. Behind him were Colin, and Mr. Aspinall dressed in a dark business suit.

Calls had been made. Under the circumstances, the Aspinalls were only too happy to look after Andy for spring break. Andy was asked, after the fact, if he'd prefer to stay with his aunt, his father's sister? But he assured them he'd rather spend it with Colin. So they left school early. Colin and Andy rode in the back of Mr. Aspinall's long, dark car with Mr. Aspinall.

They didn't speak much, Colin and Andy sitting in silence as Mr. Aspinall read through papers from his briefcase. Before long though Mr. Aspinall was dropped off at his office, shaking both the boys' hands as he got out of the car. Colin directed the driver to take them to the mall.

My father just greased us. Look. Colin held up two hundred-dollar bills. It is his way of saying that we should go and have some fun. Try to take our minds off things for a while. He substitutes dollars for words when he's not sure what to say.

Andy handed Trudy her wine.

At the mall, Andy followed Colin into the Hudson's Bay Company. Colin's strategy to get into the change rooms with women's clothing was all bluster and bravado. He would pick up a dress or skirt or blouse, along with a pair of jeans and go into the change room. If a clerk looked at him, he would smile and say his sister was in there somewhere and she was waiting for him with different sizes. Then he would try them on and wriggle about in front of a full-length mirror. He had no intention of buying them; he simply left on the ones he wanted and pulled back on his own clothes over top.

Please hurry, Colin, said Andy in an anxious whisper, as each piece of clothing was tried on, was examined from the front, from the side. Why are you fucking doing this? But Andy's protests would make Colin more theatrical. His father had not been dead twenty-four hours. How had he found himself in the unlikely situation of standing in the change rooms at the Bay, helping Colin Aspinall steal women's clothing?

Later, they ate pizza together in the food court. Colin only liked cheese on his. Nothing else. He always had food made special. He never ordered an item off any menu, even fast food, without asking for substitutions or changes to the predetermined ingredients. In this case, they made a whole pizza especially for Colin because he only wanted cheese.

We'll have a great time this week, Andy, Colin said in a quieter moment. Then, gently, he added, I'll come with you to the funeral if you want.

Andy had cried then. Deep, silent, hard sobs that hurt his chest. The food court in a mall was a terrible place to break down, but, somehow, he didn't care who saw him. Across from him Colin touched his forearm in sympathy. He let it all out.

After a time it passed, and Colin spoke. Andy?

He looked up. Yes, he managed.

I cry all the time.

Why?

Because I hate my life. I hate how I can't control anything I do. Except lately. I've been happier this year. Since we met.

About them the shoppers strode or meandered between stores, running late or taking their time. It had been the taste of chocolate milk. He hadn't ordered it on purpose but it took him back to the grease and metallic smell of his father's garage. Then, as easily, he was on the ice bursting through traffic, glimpsing the man's smile of encouragement as he skated at the boards, eyes drifting from the puck for only a moment to register and refuel upon his father's total absorption in him: *that Kronk star*, as he took a quick wrist shot from the point. He scored. His father's dreams of his son were dead.

◆ ◆ ◆

As daylight faded Trudy asked him to recall that first summer he'd spent at Huntington. Andy closed his eyes to Huntington House, its lawns groomed right to the lake's edge. He could see the view from the upstairs drawing room — Mr. Aspinall's room.

He turned. Behind him two red, leather wingback chairs faced each other with a Stickley table in between. To his right was the door. Deep bookshelves lined the remaining walls. They were not solely filled with books though — there was a library on the first floor of the house. Mr. Aspinall collected antique chess sets, and this was the room in which he kept his most valuable pieces.

Outside, the garden pathway that led down to the water's edge had a short flight of stairs every hundred yards or so; a fountain with a statue of two Victorian nymphs was positioned about halfway between the house and lake. The lawns were framed with box hedge and flowerbeds.

It was during that week following my father's death that he called me into his drawing room for a chat. He was in corduroy trousers, green cardigan, and slippers. He asked me how I was finding my stay, if I was comfortable.

Were you?

I was.

Then what?

He asked me if I knew what Colin was. He used the word homosexualist. It was the first and only time I heard him say it. It sounded so clinical coming from his mouth — as if it were a diagnosis of some kind.

What did you say?

I didn't respond. It felt like a trick question. So I sat there, stunned.

Andy was there once more, his hands squarely on his knees. He'd been asked a question and the ticking of the grandfather clock down the hall was audible and made the silence measured.

Do you have an interest in girls, Andy? A girlfriend perhaps? Mr. Aspinall asked.

His mind raced across the girls in his class. They were all candidates in his mind. Lately their breasts were pushing against their blouses, their winter coats away and blazers cast off. He'd have taken almost any one of them. He focused in. A name. He needed a single name. Something he could get behind, someone plausible. He looked up and said, Sarah Ramsey. It startled him. Then pleased him. She wasn't out of the realm of possibility. But he quickly added, We're not quite . . . you know.

I do, he said. I remember all too well the vagaries of girls at your age. There were no girls at LSC when I was there, of course. They were an enlightened addition relatively recently — not too long before Fiona was to enter high school, fortunately for us. Back in my day though we had to sneak off under the cover of darkness for an evening out. But a young Ramsey, eh.

Yes. More or less.

Then Mr. Aspinall leaned forward. Andy, he said, please consider this your home from now on. I know you are on scholarship but I will arrange to look after your incidentals. You will have everything that you need.

Andy did not know how to respond except to say thank you. He had wondered lately what would happen to him, if his father's death would somehow change his arrangement with LSC. On the surface, he didn't see why. But his father's absence created an unknown. He so desperately didn't want to leave. He forced it from his mind, hoping something would shore up his status. Here it was, solid as money.

I would like something from you in return, said Mr. Aspinall.

Of course, said Andy. Anything.

And the man leaned in and spoke to Andy in a low voice with a serious tone. You are normal; I can see that. Help me keep my boy safe. I need to know that much. You'll report back to me. Let me know what he does, who he sees, where he goes. Can you do that?

Yes.

Just between the two of us, then. Never tell Colin. Do we have a deal? Andy nodded and shook the man's hand — his grip was powerful and present for Andy even now, as if it had happened only yesterday.

Trudy had a gentle enough expression, but she was prompting him further without speaking. But he would not tell Trudy these details of his conversation, or to what he had agreed. Not yet, at least. So he moved the conversation on.

It was exam time, he said. I had to get extra help after class. Colin would join me even though he didn't need it. Colin didn't play sports — which were compulsory. He got out of it. He'd devised a brilliant scheme. Instead of purposefully failing to sign up for a sports team, and trying to keep a low profile so as not to be caught, Colin did the complete opposite. Feigning overenthusiasm coupled with a desire to try out for everything, he would sign up for three sports at the same time. Then, after a week or so, once the lists were submitted to the sports director, he would approach each coach and apologize for missing practice, but that he'd switched to a different sport. He'd tell basketball he'd switched to baseball, and baseball that he'd switched to track and field, and track that he'd decided on basketball.

None of them minded. He was uncoordinated and inept. They'd rather have the benching of Colin Aspinall be another teacher's problem. It would take the sports director most of the term to unravel Colin's series of switches. Meanwhile, he would hide in his dorm and read, or else sneak off campus.

What was he reading back then?

It's hard to recall. He read so much. He did go through a long French phase. The one cool French teacher got him hooked on it. Gide. Rimbaud. He slept with Camus's *L'Étranger* for more than a month one summer I remember. He could quote Oscar Wilde. Books were what he talked about most.

Was he ever in trouble for not playing a sport?

When he was finally caught, he would complain that none of the coaches wanted him on their team — which he knew was true — and so he felt completely at a loss as to what to do. He would then be lightly reprimanded for not coming forward on his own, and sent off to intramurals. Intramurals was supposed to be a kind of punishment.

But it wasn't?

No, this was Colin's end goal. It was a hodgepodge group of students who were too injured, or too asthmatic, or in Colin's case too delicate, for regular team sports. It was run by a senior student who needed a community service credit. Inevitably,

Fiona would have a word with this student and Colin's presence would not be missed. So, ultimately, he never did sports for more than a week or two a year. I said to him once that if he'd put as much effort into doing a sport as he did in getting out of it, then he'd be a star.

Why did he hate sports so much?

Rules. He hated abiding by rules.

I'd like to backtrack. You began by talking about the exams, at the end of the term. You said that Colin did not need special help?

No. Colin was bright. He told the teachers that he needed help so he could hang out with me. He helped me quite a bit in fact. I wasn't a strong student in the beginning. Got better by the end though.

What was Colin's best subject?

English. But he liked drama the best. We could take either art or drama as our only elective each year. He and I chose drama. At the end of term, our drama class was broken up into four groups and we had to put on a play, or an act of a play, in front of the whole school after lunch. It was a tradition. Most groups needed help in choosing what play to do and the teacher would intervene and help them put on, say, an act of *Macbeth* or *Henry IV.* One year a group did quite a bit of *The Crucible* and it was good. But, I was in Colin's group, and, at Colin's insistence, we read Act III of *A Man's Castle*.

Goodness!

You know it?

Yes, I've seen it.

It's Canadian.

I know.

It's supposed to be about the Aspinalls.

I know that too.

Well, Colin played the patriarch — his own father, in other

words. You can imagine that this shocked the school — or at least those in the know. I didn't know anything about the play until afterward when we were dragged into the headmaster's office and asked to explain our behaviour.

He was quite naughty then?

Oh god, yes.

Did you get in trouble?

We had been allowed to choose whatever play we wanted. Somehow, the stupid drama teacher was completely unaware of the play's provenance. He applauded us for doing a contemporary Canadian production. What an idiot. Colin had one-upped the teacher, so I don't recall any unusual punishment. Fiona thought it was the funniest gag she'd ever seen.

What did Mr. Aspinall say when he found out?

Oh, that's the best part. Parents came to the production. He was there. It was set up as a kind of dinner theatre. So there he was, sitting at the back of the dining hall with the rest of the parents. . . .

Good lord.

Yes. Can you imagine?

Had he ever seen it before?

I have no idea.

But he knew, obviously, the content.

Of course.

I wish I'd been there.

Fiona yelled *Bravo* at the top of her lungs at the end. Colin curtsied. It *was* incredibly funny — looking back on it.

Who were you?

What do you mean?

In the play. What character did you play?

Oh, the son. I played the son.

I don't recall that character.

He only appears once and is never named. He doesn't have

any lines. I didn't want to act and be onstage. Too self-conscious. So I thought it was great. I just had to be there in the background. I went almost unnoticed.

◆ ◆ ◆

Andy left Trudy on her own for a few minutes so she could telephone her daughter one last time — it's her bedtime she told him. He was making coffee and preparing dessert. Outside the light was fast fading. He could hear fragments of Trudy's conversation, her tones sounding like a mother: soothing, over-interested, assured.

As he scooped ice cream and fresh blueberries — bought yesterday — into two bowls. He felt tired. Thinking so much about Colin had made him ache. They'd loved one another back then. Are some boys lucky? Do some know what this kind of love means — how important it is? Do they accept it, own it, and keep it private, unspoken, and tendered? It's an aggressive love, Andy now knew, and it throws down deep roots, ensuring its return wanted or not — year in, year out.

He could describe it like this to her. But there are some things, he thinks, that maybe women cannot, and therefore will not, accept about men. At its heart is a kind of violence. Once love is pronounced, this threat becomes irrevocable, inevitable.

Andy licked ice cream from his spoon. He made small talk with Trudy. From deep within him, those early days at Huntington House produced a longing. Together, he and Colin had been brand new. Once Colin returned from England, that they could spend much of the summer before them in each other's company was thrilling. Scarborough was another lifetime. Who had he been back then? There was Andy Kronk, striding the hallways of Lord Simcoe College — spending his summers at Huntington House. At night, instead of watching hockey or working out with weights, he and Colin Aspinall, his new best friend, would sit up and read.

You must read, Andy. Books are what separate us from the animals and the masses. Colin would force them on him one after another, reading sections out loud when he came to a particularly cutting or deviant passage.

At the end of Andy's first week at Huntington, his father's funeral only the day before, Fiona had a pool party. Mr. and Mrs. Aspinall were in Montreal for the evening. Fiona told Colin and Andy, in no uncertain terms, they were not to come outside.

In his eyes, it was not a big enough group to be properly called a party. Through the window of the upstairs bathroom, Andy saw several guys from his hockey team, and a few other seniors whom he recognized, drinking and smoking cigarettes, showing off in front of about the same number of girls. They were all friends and they were entering their final few months of high school together. They were sombre, and it was evident to Andy as he looked on, how casual and comfortable they all were together. *He* would have this too. Bonds that run deep, that permitted him a lifetime of sure-footedness because of what he'd shared with his classmates.

What are you doing in there? It was Colin banging on the door.

Andy opened it. Colin came over to the window and looked out too. They stood for a moment together, looking down at Fiona and her group of friends. One of the girls was French braiding another's hair. Several others looked on as one played guitar and sang a folk song. Fiona stood and slid out of her loose shirt and shorts. The boy stopped singing, but continued finger picking. She was without clothes. She slid into the water. The moon was out; it was a warm, early spring evening, and steam rose off the heated pool. One by one, they all climbed out of their clothes. Colin put his hand on Andy's shoulder. It was the first time Colin touched him. He let himself be touched.

She's going to McGill next year, Colin said softly. Montreal. That's why my parents are there this weekend. They are buying a house for her to live in with her friends. She didn't want to live in residence.

Will you miss her?

No.

Why not?

I've got you.

Outside, one of Fiona's friends, Kimberly Payne, resisted nudity and had been thrown in the pool. There were coy screams and laughter, coaxing and good-natured taunts. The boy on the guitar sang again mournfully. Again, they all quieted down. One or two came together and embraced. The pool lights shone and shimmered, and their bodies floated about on the water or lay at ease on reclining chairs. The clouds in the night sky were black shapes that moved in inches, outlines lit only by the moon.

Andy's memory held this tableau of bodies suspended in youthful litheness. He'd caught them at a precise moment — when youth, what was supposedly to last forever, had begun to pass them by. They were not living, they were memorizing. This was the final exam. And in the centre of it all was Fiona — a seated nude. Her foot gauged the water's temperature while she rested back on her outstretched hands. She assumed the focal point — as if one of the boys might be inexplicably compelled to feed her grapes or rub her feet with oils.

Come on, Colin had said after a time. Andy's memory remained clear and sure. I'll give you a new book to read, Colin had said next, and he had begun to back out of the bathroom.

But Andy didn't move. Colin reached to his face then. Touching it, running his fingers down over Andy's cheek, his neck, and resting, lightly, on his chest. Colin's body grew electrified, undergoing subtle shocks and tremors. Andy pulled off his T-shirt slowly, swirls of his chest hair, his pectorals, tightened nipples, looking down at Colin's hand now on his bare skin.

Colin, he had said, you can do what you need to do. I don't mind. I understand.

◆ ◆ ◆

A few more questions, then, I should let you get some rest, she said. How would he be able to sleep?

Trudy was nursing a coffee. It had all gone well. As well as could be expected. Better than he'd hoped. He was enjoying himself, in a way. He liked her, how she listened so carefully to all that he'd said, picking up on points that he wouldn't have thought important or even interesting.

It had been early June and school was almost out. He and Colin wrote an exam right after chapel. Instead of waiting around to go to lunch, they'd hitched a ride with Fiona to Huntington for the afternoon. They had to be back before dinner, hoped no one would miss them. They were desperate to start the holidays.

The day was the first hot one of the summer. Fiona drove quickly, weaving around slower motorists on the highway. The car was bright red. She had the radio up loud and the top down. Then flashing lights. The policeman's stern face changed when he leaned over Fiona and looked into the car. She had her school uniform on and her kilt was pushed up, lots of leg on show. The cop forgot what he was supposed to be doing. He managed to gather himself and begin to write her a ticket, but when he read her driver's licence something clued him in to her last name, or address, as he just looked up to the sky and laughed. She was given a warning.

At Huntington, Fiona, Colin, and Andy had climbed through Mr. Aspinall's study window on the top floor and stepped out on the roof. They had towels and a radio, suntan lotion and magazines. Their mood was high, having escaped both school and the law, and Fiona was only weeks from graduation. In between two turrets was a flat section of roof, completely hidden from the ground. It was Fiona's private spot — until Colin caught her leaving via the window. Now they shared it.

But Fiona didn't have long that day. Though she spread out her towel, hitched up her skirt, rolled up her sleeves, and lit a cigarette, she spent less than ten minutes with them. Her mother was taking her shopping for a prom dress.

I'll be back in a few hours to pick you both up, she said. You'd better not be late for dinner at school or they'll know for sure you've been off campus. And she left with a smile and a raised hand, flicking her cigarette into the air to fall down somewhere below. House fires, the law, Fiona was immune to everything.

Colin took off all his clothes. He was thin and white, a boy underneath his collared shirt and tie, blue sports jacket, and grey flannel pants. He did not say a word as he did this. Andy watched him. Andy was used to seeing young men naked. He saw them every day at school in the shower, in the locker rooms before and after hockey practice. But he'd never looked on purposefully — as he was permitted to, expected to, now. Colin chattered on about the exam that morning, the chapel sermon they'd suffered through. He lay on the towel, his buttocks upward to the sun.

It was clear what he must do. Taking his clothes off as matter-of-factly as he could, Andy lay face up next to Colin, the sun warming his thick chest and face, his thighs and cock. After allowing himself a fleeting glance, Colin resisted looking at him further. Instead he remained face down and began to talk in rapid-fire about the upcoming holidays, whether or not he'd still go to Paris, then England, as planned. He told Andy all about his father's friends who lived outside London.

As Colin talked on and on, Andy felt the power he had. It was the same power Fiona had over the cop. Andy could not help but look at Colin's thin, boyish body. He wished Fiona had not left so soon. Surely she did not take off her clothes up here too? Colin's body was like his own had been two years earlier. A fine down of hair on his thighs and calves, his back was smooth, and his arms slender and without any muscle definition: this in complete opposition to Andy's own body. He lifted weights in the school's gym and his chest was even more solid than it had been six months ago. They were both fifteen and while Andy's body increasingly looked like a man's, Colin was frail, fine.

Eventually, Colin managed to make him laugh. Colin looked up. They shared one of Fiona's cigarettes that she'd left. Andy coughed. For a while they dozed, the sun warming their private world, the sky hard and deeply blue.

I'll miss you if I have to go to England, Colin said. Andy wasn't sure how awake Colin was when he spoke. Later, completely asleep, Colin rolled over. The movement prompted Andy to open his eyes for a moment to see his friend's dreams standing proudly before him.

A secret life was beginning; he could feel it. Andy accepted it as his fate, just as he understood that his father was no longer breathing and in this world, this too, his new life here at Huntington House, was his to obey.

A cloud passed in front of the sun and it took much of the

day's heat with it. Colin woke with a start and reached for his clothes. Andy dressed as well, but they stayed on the roof, Colin reading a book, Andy wandering to the edge to look over the grounds at the driveway, which wound down toward the end of the property.

Listen to this, Colin called out. Andy turned and faced him, and Colin read aloud from his book.

To know and love another human being is the root of all wisdom. Andy, isn't that a perfect line.

Their world, like the rooftop hideaway, was closed off. Nothing and no one could see or change them.

Was Mrs. Aspinall as open to your presence as Mr. Aspinall? Trudy asked.

Andy felt exhausted now. It overcame him in an unexpected wave. Remembering all this has taken it out of me, he said.

We'll stop after this then. I should get back to the B&B, said Trudy.

Mrs. Aspinall? he said, trying to concentrate. She never took much notice of me, he offered. There's not much more to say I'm afraid. She was a well-groomed woman. Tall, thin. Proper, in a way. But not always. She gossiped too. Andy looked out the window. It was dark now.

Mrs. Aspinall had been there that day after they had climbed down off the roof. In the kitchen where he and Colin had been eating. Fiona and Mrs. Aspinall arrived home, and Fiona tried on her prom dress once more, to show Colin. She called down from upstairs for Colin to come to her. That was the first time Mrs. Aspinall and he had spoken alone.

Tell me Andy, said Mrs. Aspinall, tell me about Colin's other friends. Who are his other friends?

Everyone is friendly to Colin at LSC, he'd answered. Mrs.

Aspinall leaned against the kitchen counter, scribbling something down on a notepad, a shopping list for their maid, or something for the gardener perhaps.

He doesn't have other friends, does he? she asked.

Not really.

You're it.

We're best friends.

You and I are going to get along famously, she'd said. Is Fiona going to drive you two back?

Yes.

Andy, I'm glad to hear you are going to be with us this summer. Together, we'll make sure Colin is happy.

The next day in chapel Andy had shuffled in next to Colin. He nodded by way of greeting. Colin, haughty, ignored him for the rest of the service. Andy confronted him on the cobblestone pathway outside.

What's wrong with you today? Andy asked.

What did you say to my mother yesterday?

What do you mean? I said nothing. When?

When I was upstairs with Fiona.

Nothing.

I heard you. She was listening to you say something.

I didn't say anything.

They mustn't own you too, Andy. You have to be mine and mine alone. They own everything, and everyone, and all I've ever wanted is something, someone just for myself. That's you, Andy. You're mine. Keep everything between us. You must agree.

Yes. Of course.

Colin looked up at Andy. His fringe was long and blond and was in his eyes, and so he pushed it away, but it fell back down again.

One more week to go. Four exams. Then freedom, said Colin.

I have to play hockey all summer.

I thought you liked hockey.

I do, I just wish. But Andy stopped himself.

What?

I wish I could come to Paris and England with you. That's all. But I've got to practice, get lots of ice time.

I'll write long letters and describe everything, don't worry. It's only for a few weeks. We've got two months off.

Summer was almost within reach.

◆ ◆ ◆

Trudy left for her B&B and Andy locked the door to the cottage out of habit. Sitting on the toilet, his bowels loosening, he wondered momentarily why he could not recall even one of the many times he must have shat at Huntington House. He tried to recall one of the bathrooms, its decor. He caught glimpses of wallpaper pattern, but that was all. How could he remember almost verbatim conversations from years ago, but not be able to picture the exact details of a small room in which he must have, over the course of several years, spent hours?

He climbed under the covers of his bed and lay still on his back. What did he leave out? How much had he forgotten? Countless time spent trying to decide what to eat, or wear. The myriad of minutes scattered throughout each day spent having no conscious thoughts at all. His sheets were clean. He did all the washing before Trudy arrived. Sitting in front of the dryer at the Laundromat he'd caught himself daydreaming of the weeping beeches. This was not a tree he'd ever seen, but it was one Colin had described in a letter that first summer during his trip to England. Colin's description was so precise Andy had felt as if he were there too. Now, years later, he recalled the tree as if he, and not Colin, had been the one to see it in person. The great solid arch of branches reaching out and down to form a series of perfect tunnels. But then, Colin's voice breaks through. They are like the catacombs, Andy! You can duck down inside them and come out in a completely different spot. It's so wonderful to be hidden by the branches. Do you miss me? Is it too hot on the roof? I've not fallen in love with any English girls. They are of no more interest to me than the Canadian versions. Far as I can see, girls are all the same wherever you go. Insipid, self-absorbed, cruel.

Andy fell asleep, dragged under the weeping beech. Pieces of light, streaming and broken, passed through the cathedral of it, through leaves and branches, reaching them hidden — in sanctuary. Alone. Together. The cool dirt on bare feet and absolute privacy. A faint smell of honeysuckle. This is home now, said his father's face, having joined them. The weeping beech vaults over them. A bursting of pleasure. Colin describes what happens to the mind as it drifts into unconsciousness. How do you know that? And they laugh. Shake my hand, Andy. Yes, Mr. Aspinall. Look, Andy, at those in-between places, those dark patches that give perfect shape to the light. Fiona's face comes at him, lips pressed together in a kiss. Her tongue flickers on his as might a snake's. He runs through the tunnels under the weeping beech, passing waves of defeat, regret, hatred, guilt, yearning, and a kind of absence that has no proper name. He runs free, again and again, around and around, disgusted, disappointed, sombre, afraid, overjoyed, content, alive. He draws closer to Colin's face coming out of the bark itself at a knot on the trunk. His lips are as cracked as the bark, he steps from the tree and he is blue and cold and he speaks low, with the voice of Dr. Tilford, the weight pressing down on Andy overbearing.

Andy gags. Colin laughs at Andy. Then Colin speaks again, this time with his own voice, but the words do not mean anything. Andy is desperate to hear, but the harder he tries the less audible are Colin's words. Colin is only an arm's-length away, yet he is vanishing from Andy down a tunnel that he cannot follow. It is a void into which he cannot pass. Colin slips away.

PART THREE

Trudy woke to damp sheets and the sun streaming in through the window. The lake's sparkling surface, in reflection, danced on the ceiling above her bed. Trudy leaned over the side of the bed and went through her bag. There was a photograph and write up of Huntington House in here somewhere. Andy's story had brought Huntington to life, but all she knew of the house itself was a projection — gleaned from other people's accounts, and partly imagined on her own part, along with the stage set of *A Man's Castle*. Hardly accurate. Then she found it: two pages photocopied from a recent enough book on the architectural history of southern Ontario.

Huntington House has thirty-nine rooms and almost one hundred acres of forest, field and, closer to the house, English-style gardens with mature perennial beds. Built in 1908 by Stuart Aspinall esq. for his second wife Isabel (née Hill) as a summer home on the lake, Huntington House was modelled on an estate constructed in New England about fifty years earlier, which, in turn, was based on Gosfield Hall in Essex. The neo-classical facade, a later addition, is said to have come from Stuart Aspinall himself who was something of an amateur draftsman.

In 1931, the family business suffered significant financial losses under the stewardship of Stuart Aspinall II — or Stuart Jr. as he was most often called. He sold their two Toronto properties and relocated the family to Huntington House, at which time it became their permanent residence. During the Second World War and its aftermath, business once again flourished for this great Canadian family paving the way for the success they are known for today. Following the early death of his father, the current Aspinall patriarch, then a young man freshly back to Canada from Cambridge where he read history, gave Huntington House a large renovation and addition. At this time, the pool, tennis courts, and out buildings such as the stables and boathouses were also added.

Life at Huntington during the sixties and seventies was opulent and the pinnacle of Canada's social scene — playing host to visiting dignitaries, business elite, actors, and musicians.

By the early nineties, time had marched on. Amid a business climate of widespread downsizing, with its owner now "of an age," and neither offspring yet continuing on in the family company, Huntington House was almost sold in 1993 along with most of the significant Aspinall Inc. interests. It was rumoured that Mrs. Aspinall was the one who saved the house, deciding to keep it in the family for future generations.

When asked why he would not want to save such an important historical house from the wrecking ball, Stuart Aspinall III joked with the media (as is his typical way) reminding them that, in fact, the house was only ninety years old and in Britain that would be considered still new and very probably ugly, and besides,

Canadian property taxes were prohibitively expensive even for him. Still, he remarked, my wife always gets her way. Huntington lives to see another day.

It is worth noting that at the time of printing, the Aspinall family's personal net worth is said to be in excess of four billion dollars. Moreover, while time and needs change even for our country's greatest families, the proposed demolition, then saving, of Huntington House was seen by most architectural historians — including this one — to be a significant crisis averted in the fight to preserve the very best examples of Canada's rich, if short, post-industrial architectural history.

◆ ◆ ◆

Trudy heard the B&B's owner moving about in the kitchen. Coffee was spluttering and there was the smell of toast. She slipped the papers back inside the dossier and into her briefcase. She reached for her cellphone.

It's me. Is Veronica awake yet?

No, said Patrick, audibly swallowing liquid. Probably tea, she thought. That was what he drank. Not yet. You talked to her last night, right?

Yes. But I want to speak with her again this morning. I'm the mother. She hasn't ever spent this much time away from me.

Or you from her.

They often sniped at each other when they spoke on the phone. They always had, even when they were still together: the mornings especially. But lately she'd been noticing them at it more often than usual.

Yes, you're right. And she forced a thin, light-sounding laugh.

When they had first become a couple, their differences emerged. While she loved watching him drum onstage, that he would practice — on every surface, with stick substitutions ranging from his index fingers, to pens, to spoons — had never occurred to her. Also, it took Patrick much too long to wake up. He had a sleepy head at noon.

At times such as these, she used to remind herself that he had many good qualities too. At some point though, she stopped. Patrick became little more than a sum total of his irritating tics and frustrating habits. Eventually these formed part of her reason for leaving. Her other reasons were that he did not listen to her, and was absent-minded. Both stemmed, she suspected, from his drumming. Even when sitting still, ostensibly doing nothing, he was hearing music around him. He drummed along to it — literally and imaginatively. She would talk, he would be hearing *ta, ta-ka, ta-ki-ta, ta-ka-di-tah.*

Yet still Trudy awoke to thoughts of his body next to hers. He was on her mind as she fell asleep, and was in her dreams when she first opened her eyes. He'd had a kind of warmth to him in the mornings that lingered after they rose. It was this precise trait, his slowness to react before noon, which used to bother her. But now — now, lying in a strange bed at a B&B on a lake up north and very much alone, she acknowledged in a fleeting moment that she missed it. She missed him. Perhaps it was his voice on the phone. She did not usually talk to him while she was still in bed.

You okay up there?

Yes. I'm fine. He's a talker. I'm getting mostly background so far. Bits pop out in unexpected ways. Does she miss me, do you think?

Of course she does, Trudy.

She talks about you all the time.

That's nice to say.

She does. I mean it.

What's it like up there? I've never been to Broad Lake. Up in the middle of nowhere, isn't it?

She could tell Patrick was working hard to be coherent, to not get on her nerves. He was well aware that he bothered her in the mornings. He had always respected her work. His extra effort today pleased her.

There's a town, she began while trying to get a grip on herself, not far I think. The lake is pretty. Fairly deserted. Perhaps a few more people will come on the weekend to their cottages: still early in the season though.

Trudy jammed the phone between her shoulder and ear, freeing her hands to push herself into a sitting position. Then she climbed out of bed and looked out the window. The wind on the lake brought the surface alive, the light glittery and delightful. She wished Veronica were with her.

I'm glad, he was saying, I'm glad it's going well for you.

His voice was present and kind. It was unconscionable they hadn't been able to work it out. They were still in love.

There's that canoe again, she said suddenly. Out on the lake. I'm in a bedroom and the window looks out onto the lake. Yesterday, at Andy's place, there was a canoe with two people in it. They circled about the lake for most of the day. They're bird-watchers. That's what Andy had said. A man's sitting in the back, and it's a woman in the front. Now they're down here, at this end of the lake. I wonder if they are headed back up to Andy's stretch of the lake again?

How are his J-strokes?

Nice, she said and laughed freely. Yes, firm J-strokes.

He has an even touch? he asked. He's patient?

He is, she said smiling. You can't rush a J-stroke.

They'd canoed in Algonquin Park that first fall after they'd moved in together. Having driven up on a whim, they rented equipment from a local guy. He'd charged them hardly anything because Patrick had told him — impulsively, outrageously — it was their honeymoon. He then proceeded to make up a long, and completely fictional story about how they'd eloped, got married in Las Vegas only the weekend before, and how they were forced to these ends because Trudy's father refused, *categorically rebuffed me when I approached the man to ask for her hand in marriage.*

With Trudy's mouth agape, and the man believing every word, Patrick's tale got worse. They'd spent most of their money, he told the man, and all they could afford for a honeymoon was a camping trip. The man, it turned out, was an old softie and threw in all kinds of extras, taught them the importance of a firm J-stroke, giving them a dry lesson right then and there in the shop, and wished them all the best.

Patrick told her later, once they were out and paddling on the lake, that when she was in the washroom the man had taken him aside and said how brave he was to have taken the matter into his own hands and regaled Patrick with a story of his own — one where he, unfortunately, had not been so brave.

You're terrible, she'd said. I can't believe you made all that up.

It was harmless. Besides, his prices were overinflated. Brought them down to market value. Call it bartering.

From then on, any opportunity to comment on someone's J-stroke was never missed, and when someone, anyone, was turned down, in their own private idiom it was that they'd been *categorically rebuffed.*

I'll call Veronica at lunchtime. Tell her I love her, okay?

Of course.

Make sure she eats breakfast.

I promise I will keep her thriving.

Thanks. Thank you, Pat. I mean it.

She turned off her cellphone. Outside the window, the paddlers were now almost lost to the distance and the morning haze. She dressed, ate an English muffin with honey, and drove the five minutes back to Andy's.

The light in the morning off the lake is so beautiful. I can see why you live up here, she said.

It didn't wake you up too early?

It's just what I'd hoped for. Is that coffee?

It's a long way from a latte.

Do you think I could go for a swim?

The water's cold still. But if you're game, it's deep off the end of the dock.

In her bathing suit, she made her way back down to the dock in bare feet. It was early enough that the grass still had its dew. As it was unfamiliar terrain, she found herself overly cautious of where she was stepping, protective of her feet, which looked alabaster in the brightness.

Her body exploded into the water. She opened her eyes to a streaked and fertile forest of weed. The water was cold but a clear deep blue. Rays of light appeared to grow up from the depths as if birch trunks. Her heart beat ecstatically at the cold shock. As a kid, Veronica's age, she'd have sworn that the cold meant nothing to her — such dishonest moxy.

On their trip in Algonquin she and Patrick had made love underwater. She knew this was a supposedly bad practice for a woman, dangerous for one's gynecological health she'd once read in *Chatelaine*. But as they clung to each other, suspended in the lake, she suspected many had thrown caution to the wind in the same way. Besides, didn't women give birth in water these days?

She was swimming now, a languid backstroke, kicking small, toe-pointed steps as if a faltering ballerina. She had clung to Patrick that moonlit night. They were treading water — swimming just enough to keep them from sinking, from drowning. The round moon bobbed above, disappearing and reappearing. Patrick swam them in to the shallows. She stretched out and floated on her back, letting herself coil up inside and holding her breath until she shuddered and sank. The lake had been warm, and they were the only break on its surface.

This morning the clouds floated by, or was she propelling underneath their stationary watch? She was not far out yet, but she kept her eye on the shoreline nonetheless. Andy was back down at the dock. He was holding a towel and a steaming mug. He waved at her. She returned it and then continued on for another few strokes.

She rolled over and pushed under the water, gliding through the beaming birch forest. She'd been late giving birth to Veronica. They'd induced. She remembered Patrick's breath as the contractions mounted from within. It had smelled of coffee. Then she lost Patrick somewhere during those almighty heaves, as she pushed that new life from herself in waves of . . . it hadn't been pain, not the usual kind anyway. She'd found it too total to call it just that. For a moment, when she felt she could not go on, that she had failed, been defeated by the essential act of womanhood, she sank within herself, unable to evict her baby.

She swam, pulling the water past her body. What had kept her going — defeat itself? She wondered. Where motherhood was taking her had never been clear. But she had found a new spirit after Veronica's birth. After all, what could possibly be harder? She banked on this when she and Patrick split. She could go it alone; she'd been through something harder.

Her hand hit a stick with a wallop. It was a piece of drift-wood, smooth and grey.

As a girl, she read books so she could feel alive. Next it was studying history. Then it was Patrick who took on that role. Finally, after giving birth to Veronica — this little bundle of growing needs and wants — motherhood became how she knew she was alive, important, loved.

Veronica no longer required her as much as she once did. Soon — two years, five years — Veronica would turn and look at her with disgust, or pity, or disgrace. That very being within whom she found her ultimate strength would cast her aside. Was this why she had begun to think again of Patrick? Was it him she needed? Another baby? She'd have liked that, but was too old now. What then, effortless love? Day-to-day camaraderie? Deep friendship?

Back at the dock, Trudy's hands gripped the rungs of the ladder. They were green with a film of algae. She wrung her hair out and dried herself off with the towel. Took a mouthful of coffee. Looked down at her legs. They were not the legs of a young woman anymore. She didn't much care. But, when they *were* at their best she didn't wrap them around enough young men while suspended in warm lakes. At least she'd managed it once.

She caught sight of an osprey soaring into the sky. She looked up and saw its feathers, individually, which were surprisingly clear to her. Trudy dressed quickly, slipping her bathrobe over her bathing suit. She turned to head back up to the cottage with her coffee spilling as she hurried. She felt, strangely, that she was being watched from behind.

How was it? asked Andy as she shook her head to the side trying to dislodge water in her ear. You're brave! he added. She entered the cottage. Her teeth were actually chattering.

I'll be with you in a few minutes, she said to Andy. Get settled and we'll start right where we left off. Thanks for indulging me.

In the bedroom a stack of old towels, blankets, and sheets lined the single shelf as if sedimentary layers of changing twentieth-century taste. Bright pinks and aqua paisley, houndstooth, tan and black tartan, chocolate brown, hunter green, primary reds and yellows. They must have come with the place, she thought as she unfolded one to use. On it were members of the Toronto Blue Jays from a different time. She wiped herself down with Willie Upshaw, Ernie Whitt, and Jesse Barfield. What was Andy doing up here, she thought as she wrung her bathing suit out the window and hung it over the ledge. She was cold. Goosebumps spread across her flesh in gusts. She dressed and brushed out her hair. She must make this a good day. Perhaps she could leave tonight if she got everything she needed.

Andy watched as Trudy settled herself, with her coffee in one hand, pushing her hair in behind her ear, and running her index finger down the top page on her clipboard looking for where she'd finished up the evening before. He heard the click as she pressed record, and the quiet winding as the tape began. She looked up at him. He knew exactly where they'd left off.

That summer between grade nine and ten was the first of three summers he'd lived in one of the guest bedrooms at Huntington. There was a small bathroom off the side of his room, and bookshelves that ran from ceiling to floor down one whole wall. Stuart Aspinall's chess collection had spilled over into this spare room and he'd occasionally stop in and polish them up so he could display them in other rooms. Mr. Aspinall played chess most days with Colin — when he was home from school. They'd played together since he was five or six. It was one of the few enjoyments they shared. They didn't talk much. Just made moves.

Colin and I took windsurfing lessons down on the lake. It

was during the next summer, after grade ten, because Fiona was home from university. Colin was too scared to go on his board alone. He would stand on the back of my board.

You took lessons at the lake frontage of Huntington House? They'd been lumped together with a group of younger girls. There was a lot of giggling. In the morning, one of them would arrive with a crush on one or both of them. Inevitably, it would dissipate by the afternoon. The instructors were two friends of Fiona's from university. They stayed in the boathouse, were employed by the Aspinalls to run sailing and windsurfing lessons, and to help the gardeners. It was an undemanding summer job.

And the younger girls? Trudy asked.

From other wealthy families. Friends of Mrs. Aspinall. It was babysitting. Fiona had done it the two previous summers. She had convinced her mother to hire her replacements, so she could be free.

Andy could feel Colin behind him on the windsurfer, the wet rubber grip, the sail taut, and his friend's arms around his waist. Colin would shriek as each bit of chop approached. The farther out they sailed, the closer Colin would pull himself to Andy. They would fall in often, tread water out in the deep and float a while, catch their breath, before Andy would stand on the long board and haul the sail up. Colin would then climb back up and crouch until they were sailing along once again.

I take it Mr. Aspinall was away at work most of the time? Was Mrs. Aspinall out much of the time too?

She was mostly home, he said.

The hard rain pelted down, bouncing off the cabin roof. In the dank about them, varnished wood trim, the stale smell of folded canvas, faint wisps of booze and coconut oil, it had been quiet. Andy remembered Fiona, as she lit a smoke, draping her tanned legs over the small table. She held Colin, he was whimpering.

C'mon Col, she said. It's just lightning and thunder.

Andy had never seen Colin get so worked up. Fiona was soothing her brother — but all the while looking over at Andy.

After the storm passed, the rain petering to a light shower, then to nothing at all, Colin looked up suddenly and was embarrassed. He rose and went outside. Andy followed him up the ladder, but Colin had already jumped off the boat and was wandering away down the shore. Colin had picked up a stick. Dragging it behind him, he left a light, snaking line in the wet sand. His shoulders sank down. From the cabin below, Fiona spoke.

He's been scared of thunder all his life. It's quite normal. I know you would never tell the boys at school.

Andy climbed back down the ladder and sat down. Fiona dropped her cigarette into her pop can to a split-second hiss, then moved over next to Andy. She pulled Andy to her quietly, taking his hand in hers and placing it on her stomach first, then inching it almost up to her breast, slowly. He felt her skin, its smooth heat.

I know you, Andy, she whispered. His mind was spellbound. His limbs were paralyzed. I know I can rely on you, she said. Look after Colin. Tell me if anything bad is going to happen to him. Promise me.

He did. He promised. Fiona brought her face to his, as if . . . but she did not kiss him. Not then.

What about Colin? asked Trudy.

Some mornings Colin's desire to escape Huntington would rush forward from nowhere. We would climb into one of the boats and row it out until it was just far enough away so we wouldn't wake anyone. Then we'd pull the engine cord. We'd be gone for hours. We did stuff like that. Teenage stuff.

Careening across the glassy lake, their wake cut the first disturbance of the morning. Huge granite rocks formed whole islands in the middle, many of which had coves and nooks. They would strip down and swim, then lie on the rocks, drying off in the early morning sun. They would look for patterns in the clouds, see faces, make words. From time to time, they would hear another boat coming, and have to duck in behind a tree, or lie still, face down, until it passed, hoping that its occupants would not see their boat tied up in the shadows, decide to come over and investigate.

There was a recklessness to Colin, said Andy. He'd manufacture, well, not quite danger, just excitement. He liked the rush. It was false bravado.

He could not tell her that Colin was forever taking his clothes off, and encouraging him to do the same. Or that he would steal money from his parents. He would take the spare key entrusted to his mother and break into the neighbour's place when they were in Florida. He would try on dresses and siphon off liquor. Once Colin "borrowed" a car from his father and made Andy drive fast down side roads. Colin climbed out the window and sat on the door with only his legs inside the car.

You ever dream you can fly? Colin screamed into the car at him.

What? Get in Colin.

Go faster!

Let's go back.

Take this corner fast! He laughed hysterically. It was mad, dangerous. The trees rushed by, and another car came around the corner.

Please come inside, Andy pleaded, and slowed down the car.

Colin wriggled back and they took the corner patiently, the driver of the other car passing them and shooting them a look. Andy didn't even have his licence at the time.

Of course, Trudy said. All teenagers go through difficult stages. Did Colin rebel against his parents because they didn't accept him, who he really was?

It was more complicated than that. Colin didn't fit in anywhere. He should have been the centre of the world: the only Aspinall son — and all that.

But Colin realized, said Trudy, pressing him, he was never going to grow into the right kind of man, that he was, what, trapped by the Aspinall name? Is that why he grew rebellious?

I think so, Andy said. Yes.

Late in the summer following grade ten, they caught the GO train into Toronto. Colin wanted to go: anything to get out of Huntington and away from his family. They were going to see a movie, to walk around *midnight madness* at the Eaton Centre. They blended in, as if they were just another pair of teenagers.

Sitting in the food court, eating a hot dog and sharing an Orange Julius, his and Colin's minds were far from the shopping crowds. They skipped the movie, deciding instead to walk up and down Yonge Street. About them the music had throbbed from freshly repainted cars driven by slick-haired boys — in for the night from Etobicoke, Mississauga, and Markham; and girls with big hair walked the streets, hanging outside Sam's; drunk groups of Ryerson students talked loudly with mouthfuls of pizza; skids sold hits, or mushrooms, or cartons of American cigarettes smuggled in across the border; homeless people, oblivious to it all, walked upstream through the crowds in deep conversation with themselves; throngs of preppy high school kids, from Barrie, Oakville, Guelph, and Cobourg, high on the lies they told to get away for the night, were all urgently on their way to nowhere. The night had been young, hot, and alive. They retreated into the mall to catch their breath.

You fellas looking for a party to go to? The man was not old, twenties maybe, shaved bald, with thick, muscular forearms.

He was clean-looking and wore a single earring. His name, he told them, was Stevie, and Stevie's tone was familiar and friendly. He quickly picked up on their desire for adventure, for risks, and their frustration at not ever being able to find, let alone seize, those opportunities. There was an energy about this man to which Colin, especially, was immediately drawn.

During their conversation, Andy saw how Stevie, casually — almost as an accident — touched Colin on the back of the hand with his thumb.

There's a cool party happening at a club a bit later. You guys like me to take you?

Andy could tell within minutes that Colin would follow this man anywhere. So, to keep an eye on Colin, he went along.

The place was thick with smoke, and dark, with thin bands of pink neon light moving erratically. It was still early and the club was far from full, but later, assured Stevie, the place would be packed. This place was *the* party club.

Music thumped, taking over the natural rhythms of their bodies. They sat in a corner booth and Stevie ordered beers for them all.

I'll be back in a minute, he then said. I'm going to find some of my friends.

Colin was electrified by the music. His head spun left and right, gorging himself on the groups of men drinking beers or cocktails, touching each other with such ease. Against the back wall a man was dancing by himself. He wore bicycle shorts and no shirt and didn't seem to care what anyone else thought. Andy loathed electronic dance music. On the other side of the booth Colin wore a glazed look, as if put under hypnosis by it.

Colin, I want to go, he'd said.

So go.

I can't just leave you here.

Why not?

Still underage, Andy had been inside so few bars of any description that walking into this place made him feel much the same as he had when he'd been into others: conspicuous, nervous, in the wrong. He made a face of disgust at Colin that came more from these feelings than anything else.

I'm going to the washroom. Then we should go.

In the hallway leading to the Men's, Andy encountered Stevie who was talking with another man.

You still here? said Stevie when he saw Andy. The music was loud so he leaned in to whisper something to the other man — who was tall and wore a suit. Then he said to Andy, smirking, This is Tiger. The man laughed at the name he'd been given and began to mouth along theatrically with the words: *it ain't necessarily so.* This second man looked drunk, Andy realized.

Now Andrew, or Adam, or whatever your name was, don't be the little alarmed straight guy, but I'm going to fuck your friend back there because he's good and ready for it, so unless you're going to loosen up and let Tiger here do the same to you, you should probably go home.

Then Tiger leaned in to Andy and spoke so Stevie couldn't hear, his breath close and boozy, but he sounded suddenly serious and trustworthy. *You can go home if you'd like. Your friend will be fine. Stevie is all talk. He's just trying to impress me.* Then it was Stevie's turn to sing along, and he did so, throwing his voice into high falsetto, which made them laugh, slapping each other's backs and making their way past him out into the bar.

Andy went to the washroom as quickly as he could. There were two men in the stall next to him. They stopped talking when he closed and latched the door. He'd recently learned at school that you could not get AIDS from going to the bathroom, or from saliva, but he didn't want to miss the next hockey season so he hurried his piss out, just to play it safe. When he returned, Stevie, Tiger, and another, much younger guy — closer to their own age — were all sitting in the booth with Colin. He was laughing, effortlessly, along with them.

Andy slipped away without speaking again to Colin. The night air was ripe; Toronto pounded with life. A Firebird pulled over to the corner, Honeymoon Suite blaring. These men had taken Colin's attention so easily, taken it from him. On the sidewalk ahead two girls strutted and a car full of guys smoking and whistling called out gentle sexual taunts to them. On the street corner, a guy with curly hair was selling books that he'd written himself. Two Jamaicans were playing kettledrums. Andy walked for a while and went to Lime Ricky's where he had a chocolate shake.

Hi, said a girl about his age. She was standing in front of him. He hadn't seen her. He realized he hadn't noticed anyone around him. He smiled. You look lonely, so my friend dared me to come talk to you. She pointed to a younger-looking Asian girl eating a float — she waved at them shyly. My friend and I are going to see a movie — late show, continued the girl. We're just sitting there. You waiting for someone? she asked.

My friend took off with a bunch of other guys, he confessed.

Where do you go to school? she asked.

LSC, he said.

That's a private school, she said.

Yes.

What are you going to do? she asked.

He didn't know, hadn't thought about it, so he shrugged.

I'm Jane, she said.

In the movie, dark, slunk down, he held her face and neck as they made out. He slid his hand slowly down and felt her breast through her shirt. At one point he heard Jane's friend whisper to them, *I'm going to move down in front. See you after the movie. I'll tell you what happens.* They sniggered at this through their tongues and lips. They were alone in their row, up the back and he forced her hand onto himself. She rubbed him for a while, but stopped. He put her hand back on and she whispered, *Don't.* He grabbed her by the wrist and when she tried to pull it free, he tightened his grip. *Please,* she said. *I thought you were different.*

He let her go and she sulked down to the front. A few minutes later, he watched as Jane and her friend left the theatre, arm in arm. Jane being comforted. The friend looking over at him with a tense, disgusted face. Fuck her then. Fuck this. Fuck. He was losing Colin. This was the beginning. Where the ending starts.

He caught the GO train by himself and grabbed a taxi at the station back out to Huntington. He covered for Colin. They'd met another friend from LSC, he said vaguely. Colin was with this guy seeing a late movie and would be home in a few hours. For his part, he wasn't feeling well, and wanted to come home early. Mrs. Aspinall seemed to believe him. He fell asleep apologizing to Jane — wherever she now was in southern Ontario, curled up in her bed awake, running the mistake she'd made over and over in her mind.

Colin began to go into Toronto as often as he could. Andy didn't join him. In the beginning, he'd asked Colin about where he'd been, with whom. But Colin shrugged, was not interested in answering. Then school started once again.

Andy, who'd been playing hockey all summer, was thrown right back into training. He was already fulfilling his expectations as the team's star player. But now, in junior year, the school work became harder. Colin and Andy, in separate houses, had less time for one another.

Come on. Let's go out for a walk, said Colin, who'd arrived at Andy's room late, just before lights out. It was nearing Christmas.

You just want to smoke.

Come with me, Andy, said Colin in a pleading tone Andy had not heard for some time.

And so Colin and Andy snuck down to the lakeshore. They'd been sitting next to one another in classes as usual, and Andy still returned to the Aspinalls' each holiday and long weekend; in fact no one but them would have noticed the forming rift.

Over there, those lights are the States, said Colin. We could swim it.

Together they watched the lighthouse at the end of the long pier blink green and red. The wind whipped in cold and wet. They dug their hands into their ski jackets, ties loosened but still on, toques pulled down hard over their ears. Great thrusts of ice had built up and climbed into the air at the shoreline as if tectonics, rather than sheer Canadian cold, were at work. The sky was vast and dark and fast moving. Colin smoked.

You're mad at me, said Andy.

You're holding it over my head.

What?

My life. Who I am. You keep the secret and because of that, you think you own me. You're just like my family.

I'm your friend.

Then they fell silent. After a time, a ship, impossibly, moved way out on the lake, a single light beam stretched out as if it were the centre of all things. Then, Colin spoke to Andy. Softly. Almost inaudibly.

I love you, he said.

They stood together. About them, crisp quiet.

Colin, I . . . but he didn't finish the meaningless thing he would have said.

I know what to do now, said Colin. I've done it. I know all about it. I think I've got a boyfriend.

Stevie? asked Andy.

Who?

From the Eaton Centre.

That guy? He laughed. No, I haven't seen him since. There's a whole village there, Andy. I've been going to a teen group that meets above a bookstore. We drink coffee and talk . . . about what it's like.

Do they know who you are? asked Andy.

No. But they know me better than anyone else. Andy watched him look up, realizing what he'd just said.

I get it, said Andy. I'm still your best friend. I still want to be that. If you'll let me.

Yes, said Colin.

Can I meet him?

My boyfriend?

Yeah.

Not a chance.

Why not?

You're too fucking beautiful, Andy. He'd think something more was going on. They laughed a bit then. Andy kicked at a crabapple husk in the snow. Colin lit a cigarette and inhaled, exhaling a ring of smoke that hung in the air before him. The ship had not moved.

Just think, said Colin. Next year at this time, we'll be only months away from being out of this place. Andy reached over and took Colin's cigarette from him. He inhaled and coughed a little. What'd you do that for? asked Colin.

Thought I should try it a second time, he said. Make sure I didn't like it.

Trudy insisted on making lunch. Pancakes were her specialty. Well, she admitted, she was a terrible cook, but her daughter did love her pancakes. Andy had leftover blueberries to put in them, and maple syrup too.

Are you sure you want to bother? he asked.

It would be my pleasure, she said.

Andy, it's just me. He opened his eyes. Fiona stood before him in a T-shirt and men's boxer shorts. How long had he been asleep? Move over, she said.

Andy shuffled his body over toward the wall. Moonlight reflected off the concave surface of the bedroom skylight, giving her skin a pale wash. She was next to him now, he on his back, she on her side facing him; she moved closer and placed her head on his shoulder.

I need something, she said.

This was not the first time she'd acted like this. There had been the boat. And, last Christmas, quite drunk, after an evening when she and several of her friends had been out, she'd crept into his room. She'd wanted to talk that time.

I'm too awake, she said. She lay on his bed. He sat on the floor, nodding, asking questions to spur her on, to ensure she wouldn't grow bored and leave. At about three or four in the morning, she fell asleep. He slept on the floor. When she woke in the morning she placed her hand on his face, gently, to wake him.

I'm going back to my room, Andy. Get into bed now, she said. And she had left her hand on his cheek, slid it down onto his chest, and held it there. Thanks for listening, she said, patting him.

What had they talked about? Nothing important. She had spoken about her boyfriend, that she didn't love him anymore, that she was thinking of ending it. She made her mind up as she talked. She would do it as soon as she got back to university. Andy had listened: that was all. It was as if she'd practised her arguments on him. Andy was a courtier. As she'd talked, his body ached for her. Why did she fail to see that the answer to all her needs and wants was right at her feet? Oh, her feet. Her feet were sculptures, copied from a statue of Venus. Her legs were those of a movie star. Her neck, her breasts were . . . Please god, he willed, as she blathered on about what so-and-so said to whomever, please let me be with you before I die.

Now it was the summer, she was in his bed, it was late, and she wasn't drunk this time. She also was onto a new boyfriend, whom Andy had met — she really liked this one. And so Andy lay still, feeling the heat of her next to him, waiting.

I don't know what to do, Andy, she said. Not exactly. She brought her eyes to him and placed her mouth on his. He slept naked. Twice he'd tried to speak, to ask for an explanation, but she would not let him, pressing his lips closed with her fingers. *Please*, was all she said as she guided him on top of her, to enter her.

He and Trudy swapped spots in the kitchen. She hummed as she worked, preparing the mixture for the pancakes. He retreated and sat on the couch, looking out the window at the lake. About halfway out, there was a canoe.

He'd had to wait fifteen or so years to learn why she'd climbed into his bed. After two glasses of Chardonnay at a restaurant in New York City, Fiona leaned in.

I'd shot my mouth off, she said broaching the subject for the first time. Bragged to that boyfriend, you know, when my abilities and experience were non-existent. I'd been teasing him, but it had gone too far. This was going to be *the* guy, I'd realized. He was going to go where all others before him had been denied. She laughed and nodded to the waiter to refill her glass. They waited while he came, poured, and left. I wanted everything to be perfect for my first time. Problem was, he was under a completely different impression. So, rather than wreck it, I figured, I'd practise first with you.

Andy knew this much already. In the morning, he'd found dabs of blood in his bed and matted in his pubic hair.

It was my brashness, my big mouth that always got me into trouble. It all worked out for the best, though, wouldn't you say? You weren't overly burdened by the obligation, if I recall, she said.

He shrugged. It had been everything he'd wanted, a fantasy playing itself out for real, but it hadn't gone how he wished. She'd lay beneath him, still, gazing up at the ceiling or off to the side. She looked vaguely put out, as if she were having a minor operation: a necessary thing to endure. At one point he lifted himself off her. Prone with legs splayed, skin taut and sweet, body lithe and full, it was her alright. But that was all.

Trudy interrupted his thoughts. So tell me, she asked, what happened to Colin after you both graduated from LSC. Had he grown more distant?

I was completely focused on hockey in my last year. That and school work. I was still spending time with Colin, mainly in the library. He and I helped each other study. We were too tightly connected by this time, but by the last months of high school we were both getting ready for some well deserved distance. So, we studied together. Perhaps that way we didn't have to speak about anything that much mattered.

Had he changed?

Colin had grown into himself — he had other friends, outside of LSC, by then, said Andy before falling quiet. Andy remembered how Fiona had asked him to follow Colin into Toronto. They'd graduated the week before. For his part, he'd been eager to plant trees for the summer, make some money. He was about to be on his own. He would have student debt ahead of him. Meanwhile, increasingly, Colin was spending nights in the city.

I'm worried about him, Fiona had said. I want to follow him. Let's go in my car. Make sure he isn't into anything bad.

Fiona, that's a ridiculous idea. He's eighteen.

This is Colin we're talking about.

Let me go. I'll catch a ride with him. See if I can find anything out. I was thinking about going shopping for tree planting gear. I'll talk to him. I'm sure everything is okay.

Andy and Colin had sped along the highway in good spirits. One by one, their classmates were already dispersing across the globe. And with each departure, each final farewell party, life inched open for them both. Soon they would enter different universities. And it was this newness that Andy and Colin felt as Colin floored his car along the highway, downtown Toronto approaching, a silver lure flickering at the horizon.

You can drop me off anywhere, Andy said.

Colin parked his car off Yonge Street. They parted ways, smiling at one another. Andy watched, furtively, as Colin disappeared down Charles Street. He would have to tell Fiona something, so he followed, staying well back. At the next corner Colin went into a coffee shop where he took a seat in the window. He looked to be waiting. Andy stood at a bus stop and leaned, out of Colin's range of sight, behind a telephone pole. Before long Andy saw Colin stand and greet a man. They sat down together and were talking, when, about five minutes after that another younger guy approached. Colin rose and hugged this man quickly, and they held hands as they sat next to each other and talked with the first man. Colin looked comfortable and in good spirits.

What did you see? Fiona had asked as soon as he'd returned. They were in the library at Huntington. The books were all off the shelves in great piles for their annual dusting. They looked like a series of unmanageable, impractical staircases. Fiona sat on four large volumes awaiting his answer.

Nothing I'm afraid, he said. I lost him right away.

Where did he drop you off?

Yonge and Bloor area.

Well, that's no help.

He's fine, Fiona.

He's not fine. I think he's gay.

Of course he is, Fiona. You know that.

What if he gets AIDS and dies? Is he with some dirty old man, Andy? You have to tell me. We can make him stop. We'll tell Dad. He'll know what to do.

Okay, fine. I did see him for a few minutes. He was drinking coffee with some friends. And they were young, and very clean looking. He looked at home in a way he never has at Huntington, or at LSC. He seemed free.

Free. Her voice was strident. What would you know about free? Freedom is *this*, and she flung her arms out gesturing to the room, books, and house. As if to say, *he's an Aspinall*. It doesn't get any freer. That's something, Andy, you will never understand.

Fiona, you're upset. Andy was about to say more, to say some words to make her calm down, to think about all this more rationally, when she turned at him, tears now streaming down her left cheek, eyes red.

Haven't you taken enough? I mean — sorry your father died, Andy, but we've done all we can. It's time for you to go, to wherever it is that you belong. You're like a leach, just hanging on and on. When are you going to get it? She was shrieking. A piece of her hair was caught in the corner of her mouth. Her face, cheeks, neck were blooming in patches of rose. You are worthless now. You destroyed Colin. It's your fault. She was wild with her anger. He could hardly breathe. Her words were piling on top of him, burying him in their crush. She could see their utter effect. At one point, she laughed at his hurt. Before he could speak again, appeal for mercy, she turned and was gone.

So you left Huntington then, that summer — for good? Trudy picked up her pen and notepad and made herself a note.

Yes, for the most part.

Andy, she began with a serious tone, it's public knowledge that Colin was arrested for cocaine use at about this time.

No, he said, no that was later. I was already in university. I read about it in the newspaper — along with the rest of Canada. I called Huntington and left a message but no one called me back.

You weren't still in contact with Colin after you went to university?

Colin's arrest happened in New York. He'd already moved there. I think it was my third year of university when that happened. I knew that Colin had taken a year off because we'd seen each other at Christmas. I went to Huntington for the holidays. That was the last time I was there.

Tiny white lights were strung across the facade at Huntington. Two spotlights, one red, one green, shone single beams of light on either side of the house.

Maclean's is here, Fiona said as Andy stepped from his rental car. She'd kissed him on both cheeks as if they were greeting one another not after a fight, but merely an inconvenient absence. They are photographing us for a seasonal article on how the celebrated celebrate. Dad said to them on the phone, *Oh, you must be mistaken, we're not so much celebrated as evaluated.* They came anyway, she finished with a laugh, and took him by the arm.

Andy was left in the hallway, behind the photographer, who was taking rolls of film of the three Aspinalls arranged on the spiralling staircase.

There's Andy Kronk, said Mr. Aspinall when he saw him. Come on, Fiona, get back in here.

Won't be a minute, Andy, called Mrs. Aspinall. They were all smiling. Even Colin, who was dressed in a pair of ordinary pants and a white button-down oxford. He looked like a younger version of his father.

Andy looked about him to confirm nothing had changed. The door to the library was open. The books were all in their place on the shelf, but everything else was exactly as it had been two years before. The photographer let them go. Colin came directly to him.

Ah, said Colin, taking him by the arm, Charles has returned to Brideshead.

After Fiona had said what she had, Andy had gathered his things and had stormed out. He called Colin later that week to tell him, but was only able to leave him a long message on his machine at Huntington. Andy left for tree planting with no idea if Colin had ever heard his side of the story. It turned out that he had. Colin spent the summer at Huntington and did not speak with Fiona. When he left for university, they too had had words.

You did the right thing, said Colin over the phone to him

during the first week of university. Let's just forget all that. When can we see each other? How far is Guelph from Kingston?

Few hours' drive.

Let's plan to meet next month then. I've got lots to tell you.

They talked on the phone every few weeks that first year and saw each other, but not until the spring. Andy caught the bus to Kingston where he slept on Colin's floor in residence for two days. They drank vodka and smoked.

I'm dropping out, said Colin.

What? Why? asked Andy.

It's so dull here. Everyone is so eager to be my friend. It's high school all over again. I'd have gone to McGill if Fiona weren't still there. He was drunk and slurring. Andy did not believe him. But Colin did not return to university after that term. He took an apartment in downtown Toronto with a friend. Colin and Andy had an even more difficult time staying in touch over the summer and the beginning of the next academic year.

Then Andy's roommate knocked on his bedroom door. There's a guy at the door. Fella, I should warn you, I think he's wearing a cape.

Colin and Andy embraced on impulse. To Andy, Colin looked thin, older somehow than himself. This was what shocked him the most. Colin had always been so fragile and lithe. But his smile was the same.

I need to talk, Colin had said after they'd finished with their hellos.

They walked to a nearby park, Colin slinging his arm inside his own as if they were an old couple.

I've been spending most of my time with an American, said Colin. Andy, he's great for me. He's older. And from New York City. I'm going to move down there. I'm so excited. Finally, I'll be away from the family and live my own life. You know he still checks up on me. I swear he bugs my phone, reads my credit card statements.

You sound paranoid.

You don't know my father. Who cares about him? I've come to see you, Andy: to tell you my good news.

I'm happy for you, Andy said and smiled. You seem to be doing great.

I miss you though. Seeing as I'm going, would you do me a favour? Spend Christmas at Huntington with me? I've already told them you'll come. Fiona feels terrible about what she said to you. *Water under the bridge.* That was the exact cliché she used, so she must mean it.

Colin's long dark cape, the one he'd worn from time to time at LSC looked as odd as ever on him — but it too was showing its age. Colin's hair was longer than it used to be, it covered his ears and extended down his neck. It was still as blond. Andy didn't pay much attention to Colin's new plan. There had been others back when they'd been in high school of course. He'd thought this one too would pass, turn into a wild and wonderful story with an ending that involved his family's meddling somehow — more fuel for his next fire, another reason to continue on along the same path. It was self-fulfilling.

Promise me you'll come.

You know I will.

Don't tell my family about my New York plans. Especially Fiona, he'd said. She'd just come down and ruin everything. His smile had been warm.

Let's go for a walk down to the shore, said Colin and steered Andy toward the front door, the photographer packing up his equipment, the hubbub dispersing.

Aren't you going to let him take his bags up to his room? said Fiona, cutting them off.

We'll do it later. We have to catch up.

Arm in arm again with the snow coming down lightly, lights strung on the box hedges warning of an impending Christmas, it was like old times — as if the world had re-aligned and returned back to the way it was supposed to be. Down at the shore the boats were under tarps for the winter. The shoreline was thick with ice and the sound of the snow crunched under their footfalls.

I'm glad you came, said Colin as they stared out to the horizon, lighting a smoke.

I'm not sure I can forgive your sister. She's acting as if nothing she said matters.

From her perspective, it doesn't. You'll forgive her. You'll do it for me, he said, exhaling.

Are you really in love? asked Andy.

Are you really going to law school? said Colin. And they laughed the way they used to when they were alone, as if all were still easy, and up to them.

◆ ◆ ◆

Trudy pressed stop on her recorder, the click of it sounding abrupt. The mood here this morning with Andy had shifted. She rose and worked up a smile for him.

I have to make a call, she said.

She dug her phone out of her bag, and walked out of Andy's cottage and down to the dock. It was another clear morning and the water felt cold but good. A breeze moved across the lake in short gusts, bits of white water on patches of lake, then stillness. Jack pines, cedar, and sumach rimmed Broad Lake's shoreline. At sundown the bugs had swarmed. They were not out this morning though. In their red canoe the birders floated out on the lake. They were, she thought, as dedicated to a passion as they come.

Officer Nyland?

Is that Trudy? You're faint.

It is. She walked to the end of the dock. I've moved. Is that any better? She was not speaking loudly as Andy was only one hundred or so feet away — sound travelling easily over lakes.

Yes, I can hear you now.

Oh good. I just wanted to let you know things are progressing. I should be able to finish by late this afternoon. I can't talk right now. May I call you this evening? After I return to Toronto?

That's fine. Then she lost him for a moment. He returned and was saying, I'm glad it's going well.

It might be late by the time I'm back, she said. Do you mind if I call late, or would you rather I not?

Anytime is fine. I'm always at work, one way or another. Can I quickly ask about Colin? Have you turned up anything unexpected on him? His whereabouts? I'm following a new lead.

We're not quite there yet. I'll be sure to ask Andy.

Please be careful.

He's talking comfortably. I'll see what I can get.

Trudy turned off her phone just as a large fish jumped out of the lake in a belly flop. The wind stilled. The fish's disturbance sent concentric rings out across the surface of the water. She looked up to the sky, then outward. A large rounded rock jutted off the far shore. On top of it stood a single maple tree with a tire swing hanging from it. Soon, kids would be up at the lake for the summer. They would heave themselves out on the tire, pumping with their legs for more speed and greater distance, until finally they released their hands. The sight of them entering the water would arrive here on Andy's dock well before the sound of the joyful squeals and splash. She missed Veronica.

◆ ◆ ◆

Can I speak with Mr. Aspinall, please?

He's busy right now. May I ask who is calling?

Jim Nadeau.

Is there a number where he can reach you, Mr. Nadeau?

He has it.

Is there a message?

Just to call me.

It was more than an hour later before his phone did ring.

I just spoke to Trudy, began Jim. She is getting on well. She thinks she'll have it wrapped up this evening. She said she'd call me when she got back down to Toronto.

Good. Well, I look forward to hearing what she has to say.

When should I call you again? Tomorrow is Sunday.

I won't be at the office. I will call you on Monday, said Mr. Aspinall.

Okay, Jim said.

◆ ◆ ◆

Andy watched Trudy walk down to the dock, dip her foot in. Figuring she'd be a few minutes, he stretched out on the couch and stared up at the pine ceiling boards. The breeze swung around through the open window and cooled him. His mind tacked off one way then another. No wonder his sleep had been so troubled last night. The wind was unexpectedly soothing. What sleep could there be for him after two days of recollections? His waking hours were indistinguishable from his dreams. He'd begun to occupy the past so steadfastly it had become the present.

Now, unexpectedly, sleep came to him; its slippery state took him home. He was a child on roller skates. Shoot a few more son, just a few more. But, Dad, I can't see well. A red outline was painted on their garage door the shape and size of a goal mouth. He works another slap shot at his father, its defender. It misses. The light was dim. It was late summer. Was that a look of disappointment from the old man? He'd only just missed the top right corner of the net.

Try harder!

Later, they ate Kentucky Fried Chicken. He asked a question that he'd had on his mind of late. He worked up to it, not knowing if it was off limits.

Dad?

Yes, son?

How come you never got married again?

No answer.

There had been lovers. He'd heard the man come home late once. He'd pretended to be asleep on the couch — the TV still flickering blue with a late-night show. His father had stumbled in, drunk, with a woman. *Shhh*, they'd laughed, and begun to kiss beside the kitchen table, Andy, peering out through a slit in his left eye. How long until they'd notice him there, not ten feet away? For a while he watched his father. The man's hand running up and down this woman's body as if it was the hood of a Mustang. His old man's hands — fingers that could fix anything — were struggling helplessly with her clasp or zipper. Finally she was free, rolls of white flesh and sag being thrown up on the melamine table top, her legs flung out in the air as she grabbed at the back of his dad with her one hand, and the other, biting on his shirt cuff and playfully shaking her head about as if a dog, saying only, *it's about time, John, it's about time.*

Then his dream digressed into partially fictional tangents. Andy was in his father's factory. Miss June's smile was clear and unchanged, and she was before him, wearing a baseball cap and jean shorts. She sat on the fender of the Ferrari Dino 308 GT4. Leaning forward, hands between her thighs, breasts pushed together, she was laughing. *It's about time, it's about time,* she said again. I think about you. I haven't forgotten you, Colin.

But I'm Andy.

I know, I know. It's okay, Andy. You are having a bad dream. And Fiona climbed out the window onto the roof. The sun was warm but the breeze was cool and nice, and it swept across them as they looked out over the grounds to where she'd parked her car down below.

Why did you decide to race cars? he asked her.

You've never understood me, have you? They were on the sailing boat now. The wind, moving in gusts. Andy liked it out there. Lurching left, then right. Then he felt unstable, as if he might fall in. But his balance was regained. In the distance, Huntington loomed large and proud, and together he and Fiona waved to it in big, wide arcs through the air. He controlled the sailboat with his mind, his toe a rudder that he could drop down into the water, the lake pressing against the boat, propelled across the day, bright and clear. He looked back once again, and Huntington was still there, the same size, not moving, not changing even though he was willing the boat onward.

It's the wind. It's not strong enough.

You don't know anything about wind, Fiona.

Your foot's not working anymore. We aren't moving.

He leapt off the front of the boat, across the top of the water, pushing his legs side to side, skating across the top of the unfrozen lake leaving the boat behind him as easily as if he'd always been this free. His arms spread wide, he began to fly in swooping circles over the lake, the boat tiny now below him, Huntington as if a doll's house, and in the distance Toronto, the CN tower, and beyond that flashing lights that were America. Who could reach him up there? How could he ever come down? The wind cooled, colder and colder, until a snow-covered field appeared beneath his feet, the chill of it sinking into his bones. He thrust down into the snow, scraped away until he had reached dirt, and scraped away the dirt until he felt a face. From the eyes sprung trilliums, white with green stems unfurling, the petals soft to the touch.

Colin? asked Andy. Then he saw his friend's mouth open, the parting earth falling into its gap.

Yes.

He could not say a thing. His mind was blank. Colin looked so cold. So he said, simply, Your lips look cold.

A smile flickered across Colin's dead mouth. Then he croaked the words: Biography lends to death a new terror.

PART FOUR

He awoke from his dream startled, but a cool fatalism settled him. Everything was already over. In part, he'd felt this from the moment she arrived — from even before that. He'd felt under the regulation of future time. He'd been acting out memories. He'd been in the courtroom at his own trial. About him, lawyers reconstructed the very moments he was living. While he knew he could change what he was doing — change exactly what they would be able to suppose happened — he somehow couldn't. They were correct; the future was controlling his actions. He was powerless, without free will, and bound to a predetermined future.

In law school, he'd become infatuated with his family law professor. She'd been a married woman who did not encourage him in the slightest, who was never interested in his brooding, or his obvious plays for attention. She had several children and spoke of them often in class. It was a kind of power she had, this raising the fact of her family in the context of her teaching. To the rest of the class — to the women especially — it showed how she could have it all: career, a fine academic mind, and motherhood. For Andy it made her more glamorous, mysterious, out of bounds. She could not have been less like Fiona.

There had been a cocktail party where they had talked alone for half an hour. His professor nursed a glass of white wine and asked polite, interested questions about his future. He sipped on a beer, holding up the frame of a door so as to disguise his lack of composure. Nothing improper occurred, or was said. She drifted away from him at that party at a respectful moment, and that was all. For his part, it had been an act — he'd wanted her.

Why think of her now? Trudy had ducked out of their intimate interview to call her own daughter. Perhaps that was it? That was not it. As he'd leaned against the door frame, he'd had no sense of the future intruding on the present. If he had, or if she had, then they might have stolen away from the party, undressing each other eagerly as they threw open the door to his apartment, a hotel room, the back seat of a car.

By contrast, all he felt today was the future. Every new moment was a memory. He heard Trudy come into the cottage.

I didn't want to wake you, said Trudy. He pushed himself to an upright position on the couch.

How long was I asleep?

An hour maybe.

Oh god.

No big deal. I made coffee.

As they began their conversation again, Trudy writing down notes and recording his words on tape, Andy drank coffee. And while he grew more alert he couldn't completely shake off the skim of sleep. Could time be this uncertain, this subjective? Was every new life the signal, the certainty of its own end? Were birth and death the same? Andy sank into the philosophical inevitability of meaninglessness, of nothingness. Its dull presence in his life, underneath whatever was going on in the day-to-day, always gave him a relative comfort.

Colin disappeared after that, Andy said. The last I saw of him was that Christmas. He wore his cape the entire time those holidays. Looking back, it's kind of a forlorn image, he said wistfully. A superhero living among his fantasies of unattainable freedom, running away from a family that doesn't understand him but has everything.

And you drifted from the Aspinalls after that Christmas? asked Trudy.

I did try to stay in touch with Colin and Fiona from time to time. Fiona would, occasionally, contact me in return. Colin and I lost touch. Fiona went to Europe in the mid-nineties to learn how to drive race cars and sent me a run of postcards from Germany. I have them in a box somewhere; there are also ones from Madrid, and the south of France too. Then I wouldn't hear from her for a year or more. By the time I was articling, our contact was infrequent.

And all this time, no Colin either?

No.

So as far as you know, he's still in New York?

Andy fell into silence. He was trying to organize his thoughts in a logical sequence, or at least in the order in which they were supposed to have happened. After a long sigh that he realized must have sounded histrionic, he looked up at Trudy.

If there's more to say, start at the start of it, she said. That's the only way.

But the order of events was unstable. He began slowly at first, choosing his words from all those available to him. He tried to sound bright, philosophical.

We need families like the Aspinalls, he said. We long for their example, grace, and luxury. They remind us that life is not democratic, or equal, or just. They fuel our selfish desires; they harden our egalitarian resolve. We yearn to be them if we only could; we loathe them because we never will be. They are the beloved, the entitled, the unaccountable ones, and they walk among us, breathe our air. They both own and ignore us.

He shook his head in his hands. Tears came. He bit at his lip. Why must he say this? Surely he could leave it all where it was, where it is. But the future was about him. The truth was needy. This was *the* moment, the fulcrum.

His thoughts and memories came on hard and fast. Wanting simply and finally to be rid of the story, as if it were a tapeworm being pulled from his stomach out through his mouth, hand over hand, he talked and told, until it was all out. Until it was gone.

He'd received the call last fall — *Fiona's voice on the other end of the line sounding forcibly calm. Can we meet, Andy? I have something to discuss. It's important*, was all she'd said after they'd exchanged pleasantries. But he'd only just moved up to Broad Lake. He was full of personal fire and ambition to make his new, simpler life work out. Her call embodied the most complicated part of his past. He hedged with her, wondering aloud, in a feigned good-natured way, what this could all be about? He was rather busy at the moment and coming down to Toronto was not as easy for him as she might expect. *It's about Colin, Andy. You have to come.*

The next day he climbed into his pickup and threw it into gear. He could not believe he was doing this. He'd been forced to dig out clothes he'd packed away that would be suitable for a lunch meeting at Gorgon and Zola's. Of all the places and people he didn't want to see, the inside of an upscale restaurant and Fiona Aspinall would have been at the top of his list — if he'd even thought to have such a list. He'd been up north only three months, and was just starting to acclimatize. Now this rupture. Perhaps he wasn't able to do this? Selling antiques and living on a lake far from anywhere — was he mad? No. No, he wasn't. It was a good idea, a healthy plan for him and his life and one that would ultimately make him happy. He just had to stick with it. If his old life continued to find him up in his hideaway, then so be it. He would have to grow accepting of this and deal with it on a case-by-case basis. Just because he was in his truck driving south did not mean he was defeated. It meant he was coping. And that was all.

Andy spoke to Trudy of these doubts he'd had, as if to remind himself of them. Saying them aloud once again helped his present state of mind as well. Perhaps the future he was already sensing back then, in his truck, was right now? But did he feel the future's presence then? Or did that begin later? He wasn't at all sure now. Time was becoming even more unpredictable, distant moments calling to each other with the clarity of contemporaneously experienced sensations.

He'd been to Gorgon and Zola's before. An aquamarine blue ceiling and floor were joined with walls covered in a tiled, spiralling mosaic. Every few tiles was a shard of mirror, or piece of sea-smoothed glass. From a distance, Andy could see mermaids and starfish, buoys and sailboats. Up close it was a bright blast of colour and refraction. The tables were arranged in a wide arc, the kitchen and bar in the centre. The waiters and clients were all about the same age, and, given this was lunch, were both wearing all-black or dark suits. The potential for confusion or comedy suddenly seemed likely to Andy. He surveyed this scene with a remove and disassociation that he'd never before enjoyed. But he was well aware that at any moment one of these lunching interchangeables might wave and ask him where the heck he'd been lately.

As he waited for Fiona to arrive, he sipped on a mineral water and eavesdropped on the conversation at the table next to him. There were three thin people, two of whom were women.

The man, who seemed especially familiar to Andy, wore a dark
fitted suit with no tie. He looked distracted. The two women
were only just holding his interest. It soon became apparent he
was their boss.

Did the waiter say, African stew? said the taller of the two
women.

I thought stew was English? said the other, sliding out of
her black cardigan and hanging it on the back of her chair. With
her arms now exposed, Andy could see that she was muscular,
tanned, about forty years of age. Her bleached teeth gleamed.

I think *stew* is just a word, said the man, then added, will
the two of you be able to complete the project before Monday
then?

Yes. You're making us work all weekend. But yes, said the
taller woman.

My grandmother used to make us stew, continued the
shorter woman. Big thick chunks of beef and carrots and things.
I hated it.

Shouldn't they be more specific than African? said the taller
quizzically. There are a lot of countries on that continent. I'm
sure Moroccan stew is different from Ugandan stew or Ethiopian
stew. I wonder if they'd serve generic European stew in
Mogadishu?

Where? said the shorter.

Somalia, said the man. It's the capital.

Oh, what would they make stew from there? snarled the
shorter. UN rations?

Don't be so ignorant, Sara, said the taller woman.

This is a stupid conversation, said Sara. I just want to order.
I'm meeting with clients in less than an hour.

I've been there, said the man.

What? said Sara.

Somalia, said the man, motioning to the waiter. I went there with an NGO about a decade ago.

Why, David! said the taller woman. I didn't know you gave a shit about anything. How heartfelt of you.

How do you go from working with NGOs in Africa to doing PR for pharmaceuticals? asked Sara.

Well, you see, I met Mephistopheles one evening in Bangkok and in exchange for eternal life . . . but he petered out, as if realizing this short-lived burst of conversational energy was being misspent. The two women looked at him blankly, waiting for the punchline so they could laugh and move on. Never mind, David said.

The waiter then swooped in, shoving his backside close to Andy's face at the next table, and took their order, but not before first being asked if he could hurry their food to them as they were now in a rush. Once Sara established that it did not have chicken in it, she opted for the warm goat cheese and mixed nut salad. The taller woman ordered French onion soup, declaring to the table that she hadn't seen it on a menu in years and was glad it was making a comeback.

Do you have the trout today?

I'm sorry, we don't, said the waiter.

Can you tell me about the special then? asked David.

The African stew? said the waiter.

Yes, said David. What part of Africa is it from?

What part of Africa is your favourite? said the waiter.

Somalia, said David.

Then you're in luck, smiled the waiter. It's from there.

You wouldn't want me to eat inauthentically, said David.

Wouldn't dream of it, said the waiter bowing imperceptibly and backing away toward the kitchen.

What a prick, said David. I'll bet he never finishes that

Ph.D. he's no doubt in the seventh year of, and ends up working for me in market research. He's got the face of a sellout.

During the course of this conversation, Andy remembered that it was from his law school days that he knew this man's face. David had dropped out in *their* first year. He'd had a kind of reckless intelligence he'd admired at the time. They'd taken a few classes together, but had never spoken.

Just then, the noise in the restaurant hushed several decibels and the room's energy shifted from being decentred to a singular focal point. Fiona Aspinall was being shown to her seat.

As she approached, Andy stood, kissing her once on both cheeks.

You look wonderful, Andy, she said as she sat down. Then to the waiter who had shown her to her seat and was still hovering, Maybe I'd like just a glass of Riesling. Could you do that for me? The waiter said of course and was gone.

Fiona's hands were slender, nails manicured. On her left wrist was a thin gold chain that looked as light as only a few strands of hair. She wore a black blouse with a V-shaped neckline. Her skin was smooth and without blemish. She wore a choker that matched her bracelet. Its fine links so light as to be illusory about her slender throat.

At LSC, Fiona Aspinall had been young and radiant. She was at any moment laughing easily or fiercely cross. Her lips were always painted and pouting, her brown eyes had a look about them that was both coy and wry. In her senior year at the school's annual swim meet, when she crossed her arms, and lifted her sweatshirt up over her head and took her place on the starting blocks, the gasp was audible. It was still a moment spoken about in sacred tones by all those younger males fortunate enough to have been present. Before Andy today, he saw that same beautiful woman almost twenty years on. Her eyes ended in delicate creases, her hair had lost some of the natural lustre, her mouth was firmer and was no longer that of a girl's. When taken together though, Fiona was more perfect than ever, having matured into the kind of woman every other woman hates for no good reason at all.

You haven't changed, Andy smiled.

You've always been a first-class liar, and she reached forward across the table and squeezed his hand affectionately. At the warmth of her, Andy felt his blood uncontrollably rush.

They caught up in half-sentences and unfinished stories — the gist being all either needed. Andy relayed an abbreviated version of when and why he'd decided to move up north. Fiona listened and nodded, smiling, touching him on the wrist with a finger or two at one point, as if to say, *I'm so glad we are doing this*. Her wine arrived and, after a time, they ordered, then ate. Fiona talked about her family obliquely, and caught him up on some gossip from her friends from LSC.

You wanted to talk about Colin, Andy said as their coffees arrived.

Andy, I need you to come with me to New York. I have to talk to Colin. He has to come home. Mom has become very sick. There is a good chance she . . . Fiona looked down and bit her bottom lip before continuing, that she won't make it. She has cancer. Breast cancer. On and off for three years now. The doctor is somewhat hopeful but I've never seen her look this bad. I just think, again she paused, Colin needs to see her. He owes her that much.

As soon as he'd agreed to help her, Fiona placed a call, then and there, to her travel agent to take care of his arrangements.

He and Fiona met in the lobby of the hotel where they were both staying. Flying with almost no notice to anywhere he was told to be was precisely the kind of thing, when he'd quit his job and moved, that Andy wanted never to do again. Yet there he was. Still, could he have said no? And, after the emptiness and quiet of Broad Lake, New York struck Andy as absurd. That people would live like that, thought that a life spent wedged up against one another in restaurants and on the subway, in office and washroom cubicles alike, was at all fulfilling made his prudent decision to escape righteous.

It turned out that Colin had had almost no contact with his family ever since, in his cape, he'd left for New York all those years ago. He would, from time to time, e-mail Fiona to tell her something new about himself. Usually that he had a new address, or had moved on and was living with a new man — *someone who treated him properly!* There was a flurry of e-mails after 9/11. I'm fine. We're watching it on TV too, Fiona. In the weeks that followed, he described the sound, the smell of the place, how screwed up his friends were who lost family members, friends. His correspondence waned by the end of the year, returning to its normal, almost non-existent state.

Fiona had phoned him the night she first learned of their mother's cancer. She told Andy that Colin was distracted and unable to comprehend what she was telling him. She e-mailed him updates on her progress, her initial remission, her subsequent relapses, new treatments, support groups, her own efforts in lending her name and spirit to black-tie fundraising to find a cure. But to all this news she received no response from Colin. An occasional one- or two-line reply containing no emotion, only a vague commitment to come home and see her when he could. But he never came. Recently, she'd begun to push harder, and Colin had stopped replying altogether. It was this, along with her mother's deteriorating condition, that led Fiona to decide to go and get him. But she knew she wouldn't be able to get him to come on her own. She needed help. *Andy,* she'd said, *you're the only one Colin might listen to.*

What's your plan? said Andy after they'd greeted one another. Her face was more serious looking that it had been in Toronto only days before. She was in a navy-blue suit, and her hair was up in a twist.

We are going to see a lawyer I know. I discovered yesterday that Colin moved about a month ago. Christopher will know what to do.

How did you find this out?

Well, I sent him an e-mail, just a chirpy one the day after we met, to see if I could catch him in a better mood, to see if anything would change. The address I'd been using for him for the past year or so was one that he and his partner Nigel shared. I received a note back from Nigel informing me that Colin had moved out a month ago and that they were not speaking, that Colin owed him money and would I pay him? Well, I wrote him back and told him to itemize what he was owed and I'd see what could be done, but only if he could tell me where Colin had moved to. I received the itemized list all right, a couple of grand for bills and stolen clothes, but he had no idea where he'd gone. Apparently, they'd had a horrible fight, one of many, and when Nigel returned home from work the next night, Colin, along with all his stuff, was gone. Not even a note.

Fiona, was all Christopher Llewellyn said, and he kissed her on one cheek. Andy shook his hand. Llewellyn's office was palatial. Blond wood panelling lined the walls with black parquet detailing on the floor and a generous Persian rug. Llewellyn had a full view of Central Park. He was about their age, beautifully dressed, but his manner was relaxed and easy — the kind of guy it was just not worth trying to dislike.

After we spoke yesterday, Llewellyn began, I thought I'd just do some initial work to see how hard it was going to be to find your brother. Finding missing people isn't something I do. But there is a fellow here who does a lot of criminal work and who knows people. So we spoke, and I gave him the information you gave me. And well, all I can say is — isn't technology an amazing thing?

Andy watched as Llewellyn handed Fiona a piece of paper. She glanced at it and then looked back up at him, handing it to Andy. Andy looked down at the internal memo, with the firm's logo at the top. It listed Colin's new address, and a phone number of a shop where he worked.

How did he find this so quickly? asked Fiona.

I understand his assistant found it on the Internet in less than five minutes.

Well, that's wonderful. I feel a bit foolish. I just assumed this was going to be hard, said Fiona.

As did I, said Llewellyn. But there you go.

Well, I won't keep you, said Fiona, standing up to leave. Andy also rose. Then Fiona turned to him.

Andy, would you mind giving us a few minutes? There's another matter I need to discuss with Christopher.

Andy took a seat in the waiting room. It was like the thousand other waiting rooms to legal offices and chambers he'd been in. Yet somehow it was nicer, more spacious maybe. The receptionist offered him a beverage that he turned down. Down the hall, the door opened and he watched as Fiona and Llewellyn were finishing their conversation. They looked comfortable with one another. Fiona held her hands together in front of herself and cocked her head to one side. She was smiling. He'd seen Fiona this way before with certain men, boyfriends in high school, important friends of her father. This was the cluster of gestures she used to show she was paying attention to what someone was saying.

Outside, the late fall weather was damp and cold. Wind pushed a paper coffee cup down the sidewalk ahead of them, its opening acting as a sail.

Should we just get in a taxi and go to the address? asked Andy as he turned up his collar and hunched up his shoulders to the wind.

I need to collect my thoughts, Fiona said. Let's eat something. They sat at a small table in the corner of a busy Italian restaurant. Andy ordered a plate of spaghetti; Fiona, soup. They ate in a comfortable silence, recovering from the news and weather, mentally preparing for Colin.

I haven't seen him in more than ten years, said Andy.

Neither have I.

At least you've talked, e-mailed.

He loved you, Andy.

Yes, he said. I suppose he did.

What was that like? she asked. He pressed his lips together in a half grimace, half smile.

I don't know any different, it just was the way it was. They ordered coffees and sat, mostly in silence, trying to imagine what Colin would be like, if he would come with them.

◆ ◆ ◆

They stepped from the taxi at the address on Llewellyn's paper. The building was rundown without being derelict. The main hall was carpeted in a colour that had long ago stopped reflecting light and become shoe-dirt grey. The walls were off-cream. The number, 074, was in the basement. In the stairwell, a smell of stale sweat, of human being, pervaded the air, as if someone who didn't shower lived in there. They followed the dimly lit hallway to his door. It was thickly painted brown and had a peephole. On the floor lay a small pile of free newspapers and flyers.

Colin opened the door and stood before them, gaunt, greying at the temples, thin-wristed, and dressed in baby blue pyjamas with the waist tie done up in a drooping bow. On his feet he wore slippers with sheep's wool stuffing bursting out of one of the front seams. He had not shaved in days.

Oh bravo, he said sardonically. Someone sent the rear guard to resurrect the misanthropic fag. Don't look so shocked. You've found Wilde in Paris, only difference being I'm in a duel to the death not with the wallpaper but my own mind — so I'm to go, one way or the other.

Can we come in, Colin? asked Fiona.

To Andy, nothing about this apartment looked legal. There was only one window high up and it was covered in dark grime. The foot of Colin's mattress was wedged up against the toilet bowl. Takeout boxes and containers were piled on top of the bar fridge, which was next to a kitchen sink with its plumbing exposed. At least a dozen bottles of vodka and gin were littered about, some partially filled, some empty. On top of a dresser sat a television that was on, a talk show flickering across its screen. Fiona stepped over to it and turned it off. With three of them in the room it felt claustrophobic.

It's good to see you Andy, said Colin in a different, weary tone once they were all inside. There was nowhere to sit, other than on his bed on the floor, so they stood. Fiona lurched at Colin without warning and embraced him. Although he was taller than she, he appeared the weaker-bodied of the two. He resisted for a few moments, then gave himself to her hug, wrapping his arms about her.

You have no idea what I've been through, was all he managed after a time. Finally he began crying in long, deep sobs.

I've missed you so much, Colin. Fiona was stroking his head and neck. I've missed you.

Pinned to the wall was a newspaper clipping, yellowing and

brittle. It was from November 2000. It was about Oscar Wilde. It was the only item in Colin's room that personalized it in any way. Andy read its opening line:

Flamboyant Irish writer and wit Oscar Wilde did not die of syphilis but from a chronic ear infection that spread to the brain. Medical experts say . . .

I'd like you to come home, Colin, Fiona said. Just for a while. Then she added, besides, you don't appear to be doing all that well at the moment.

I cut up Dad's credit card a few months back. Big moment. I thought Nigel was it for me. But then he kicks me out. He said I was draining him of his money, his life. Fucker's a cokehead and a liar. You know, I can't . . . Colin stopped and looked at Andy. He tries to make up with me. He insists I stop drinking. It's never going to work. I got this place through an old friend. I'm working at his shop on the weekends. I sell loose tea. It's a specialty tea shop. It's bullshit. Did you ever get to law school, Andy?

Yeah, Andy said, and smiled. Colin was shivering.

Will you come home with us, Colin? asked Fiona.

Home? Where the fuck's that? That big house in Canada? You know the last time I was there Mom took me aside and said she had heard of a doctor in Austria who could cure me. Can you believe that? I still have this dream of my own castration at the hands of some neo-Nazi quack hired by my own mother.

Things have changed, said Fiona.

We're all going to march in the parade together?

That's not what I mean, she said.

I can't run away from my life right now. I know how it must look, but I can't. I'm turning myself around. Then, as if he finally realized or remembered why they were there he said, how's Mom doing?

Fiona slid her hotel key card in and out of her room's lock and pushed open the door. Her room, she thought once again, was too small. She used to like this place, didn't she? Maybe she never did. Perhaps she continued to come back here because this is where she always stayed in New York. It was likely no longer fashionable. She should ask Christopher where people are staying now. Oh, why bother? If she continued to stay here when in town then in another two years this place would switch owners, redecorate, and be back in style. Then she'd be able to say that she'd always stayed here, that she knew about it long before everyone else. She began to bore herself with this line of thought. Maybe she'd have a bath.

Hello? she said into the phone, vaguely annoyed.

It's your father.

Daddy.

Well?

We found him.

And, how is he?

He's nervy and sick looking. Living in squalor. He wasn't making a lot of sense. He's a drunk, Dad.

Well, get him out of there!

It's complicated.

Rubbish.

I don't see *you* down here . . .

Don't take that tone. I sent you there to get him. Tell him to stop being so selfish.

He's an adult. I can't kidnap him.

How did I bring up two children so ungrateful?

You paid the wrong people?

Silence.

Please stop barking at me, she said wearily.

I won't speak to you if you're going to be like this. I've got to go. Fiona heard her father breathe in deeply, exhale slowly.

Okay, she said. I'll see you at Huntington tomorrow evening?

But Colin will not be with you?

No, Dad. He won't. He is a grown man who makes his own decisions. She paused, and then added, He did ask after Mom.

How kind.

We're getting nowhere here.

You're getting nowhere.

Fiona hung up the phone after her father. She drew a bath, breathing in the steam of it, noticing how tight her chest felt. He always did that to her. What was she to say? Colin was the one person her father had no control over, because he was the one person who did not care what his father thought.

Yet, it hadn't always been that way. She recalled long chess matches between Colin and her father. The two of them would stare at the pieces, Colin gently moving his, looking up for the slightest flicker of disapproval. He did wish to impress him then, as a boy. But it all changed when Colin grew.

Fiona lowered herself into the bath. The water was hot and her legs became flushed and red. She scooped water up over her stomach and arms with a cupped hand, being careful not to get her hair wet. Christopher was exceedingly handsome.

Have dinner with me tonight, he'd said to her today. *Stay with me.*

I can't, she said in return. I'll come back next week. I've got to deal with Colin, and my mother. . . . My father needs me. Then there will be lots of time for us. She kissed him again and again on the mouth. I promise, she whispered. Soon. Soon.

Who's that guy you brought along? Should I be jealous?

Of Andy Kronk? Oh, she said, he's a long story — an old friend of Colin's. I thought he might be useful to me, that's all.

And was he?

She sank down into the bath, giving in to the warmth. She'd put up her hair; it was only Andy she was dining with after all. She felt like a drink. Something strong. Christopher has nice eyes. They sparkle. What would, she speculated in a moment of utter fantasy, their children look like? She took his face and blended it with her own. What did babies look like? She thought of Kimberly's children. Round and pink and often cross or upset. No, she'd adopt. That was a good plan too. He was a planner, Christopher. He was a step ahead. She liked that. She was used to that. Her father was much the same.

◆ ◆ ◆

I told Dad, said Fiona, we couldn't exactly take him by force.

How did he take it? asked Andy.

As you'd expect.

Andy and Fiona had finished dinner and were walking to the nearest corner — but where they were exactly, he wasn't sure. Earlier, Fiona had whisked him into a taxi, said the name of a restaurant at the driver, and they'd belted uptown some blocks making a series of turns that nullified his usually strong sense of direction. Walking now, before they reached the corner where he might gain his bearings, they passed by an Irish bar. From the outside, it was difficult to say what was going on inside, but it did, somehow, have a warmth to it. Fiona stopped at its front door.

Want a drink?

They elbowed their way through a mixed crowd of after-work loosened ties and students. When they spotted a table, he'd smiled and pulled out a chair for her. He went straight to the bar for them both to fetch drinks but he found himself waiting behind several other people. Before long, Fiona was at his arm.

I got bored, she said.

Next to them, a girl sat reading a large, well-thumbed novel. When it was their turn next, the bartender raised a finger to Andy and looked at the girl reading.

She's first, he said.

Jack and Coke.

Good book? asked the bartender.

I'm just about done. You read?

Ha. Some, he said.

You buy me this drink; I'll leave it for you.

Suddenly a band began to play at the far end of the bar. The music was fast and acoustic. Not quite Celtic, not quite blue-grass. The abrupt loudness of it stunned Andy who was now being asked for their order. Fiona switched her drink to the same as the reading girl.

Jack Daniels? said Andy.

Just trying to fit in, said Fiona, when they returned to their table.

How is it? he asked when she'd taken a mouthful.

Revolting. I'll finish it though.

A younger couple at a table wedged next to theirs intro-duced themselves. They were in town from Los Angeles. The man was handsome. Even Andy could tell that at a glance. The girl was pretty but not striking. They looked mismatched somehow, he thought.

Fiona soon tired of their conversation — he had a big

audition, she was along for moral support — and turned back to Andy. The couple began to kiss. Fiona and Andy pivoted away from them slightly, as if offering them privacy.

Do you remember the first time we kissed? asked Andy. She'd been in an easy mood, and somehow, after having been dragged down here, having done her that favour, he felt he could broach their past.

It was on the boat, wasn't it? she said directly.

No, I don't believe you actually kissed me that time. You almost did.

Really?

It was later, in my bedroom at Huntington, I think. She'd lost her virginity in that room. Surely she thought of it, him from time to time?

By the time they left the bar, she was in a fine mood. In the taxi on the way back to their hotel, she chatted about the girl with the book and her feigned cool banter, about the music and dumb handsome guy at the other table.

I'm sorry we didn't manage to convince Colin to come home, he said as they were entering the lobby of the small hotel. The room was dark, only a few small decorative lamps on in the corners and the signs lit up showing the way to the elevators, the stairs, the exits.

When I talked to my father today, she began, he was unforgiving. He can't understand why Colin will not come to see Mom. He's getting older. Cranky sometimes. She ran her hand up and around her neck, stopping herself from speculating needlessly. I'm ready for bed, she said.

Will I see you tomorrow? asked Andy.

Possibly. I'm going to try and do lunch with someone.

So I'll go home then, if I can get a flight?

You've been a good sport, Andy. Go back to your lake. She took a step toward the elevator and stopped. I remember it,

Andy, she said, facing away from him. Then she turned. I wanted to make sure you did. She pressed the elevator button with her index finger, waiting with her hands clasped in front of her, shoulders back, breathing deeply as if trying to control her mind and body after the three Jack Daniels she'd had. Then a chime sounded and the doors opened and closed as if a camera shutter, Fiona disappearing, leaving him with the image of her wan smile.

Andy walked down the hallway past the elevator to his room — which was on the first floor, just beyond the ice machine. As he climbed into bed, he was thinking about the handsome man at the bar. What would make someone want to act for a living: the grimacing or faux delight, the pain of waiting for other people to judge you worthy or not, and all this so you may portray a person who is not you? But then he considered it not unlike life, at many turns. Would he be able to play the part of an antique dealer? He'd failed at acting like a lawyer after all.

As he fell asleep on the soft mattress in the small hotel room in New York City, he'd thought about his cottage on Broad Lake. The absolute quiet of it, the ground a carpet of rust- and dun-coloured leaves, the itch of wool against his neck, his breath before him in puffs of cool, and beside him was Colin. Not the strung out man whom he'd met earlier in the day, but the boy he used to know. The Colin of his dreams. *Look*, said Colin, *those lights are the States.* And they were, blinking, blinking.

Andy was awake. Outside his barred, first-floor hotel window, an all-night diner flickered *Open, Open* in neon, at jerky intervals.

Andy dressed, pulling his coat about him tightly. The night air was bracing and a mist of rain just hung about him. New York, grey-dark and patchy, throbbed under its own weeping weight. As he pushed open the door to the place, he was met with a wall of smell and warmth, toast and bacon. He ordered a coffee and a piece of apple pie and sat for a long while watching CNN in silence across a TV screen mounted high on a wall above ancient signed photographs of Lauren Bacall, Mickey Mantle, and Ike.

Outside, an ambulance careened past, its lights ablaze in the dirty mist. It was half past three in the morning. He'd never been lonely up at Broad Lake. He'd never even considered it a possibility.

◆ ◆ ◆

What a busy night I'm having, said Colin at the door in only a pair of jeans. His concave chest startled Andy. Fiona was here an hour ago. His torso was pale. She came back to try again on her own. You're here to do the same?

Andy entered the room after Colin turned and stepped away from the door. The apartment had an odour to it now, in the early hours of the morning, which he hadn't noticed on their visit yesterday. It was acrid. It was the smell of vomit.

You never did make much of a team, my sister and you. Drink?

Andy nodded.

You agreeing with me, or do you want a drink?

Both, I guess.

Colin poured three fingers of vodka into a paper cup and handed it to Andy. It's the new bohemian martini. You wait, next year they'll be doing this at swanky bars coast to coast. Cheers.

It's good to see you, Colin, he said.

It's good to be seen.

You might think about firing your maid.

You think she's stealing the Aspinall silverware?

The vodka burned Andy's throat. He was leaning up against the wall. Colin lowered himself to the floor, so Andy slid down the wall to a sit. Eye to eye now, there was no way to pretend that nothing had changed. Once they had sprawled out, two boys suntanning naked and white among the turrets at Huntington; they had passed answers to math problems on small pieces of paper to one another; they had walked together around a park, thrilled to be in one another's company after a time apart. All this was behind them. Whatever they'd had back then, whatever promise lay before them, felt — on the floor of this cell-like place — well and truly spent.

You ever screw my sister? asked Colin. Andy didn't answer. How many times?

Once. She screwed me, really.

I knew it! I always thought you did. You still see much of her?

No. Until she called last week we hadn't spoken in ten years.

Sounds like my mom is dying.

It does.

I can't go back to Huntington. It's not even my father so much. The house, the whole thing.

You know, Andy began, I live up on a lake a few hours north of Toronto. I'm trying something new with my life. You can come and stay with me for a while. Then Andy added, No one would know. It's isolated.

Colin looked up at him.

Maybe from there, said Andy, then he stopped. But started again, Maybe you could slip into the hospital — see your mom for a bit. When no one else was around?

They don't respect me, said Colin taking a long drink.

I'm not following. Who?

Nigel. The others. I don't tell them *what* who I am means. They don't hear Aspinall and think Rockefeller, or Kennedy. They just hear a surname.

I thought that's what you wanted, why you left Canada.

But they don't treat me right. I work in a fucking tea shop, Andy. I serve people. I want to spit on them. Say fuck off you dirty people who came begging to this country, your hands stretched out. You are the children of sheep fuckers, or the lucky ones who avoided the machete and are now among the un-eth-nically-cleansed. I hate them Andy. I abhor them, common as dirt, and these are the ones I fuck. Andy, I have to. Why? I have to. They let me. They are the only ones who let me. They think I'm one of their ranks, and they just agree. I'm another piece of meat with a hole in it.

I know who you are, said Andy. Come with me. You should see your mother.

Because it's the right thing to do? It's a bit fucking late for moralizing now, isn't it? Look at me. Look. You see something with worth? Why should I go? Why should I?

Because it's the human thing to do.

The sliding glass doors opened for Andy and Colin, and they stepped out into the bright cold. On this late November morning, the Toronto sky was high and blue. They climbed into the cab of Andy's truck. As they made their way east through greater Toronto, housing divisions rushed by them for the first hour and a half, then petered out, to be replaced first by the rolling hills, mixed forests and farmland of Northumberland county, then by the flatter, scrappier land as they worked their way north in and around a series of lakes.

Colin had the window down a half turn and the wind made for a colder- and louder-than-necessary ride. They didn't talk much. Instead, stopping for Tim Hortons coffee and donuts, they ate, drank, and let the silences grow into comfortable long waves.

With the aid of the vodka, and plucky impulsiveness, Andy had thrown Colin's stuff into a plastic shopping bag and together they had grabbed a cab back to Andy's hotel room. There they showered, shaved, and changed. At 7 a.m., Andy began calling airlines and soon had booked them two tickets to Toronto for 9:30. Miraculously, Colin had a valid passport. It turned out in the past five years he'd twice been back to Canada to see old friends without any of his family ever knowing. On the lookout for Fiona, they'd left the hotel for the airport. They boarded the plane. In the quiet hum of the aircraft in flight, it felt to Andy a long line of easy moments, but all of which had the possibility of calamity. The plane landed. Finally, they were in Canada.

Outside the truck, the trees were leafless, the odd stubborn maple that did not get enough light clung onto a now-browned and thin canopy.

They arrived at Andy's cottage in late afternoon. Broad Lake was heavy and leaden. Together, Andy and Colin stood on its shore with their hands deep in their pockets.

I have a jacket I can lend you, said Andy.

Not sure how long I'm going to be able to stay.

I know. Let's just go day by day.

You got any booze?

No, but I can get some.

Yes, okay . . . No, wait, don't. I'm going to dry out a bit. Then I'll go see Mom. He was quiet for a moment then said, what made you come back to get me in the middle of the night?

I just couldn't sleep.

Andy watched Colin from ten feet back. Colin had stopped and was peering through a glass panel in the heavy hospital-room door. A minute later Colin pushed open the door and went inside. Andy sat down in the waiting room around the corner. There was a fair chance that either Mr. Aspinall or Fiona would come walking around the corner at any moment. They'd discussed this, he and Colin. After a few days, Colin grew restless and believed that whatever or whoever he found when he got to the hospital would be what was supposed to happen. The longer he waited, the more chance he had of being too late. And that, he came to realize, would be harder to live with than anything, even if it ruined his cover. So Andy drove Colin into Toronto to the hospital.

Andy flipped through an old *Toronto Life* magazine absentmindedly until an image of Fiona jumped up at him from its pages. She was wearing a short black dress and had a pink scarf tied at her neck. She looked French somehow. The photograph was taken at a charity gala last winter — the issue was months old. Andy looked up. Colin was still in the room with his mother. Should he go in afterward? They had not discussed this, but Andy had known Mrs. Aspinall for a long time. Should he, too, pay his respects and wish her to get well, if even briefly. Why didn't it feel right? He wasn't her son, and with death so close. . . . He stayed put.

On the wall was a clock. Time weaves around and through lives, joining together moments related and unrelated. From one hospital waiting room to another, Andy was taken back to his own father's death, but not by the similar locales. Nothing about this visit by Colin to Mrs. Aspinall had, so far, reminded Andy of his own father's death. But, as he flipped through the

Toronto Life, he was hungry. And it was this hunger that led him to wonder what he could grab quickly to eat. He thought about pizza, but didn't want that much cheese — too heavy — and then thought about soup — too messy to eat sitting in a waiting room. Then a sandwich, a tuna, no, a chicken sandwich was just the thing. These were his thoughts. Fleeting, ordinary, about only the matter at hand. Then he remembered vomiting chicken after learning of his father's death. The headmaster was patting his back, saying how sorry he was. The taste of it, hot and sour, was in his mouth. And from that the smell of vomit at Colin's apartment, so recently. Would these moments in the future live together for him in a single episode of jumbled contemporaneity? Time worked like this. Separate moments joined to one another, not by the number of times an hour-hand circumnavigated a clock face on a waiting room wall, but by the taste of chicken.

How does she look? asked Andy when Colin emerged from the room. He appeared calm, resigned. His face had a line across his cheek, as if he'd just woken up, or had had his face resting against something hard for some time — the edge of a bed rail perhaps.

Pallid. She looks like that. If that's the right word, said Colin. Let's go. Let's go get a drink.

Outside, the air was cool. No, let's skip the drink, said Colin. They headed back to the truck.

Should we just hit the road? asked Andy.

I want to go to Huntington, said Colin. I need to see it, face my father.

◆ ◆ ◆

The tree-lined driveway leading down to Huntington was unchanged. Oak after leafless oak stood resolute and familiar.

You remember climbing up on the roof, said Andy as they approached the house in his truck.

I remember everything, said Colin. That's what's not fair about it. He was looking out his window at the field that stretched from the house up to the main road. In the summer, there was a small pond in the middle and a short nine-hole golf course. But it had snowed lightly the day before and a thin cover whitened out the details. The last of the oaks gave way to the circular driveway. Another car's tracks in the snow headed around to the garage in the back.

Where should I park, do you think? asked Andy.

Guests park at the front door.

The look on Stuart Aspinall's face was of stone. Yet he took a step back and opened the door wider, letting Colin and Andy in. The foyer was even vaster than it was in Andy's memory, opening up into a wide hall from which corridors led both left and right and a staircase with a sweeping banister pushed a flight upward and downward. The floor was marble, the ceiling wood. Windows with small panes of glass flanked the staircase on its ascent. A portrait of Colin's grandfather and great grandfather hung at the foot of the first landing. Huntington had avoided time completely.

Good god. It was Fiona's voice. She was walking toward them out of the darkness from the hallway that led to the kitchen. She was carrying a tray with two cups of tea.

We were just about to have tea, said Mr. Aspinall. I should think it's a good idea that we all sit down. Nice to see you, Andy, said Mr. Aspinall. Colin stood motionless for a time, then looked up to the high ceiling.

Andy was the successful one, said Mr. Aspinall once they were all seated in the sitting room that looked out to the back garden. A woman, a maid, whom Andy did not remember, came with two more cups of tea for Colin and himself. For a time, no one spoke. The maid wandered off. Mr. Aspinall looked as if he was going to say something further, but did not.

I just saw Mom, said Colin.

Dad and I were there last night, said Fiona.

I'm there every day, said Mr. Aspinall. Again, there was silence.

Andy, I'm glad you're here, said Mr. Aspinall. Seeing as you are, could you explain to a father why his son wouldn't come to visit his dying mother?

That's great, Dad. Not only am I invisible, but you're in the third person, said Colin. This was a good idea.

You never listen to me. Why should it make any difference if we are together in the same room?

What is important, Dad, is that he's here now, said Fiona.

She wanted to see him. That was all. And he wouldn't come. Now she's vegetative. Mr. Aspinall raised his voice during the last few words, and as he began the next few at the same angered pitch and threatening volume, he rose to his feet. We are old. She is dying. And you, he said, pointing at Colin with a menacing finger, haven't grown up at all. How is this possible? Exasperation slid into his voice at the end, and he fell back into his seat, the leather giving up a soft sigh of air.

If I were to say, for example, that I have an extremely insightful observation to make about our family, what response would you have, Dad? I mean, before you've even heard what I have to say?

Games are for children. I'm not going to play games with you, Colin.

How's your chess collection, Father?

Do you know what your mother said to me when she was still able? She said, and these were her words exactly, *I don't know what I did wrong in his eyes.* She couldn't understand why you would not wish to be by her side as she lay dying. She blamed *herself.*

Finally, someone around here has accepted some personal accountability, said Colin.

For a while, there was no talk. Andy looked over at the windowsill to a blue china vase holding a half-dozen peacock feathers arranged in a fan — six azure eyes caught the light from the window above.

When she goes, so does all this. Mr. Aspinall lifted his hand vaguely. Then he looked up and across at Colin for a moment, as if memorizing his features before getting to his feet and leaving the room.

He's been saying he's going to sell Huntington, said Fiona after he was gone.

He won't, said Colin.

No. I don't think he will, she said. I'm glad you came, Colin. Andy's cleaned you up.

Yes, thank Andy, Colin said, getting to his feet, then added, we're not going to stay. I might pop upstairs. I've wanted something from my room — if it's still there. Is that childish of me? Be right back. Colin's footsteps echoed on the marble floors once he crossed the rug.

You're a magician, Andy, Fiona said, also standing and walking toward him. Andy stood. She reached up to his face and patted him on the cheek. I don't know how you did it.

Luck? he said.

Love? she said in a whispered response.

He could smell her she was so close. He'd have known her smell anywhere, but, until now, he hadn't been aware that he knew it by heart.

She'll be dead in a matter of days, said Fiona.

Sometimes they hang on for ages.

She was hanging on — for Colin. That's why Dad is so furious. He knows it too. She can die now.

◆ ◆ ◆

The Aspinalls are buried in the Mount Pleasant Cemetery in Toronto. Their mausoleum has columns that evoke Huntington's facade. In the limousine, which smelled faintly of smoke and booze, travelling backward Andy sat next to Colin, across from Fiona and Mr. Aspinall. The funeral was a private one, but, they were later told, more than three hundred people filled the church. Afterward, they headed up a long procession of cars snaking through North Toronto to the cemetery. They were older faces Andy recognized as the now aged parents of LSC friends he, Colin, and Fiona had known, but other prominent Canadians were there. Andy thought vaguely that it should have been a bigger production, newsworthy even. But no television cameras were present. When he mentioned this to Fiona, she'd said that her father had made some calls to keep them away. Then they arrived and all hands were cold in black leather gloves. Woollen grey or black overcoats were buttoned high to the neck. The words at the gravesite were brief. Later, Andy and Colin joined about a dozen other friends of Fiona at her apartment in Yorkville.

After their visit to the hospital and to Huntington, Andy and Colin had returned to Broad Lake to wait for word. Andy did not tell Fiona where Colin was staying, but, he assumed she would know it was with him up at the lake. She had his number. It would only be a matter of days. Indeed, Mrs. Aspinall had died the next evening. The funeral was set for the following

Monday. Andy took the call from Fiona and simply nodded firmly, grimly, apologetically, to Colin across the room.

I'll go, Colin said after Andy hung up the phone. You'll come?

Of course.

Andy?

Do you think we could get Liona Boyd to play at the service? They used to be friends, you know. I love her music.

You never know, Colin.

Andy?

Yes?

If you wouldn't mind, I'd like to stay for a while after this is over. I can't remember ever having gone so long without a drink. It's so peaceful up here. I need a bit longer before I go back to New York.

Colin, as long as you like. Please.

They'd slipped back into such easy friendship. In the truck on the drive from the airport, Colin had made Andy laugh and something of what they used to have returned. It was as if Colin's New York life became secondary to him, at least for now. The story of who he was, and what, and why, was clearer in Canada. Sitting around Andy's fire, the smoke of it blue and heavy, they'd spoken of the paths their lives had taken. Andy tried to articulate why he'd left the law, telling the story of Sondra and her father's watercolour regrets. Colin speaking of his relationship with Nigel, their circle of friends, his job in the tea shop.

I can't imagine you holding down a retail job, smiled Andy.

I'm pretty good at it. I like working. All that stuff I said at my apartment . . .

Forget it.

Colin and Andy had agreed that following the funeral they would get back into his truck and return to Broad Lake. But Fiona insisted they spend the night with her and their friends. They were all her friends, some of them older versions of those that Andy had watched out the bathroom window, swimming in the pool at Huntington years ago. They had been so young; everything had been before them. Now they sipped wine and confessed to the affairs that ended their first marriages, smiled as they recounted the moments of their children's first steps or words, or spoke sadly of the children they were not able to have, the husbands or wives they never did find. The central gossip of the evening centred on Christopher Llewellyn, who, Fiona announced, she'd told not to come — I told him things in Canada are sad and complicated tonight, she said. I need him to bring me up and into the light tomorrow. They drank to that.

Colin gulped wine greedily all night and seemed happy enough to speak with Fiona's friends — most of whom he'd once known well. Andy watched him, expecting him to grow more gregarious, or vain, or even upset. None of these moods emerged in him. After a while he approached Andy, who was listening passively to a conversation, and pulled him away.

I'm going to go to bed. I think if I shut the door, the noise will . . . and he drifted off toward Fiona's guest room. They'd already decided that Andy would sleep on the couch, which meant he would have to stay up until the last guest left. Gone were the days of 4 a.m. drinking binges. They'd all left by eleven, going home to their kids, partners, happinesses and sorrows.

Fiona's apartment was furnished in modern minimalism — cube armchairs, square white leather sofas, two huge pieces of matching, geometric art. Andy helped her clean the glasses and plates from the floor and side tables.

You okay? he asked her.

Funny that Colin went to bed.

He might have been disappointed he decided to drink tonight. He's been drying out with me.

Even a drunk deserves a drink when he buries his mother. Leave them, I'll do them.

You do dishes?

Only in front of people. For effect, she said with a tired smile. Then her arms fell to her sides. As if all her muscles had lost their ability to hold her up she crumpled to the kitchen floor, and wept in long hard heaves. Andy put his hand on her shoulder, sinking down to the floor and sitting beside her cross-legged, holding her against his chest. The smell of her was strong.

It's been a very long day, he said. And then said it again.

◆ ◆ ◆

Pass me the flipper, said Andy.

No one, began Colin, blowing into his hands and placing them over his ears, barbeques in minus ten, surely?

I do, said Andy.

It was February and Broad Lake was frozen from shore to shore. The sun had dipped behind the horizon and streaks of orange and blue followed it west in a trail of streamers. There was no wind, just hard cold.

Do you want to go walking out on it after supper? I have snowshoes for us both.

Back inside, they ate hamburgers. Colin liked to fry an egg and put it on top of his burger, which he also doused in ketchup.

I dated this Australian guy a few years back. He was a waiter in the Village. This was how he ate them, except he put pickled beets on them too.

What happened to him?

He went home. They all do, the Australians, the English, the Germans. They all go back to their homes.

What about us Canadians? asked Andy. Do we go back home?

The dark seeped into the sky, taking it to a bruised purple, then all-out black. They layered on Andy's warmest clothes and strapped on the aluminium snowshoes. Stars freckled bands of the night in barely discernible glimpses of unimaginable elsewhere. They set out, walking on frozen water.

Do you want me to turn on the flashlight?

Colin, who was walking a few paces ahead of him, didn't answer Andy so he flicked it on. They walked for about fifteen minutes before Colin stopped. He had his neck craned skyward.

I think that's Cancer. Remember we learned the constellations and the zodiac stories in science class. LSC was good for something.

I can't remember any of them, said Andy.

Juno sent the crab — Cancer — to distract Hercules while he fought the Hydra. Remember it nipped at his heels?

Oh, I do remember that one. He crushed it, didn't he?

Yes, but it was given a place in the heavens as a reward for its loyal service.

Show it to me, said Andy. They stopped. Andy turned off the flashlight. Around them the details of the shoreline had faded into black absence. There was no moon.

I'm not sure, but you see that one? Then there, and there. Colin pointed to star after star, linking them up with sweeping gestures. Andy was unclear on which stars Colin was pointing out, but he didn't want to dampen his friend's enthusiasm, so, with an unsure but interested voice, he did his best to follow along.

Andy had not been sure how long Colin was planning on staying with him: a few days maybe? It had been weeks now.

Colin only occasionally brought up his job at the tea shop that was, ostensibly, waiting for him back in New York. He'd called his friend — the same one who found him the apartment — from Fiona's after the funeral and explained that he would be delayed. It sounded to Andy as if Colin's job was nothing more than a favour, something for Colin to do, earn some money so he could eat, and drink. Early on, Andy had decided against asking him too much about his life, his ruined relationship with Nigel, or his still-nameless friend who was housing and employing him while he got his life back together. Instead, Andy waited for Colin to speak, and asked him questions based on what he would bring up.

After a time, their silences grew longer and sustained. They were not difficult or awkward. The winter weather was cold, but bright during the days, and deeply black and quiet at night. The radio stayed on CBC in the background. One day Andy found an old hand auger in the shed out back and, with great effort, drilled a hole in the ice. He and Colin fished for several hours before the cold overcame them. Andy spent most of his days reading about antiques. Colin leafed through magazines distractedly, but not discontentedly. At night they played cards, or walked out on the lake, or listened to the radio and watched the fire sputter and start until there was nothing but glowing coals. Andy was glad for the companionship. Colin stayed sober. Then, Fiona called to announce that she was on her way.

◆ ◆ ◆

He's selling it. These were the only words Fiona managed before she began to riffle through the bag Andy had carried in from her car and placed on the floor. From it she pulled a bottle of wine. Glasses? Corkscrew? Could you live any farther away, Andy? It took me forever to get here.

Andy sank the corkscrew into the neck of the bottle as Fiona was taking off her coat. She left on her black leather driving gloves, rubbing her hands together.

I wore these the whole way up. It's so cold. Warm in here though. This is rustic, Andy! How long have you been here? This should be decent; I brought us a few bottles. Colin, if you're not drinking, stay away from it.

Easy for you to say, he said. Colin was sitting on a deep sofa across the room. He'd been reading a mystery novel all morning as they awaited her arrival. They both knew her presence would alter their quiet existence, and so they spent the morning in silence, bathing in the last hours of solitude.

Cheers, she said. Fiona had her hair back in a single, low ponytail. She wore a designer jean jacket over a black cashmere turtleneck and black pants. After taking three greedy gulps of her wine, she smiled. Bit cold from the car's trunk, but hey, it's medicinal.

Andy moved her bags into his room. He insisted on the couch and she did not protest. Colin was already in the only other bedroom. She began the story almost immediately. She was, clearly, consumed with it.

The day after the funeral, yes, only a single day passes — that's it! — he calls a lawyer he knows and, apparently, retains him to sell Huntington. They negotiate for a month, and wait for appearances to improve, then out it comes. Of course, prime piece of land and lakefront, the guy makes a few calls to developers and there is interest immediately. Next day, it's in the *Toronto Star: Aspinall to Sell Huntington Estate to Developers*. What a mean shit. So I get a call from Kimberly, you remember her . . . Of course you do, she was at the funeral, and my apartment. She's telling me it's in the papers and she's so sorry that we have to go through this. But of course, I don't know anything about it. So I'm vague and acting like there is more to it, that I'll get back to her later. What I do later find out, because of the article, is that *more parties interested in the property are likely to surface. The property* — for Christ's sake. This is our home they're talking about.

Fiona downed the final mouthful of her wine and poured herself another glass. Andy shifted over to sit at her right, but she was talking to Colin, who remained, unmoved, on the sofa with his mystery still open on his lap.

So this lawyer, I don't know the guy, a complete crook probably, decides to hold an auction later this month. This is how much interest he's got. Colin, whoever buys it will pull it down. I know a guy who works in the same firm as the lawyer Dad's retained. He won't tell me much at all, he's a good one, he would if he could, believe me, but he did leak that it's going to sell. The price is big. One of the offers they had in was to turn it into a golf course; Huntington would be the clubhouse and event centre. Christ, weddings and birthdays of awful people from Hamilton and Unionville *pretending* in our home, taking photos of their kids in tuxes which will forever sit on their inherited Sears sideboards. So, at this point, I just can't stand it.

Have you spoken to your father? asked Andy.

Oh, I'm not even half done yet, said Fiona. I hang up from Kimberly. I'm stunned. So I phone Dad. Says this shouldn't be news to me. Confesses that this began the day after Mom died, that he went to the office the next day to begin the proceedings. It's my mother, and I was all fucked up, and crying on and off, and generally trying to pull myself together, and where was he? At the goddamned office. With, apparently, a head so clear that he's selling our family estate. Been in the family since 19-fucking-08. *His* grandfather built it. It's all too unbelievable.

And I'm just flabbergasted. I say, Dad, can we talk about this? And he says, about what? Then, then he said . . . Fiona paused. Losing composure completely, she stood and looked about for a Kleenex or the bathroom, Andy wasn't sure which. So Andy leapt to his feet and guided her by the arm to the bathroom where she stayed for several minutes. While she was in there, Andy exchanged glances with Colin.

Not sure why she's dragging me into all this, Colin said more to himself than to Andy. Finally, she re-emerged.

I heard what you said in there, said Fiona. She reached for her wine and swallowed a mouthful. Don't you care about your home? He's selling what is ours. The Aspinalls are that house. It's our birthright.

Colin sat on the sofa and wore a glum expression, but, to Andy, it looked put on. Andy had the notion that Colin might burst out laughing at any moment.

He said to me that I wasn't to worry. I'd still be given my allowance. That's when I lost it. I quit racing cars so I can take over his company one day because I think of it as my company too. It's my last name as well as his. My allowance! The fucker. I'm going to get him. He deserves it.

Colin got to his feet. Now, Andy thought, he looked genuinely concerned — as if he could read his sister's thoughts and knew what she was capable of.

I called Christopher. Andy, you met him. We're together now; it was in the papers in January. We've pulled together silent partners. It's all UK money so he'll never get wind of it. One of them is going to be the lead on the bid. We are going to buy it. I'll stay in the background until the bid goes through. Then I'm going to keep it, live in it — at least initially. I'm going to rub his fucking face in it.

How are you going to pay them back? The other investors? asked Colin.

Colin, darling. I'm starting a property development company. With a fifteen-million-dollar asset, we'll borrow more against it and make money elsewhere. We'll all do well. One day, I'll buy them out. Preferably with Dad's money once he drops dead.

You'll never see it if you do this, said Colin.

Well, unless he gives it away while he's alive, or leaves it all to you, I'm likely to still get most of it. Besides, if he's gone, it's a court case I'll win eventually.

Andy? asked Colin. Wouldn't you say old Adam Patch won out in the end of that book we read together, way back? Assuming happiness and a sound mind is at all important, that is.

Don't get smart, Colin, said Fiona.

Fine, said Colin. I'll drop the allusion and dumb it down for the blond. All I'm saying is that he'll screw you over, Fiona. You won't win this.

Us. It's going to be us, Colin. We have to go into this together. I need you to be a director of the company too. Your interests in the estate have to be in line with mine or the investors think the risk of Dad leaving his money to charity is too great. They want to know we are together, that you are not going to be the sole inheritor — when the time comes. It's got to do with risk.

Risk! Yes, I'd say risk is the right word.

Colin. This is a good plan. We'll save the house.

There's no chance. You're on your own. I don't care about the house. I don't care about my ass of a father either. This is precisely why I've had nothing to do with him for all these years.

But you care about me? asked Fiona.

Yes, but less so if you're going to be just like him, Colin replied.

How could you say that? answered Fiona who was screaming

now, her voice shrill — rising up an octave. Andy stood, moved toward her and she struck out at him with a flat hand hitting his face and neck with two slaps, Get away from me. You bring him up here; you pretend he and you are the same. That's a laugh.

Colin leapt from his sofa, grabbing Fiona to stop her from hitting Andy, who was not defending himself. Interlocked, brother and sister pitched toward the kitchen in a staggering half-fall.

You *are* just like Dad. Mom knew it too. That's why she never trusted either of you, screamed Colin in return, his voice losing its strength, climbing to a hoarse cry.

I hate you, Fiona hollered as she swayed forward, grasping at the handle of a cast iron skillet, still on the counter from breakfast. I hate, hate you, and Fiona swung her whole body around, heaving the weight of herself and the skillet, into Colin, who was still getting up off the floor.

The skillet as mallet connected with skull, the dull, deadening toll of it followed by Colin's body's taking an involuntary crack at recovery — a flash of cognitive disbelief at what had just occurred — then its total failing culminating in a single convulsion. Then nothing. Blunt-force trauma.

Fiona looked at her gloved hands holding the pan and released it. It thudded and landed right side up.

Andy was the witness. This series of events, lasting no more than a few seconds, transpired while he'd been motionless. Once over, he found himself frenzied, on the ground next to Colin, poking for a pulse at his friend's neck. Nothing. He lolled the head to its other side and tried again to feel. Nothing. He looked up at Fiona. Expecting her to speak of ambulances, to see her face full of tears. But in her mind, time was moving in the opposite direction. While he was searching for ways to undo, to revert, backtrack, fix, and heal, Fiona was speeding forward, processing facts and anticipating consequences, measuring final outcomes with self-preservation as her target, and deleting the riskiest options. Collateral damage was an unfortunate inevitability.

No one knows I'm here, she said in a plain voice. She looked down at her gloved hands.

Andy gave Colin mouth-to-mouth, slapping him on the cheek, pleading with his limp, lifeless body to respond. He felt Fiona moving about in the background. Only later was he to deduce that in those few minutes she had collected her bags from the bedroom where he'd moved them, re-corked her wine bottle and thrown it, along with the empty glass from which she had drunk, into her bag.

The sound of her car's engine starting was what first got his attention. Where was she going? Was a plan made? Had she spoken to him? *No one knows I'm here.* There would be no ambulances. No sirens or hospitals. No authority calmly, professionally taking over, taking things from here. Fiona had left him holding Colin's dead body. This was to be his sole responsibility. And he knew, as if it were self-evident, that he would honour this obligation. This was his role to enact. So Andy stood up into the faint smell of her, which hung in the still air, the way beauty does as it is getting away from you.

Andy? Trudy was still; her eyes did not look down at the tape recorder which was still on.

Yes?

You okay?

Yes, he whispered.

I'm glad you told me, she said softly.

I feel relieved, he said.

They were silent for a few moments. She smiled at him, and without looking down she casually grasped her tape recorder, pressing stop as she dropped it along with her pad of paper and pen into her bag. Let's continue this tomorrow. We'll pick up right where we left off. Get some rest.

◆ ◆ ◆

Andy descended into the raw hole. About him were the tread and teeth marks of a backhoe, the arrowhead divots of a pickaxe, bits of rock shard from the blasted-out boulder, a discarded paper coffee cup. A milky slush pooled in two corners. Under a skim of rime, leaf litter and doughy mud gave the air a peaty thickness.

The light was poor, all but dark, but from its void fell gentle sleet that settled on the wool of Andy's plaid work shirt, the steel toes of his boots, his ruddy and whiskered cheeks, the fingers of his gloved hands. Pre-dawn, back in late March, the ground was only just thawed enough for this. Overhead, skeletal birches rocked and bowed as if keening.

At the deepest end of the pit, which would soon accept the concrete septic tank, Andy stamped his heel down on his shovel's shoulder. After a time, steamy, he removed his thick work shirt and hung it on a now head-high, severed maple root, stuffing his gloves in its breast pocket. With his T-shirt, Andy wiped the dripping sweat stinging his eyes; the taste of salt was at his lip. He noticed a thin scratch line of caked blood across the back of his index finger. After two hours of labour, he had depth enough to call it a shallow grave.

He looked down at Colin's sleet-covered, dirty face and blood-matted hair. There were three pine nettles stuck to his ashen cheek. First light. Andy must finish what Fiona had begun. Andy wrapped the body in the tarp and bound it with duct tape. Before covering the head, he touched Colin's lips with his fingers. He wanted to kiss Colin as a final act, but the smell now — it had come on so suddenly. Last week he still looked merely asleep, cold. But now he was transforming. Andy looked at Colin's wintered lips, lifeless shorelines.

He lowered Colin down into the pit with a length of rope that, in the warmer months, anchored his floating dock. Nearby, a cracked ice plate on Broad Lake shifted and moaned. About him it was still dark, but the temperature, he felt, had warmed a degree or two.

When he rolled Colin in, it was only to discover the grave he'd dug was not long enough, so, as dawn grew closer, Andy worked hard to lengthen it by another foot. A blister on his thumb burst.

Then he fit. He lifted up a shovelful of dirt and rock. It made an artificial sound as it fell against the plastic tarp. Another. Again. Soon the blue of it was covered, leaving only the rough shape, not of someone buried, but of a long forgotten childhood game played at Wasaga Beach with his own father on one of their few vacations. But this time there was no squirming and giggling. He continued to pile on dirt. And then the hump too disappeared. To finish off the job he smoothed the earth flat, scattering leaves haphazardly to disguise the floor of the pit as naturally occurring, taking on the look it had, before he'd begun.

Weeks ago, Andy had taken a walk out onto the frozen lake, alone. Bright with stars and moon, but still cold, with each step and the slight give of the top crust under his snowshoes, he deliberated upon Colin's resting place. He walked rhythmically with his sights set on the diagonally growing Jack pine across the way, perched up on a bluff. Under the influence of whisky and silence, Andy etched Colin's face into every shadowy cloud that passed in and out of the moonlight. Colin's smile emerged up ahead, in the half-erased tire tracks of a snowmobile, in the windows of distant boathouses, the angles of raised docks.

How is it, Andy wondered, that we move from this world to an altogether different one? Is the end of life a single instant of sudden absence, or is it a flickering off, and on, and off? Andy's snowshoes rose and fell as if remotely willed. Perhaps it was neither.

Colin's mouth. The familiar opening from where his friend's secretive words took shape had transformed into a bolt of velvety murk. A low boom followed another shift of ice out on the lake. The end of winter here was sonic, a percussive score of groans and laments. Last night he'd dreamed he was back out on the lake. In the snowmobile tracks, he'd seen Colin's smile falling inward and the frozen plates opening up, and then sinking. The edges were then a series of splits made by the tread marks. They were Colin's icy incisors, his lips, wanting a healing lick. Then silence leached into the cavity, the dark and heavy water was slow blood. Sleet collected into a slush that began to thicken and clot the newly formed gap. To Andy in this half-light, Colin's face distorted and swelled into a ghostly lake floe, then broke apart into small, shadowy burgundy-black bruises pockmarking the ice. His own convulsive cries woke him, saved him.

A bird's cry hung in suspension. He would be always lifting another shovelful of dirt and throwing it on the growing pile. The moments of him digging would be cross-examined. A carved and painted coat of arms and the dark oak panelling of a courtroom closed in around him. The court reporter would be at the ready, the sergeant-at-arms standing motionless by the door, and there would be Madam Justice's red sash, her reading glasses low on her nose. She would gesture to Crown counsel to please begin. Is this paranoia? How would his actions, each step he'd taken, unfold? If he could just read the briefs, better still, the court transcripts, or hear the evidence for himself, then he would know what he had done. Then he could understand.

Digging now, his hands, blistering, committed more facts with each shovelful. This moment — even his thoughts of the future, would be a part of what had happened — was still underway. A pathologist would perform an autopsy on Colin. How many pathologist's slides would be put to blunt-force trauma experts? How many months spent building the case, interviewing witnesses, gathering proof, would it take to pin Andy to right now, right here? This could all happen.

But Colin was an Aspinall. The courtroom proceedings would only be the beginning. There would be widespread interest. Outside the courtroom, journalists with deadlines would stick a tape recorder in his face. *Why did you kill him, Andy? Can you tell us why you did it?* They would badger him in a scrum as he pushed his way through to the front doors of the court. *Were you and Fiona Aspinall lovers? Who are you protecting, Mr. Kronk?* He would say nothing to them, force a vacancy into the look of his mouth and eyes as photographers shot him in rapid-fire. Without an immediate admission of guilt and a covered corpse to draw the reader in, the media would begin to comb his past: interview everyone he had ever known. Day by day, they would increasingly cast their speculation as fact. Words such as "accused," "supposed," and "testified" would fall away as, like maggots, the media gorged. They would cast the day's events not as reportage, but as blueprints for screenplays. He'd had clients who had been their carrion. He'd seen it all before as a lawyer.

In the beginning, he would be sentenced daily by what was quietly omitted in the *Globe and Mail*'s reporting — its readers needing no introduction to, or back story on, the Aspinalls. After an initial blitz at opening arguments, a month into the trial the *Toronto Star* would begin to determine his guilt piece-meal through the unintentional ignorance of the different journalists sent each day to pick over and notch up the false-hoods that ran yesterday. By closing, the *Toronto Sun* would do its service to the public largely with skewed captions under the one photo of the hundred they'd snapped where, due to a shadow, it appeared he had the guilty face of a killer. On CBC radio, they would fret about what this death means to the community. Then, in journalistic bafflement packaged as egalitarianism, they would turn his case inside out, asking Torontonians what they thought. Now deputized as media, Torontonians would write, or e-mail, or leave voice messages, regurgitating what they had read in the *Globe*, or the *Star*, or the *Sun*.

Madam Justice, and her rule of law, would not stand a chance. Neither would he.

Again, the bird call sounded and his breath burst into a cloud in the cold and was gone. The sleet fell, flattening the details of the earth. A wet skim of ice covered the ground, and in the dark, all impressions recognizable as human, of those living and dead, were removed.

PART FIVE

She's leaving. Paddle closer. Get out the binoculars.

Can you see him? Take photographs of her.

Can you get her face?

Yes. Yes, I'm getting some good ones. She's popped the trunk. Her face is in clear view. Now she's getting into the car.

I see that.

She's in a hurry!

Do you see him?

Must be inside still. Crane up at the sky in case he's watching us.

I haven't seen the osprey for hours.

That's two full days of this with her now.

I think we should call in a report, now we've got better photos.

She'll want them e-mailed to her.

Yes, go ahead. I'll keep watching. Your cell charged, or you need mine?

Mine's good.

Phone her then.

I am. Shush.

Are you *shushing* me now?

Quiet. Hello? Yes, may I please speak with Fiona Aspinall? Oh, this is? It's us. We're still up on the lake. We think we've got something for you.

◆ ◆ ◆

Trudy accelerated and swerved into the empty oncoming lane, passing a much slower moving mini-van. It was a miracle she escaped. At the B&B she ran inside, grabbed her clothes and threw them in her bag. The owner's car was not in the driveway. On the bed she left her business card. Scribbled on the back of it, *Send me the bill. Emergency. Have to run. Thanks, Trudy.*

How had this happened, come to light? She'd thought she'd been winding Andy up — so he would let slip a few private facts about the Aspinalls. That was all. But clearly he needed to unburden his conscience. Once he got going, she thought, once he knew that he was going to tell it all, he almost did not take a breath. Had she heard right? Fiona Aspinall killed her brother? That's manslaughter, isn't it? The word lolled about in her head, breaking down into its syllabic parts then colliding back together.

Officer Nyland? She was driving quickly and had her cellphone wedged up under her ear as she flicked on her headlights. There was still plenty of light left, but she drove with her lights on out of habit. To her it was safer, especially now. It's Trudy. Yes, I'm fine thanks. I'm on my way back. You're going to have to meet me at my house right away. Colin Aspinall is dead. Yes, dead. That's what I said. According to Andy, an accident occurred during a fight. Evidently, Fiona killed him. During an argument they had at his cottage. Yes. Yes. No. About two months ago. Some sort of heavy fry pan. Awful, yes. It's all on tape. Didn't expect this! I was just glad I . . . About two hours away. Right. Yes. See you there then.

She pressed *End*, took a deep breath, and pulled onto the ramp that led to the highway. She should slow down.

Across the farmers' fields, the fading light bathed the tilled rows in a rusty gold. The drive was a long one. She flicked on the CBC to try to calm her mind, but she found the chattering voice irritating, opted instead for silence and simply sinking into everything she had just learned. Now she had told Nyland, the police would be making calls, likely organizing to swoop in on Andy. She felt sorry for him. She believed his story. She thought she did. Perhaps he was delusional? Perhaps Colin is alive and well, living in New York? Or maybe Colin *is* dead, but it was *he* who did it. Fiona Aspinall being cast as a crafty, heartless manipulator only to excuse his own actions?

Somehow, no. She didn't believe these alternatives. He'd been so easy with his account. His facial expressions gave no hint of fabrication. She believed him. She dug into her purse, retrieved her tape recorder. Hit rewind and waited. Then pressed play.

I blew into his mouth, you know. CPR. I'm thinking that I know how to do this because we learned it in school, right? So I'm blowing and blowing. His chest is rising and falling. But nothing is happening. Oh god, and Fiona's just behind me doing something. I think she's looking for the phone to call the ambulance. I'm thinking that I should tell her where the phone is. You know, help her. But I'm too busy blowing. Slapping his face to wake him up. And I was crying.

You were frightened?

Of course. I thought he wasn't dead. I thought we were saving him. But she was collecting her stuff! She was about to get out of there.

What did she say to you?

Nothing. No, she said, *No one knows I'm here.* Then she looked at her gloves. She never took them off. Too cold. Drank wine with her gloves on, complaining all the while like a princess. I remember that, thinking it looked funny. So I guess she was calculating that she's not left fingerprints anywhere. She's here and no one but me knows that. So she's busy collecting up whatever evidence she's left: wine bottle, her glass. And next thing I know, she's started her engine. She's leaving me with Colin's body. Takes me about half an hour after she's gone to admit all this, and several days to understand what had happened. I couldn't believe it, you know?

That she left you there to deal with it?

Well, yes, that. But, that he's, you know, dead.

Trudy hit stop. Beside her, a long stretch of cedar forest rushed by in a blur. Her book was going to be huge. She again reached for her phone. She wanted to hear Patrick's voice, make sure Veronica was okay. But she called Humphrey instead.

◆ ◆ ◆

Mosquitoes crowded about his face as he pressed the hamburger patty into the grill. Broad Lake was still. Above him, the osprey rose and fell on updrafts. What does *he* look like down here? A lone mammal. Standing before a fire, swatting insects, cooking food. To the osprey, perhaps not much had changed since the last ice age.

He ate inside, washing it down with a beer. He looked, out of habit, for the two in the canoe, but they were nowhere to be seen. On the wall hung the cast iron fry pan. He'd washed it that night. After he'd hauled Colin's body out into the shed and wrapped it in the Canadian Tire tarp, he'd come back inside. He hadn't known what to do. There had been some blood — from Colin's head. Not as much as he might have expected, the real bleeding happening on the inside, he guessed. But he washed the floor and filled the sink with hot water, soaking and scrubbing the pan. He did these things without serious thought. It had occurred to him he was removing evidence, but he still had to go on living. Eating breakfast, reading up on antiques. He needed the pan for cooking.

The night following Fiona's departure, the bitter cold of an Ontario February evening had swirled about his cottage. Andy had suited up into his warmest clothes. In the shed, he drew back the tarp for his first look. Inch by inch. Colin's face was agog. A question hung in his permanently raised eyebrows, creased forehead, his parted lips. In a plain, straightforward voice, Andy began a one-sided conversation that continued, nightly, until April — when the backhoes arrived along with the thaw.

Do you remember, asked Andy on one of those nights, the morning we met those twin sisters from Ohio out on our island? Their funny accents. The fury they'd felt toward their parents for making them come on a houseboat holiday? We'd snuck away in a canoe from Huntington. Paddling out into the lake. What was her name, the one who said you looked like a child? You took such offence. I want to say it was Karen. So long ago now. But we all made up somehow; the way you do when you are young. And we swam with them, jumping off the overhanging rock. They were simpler than us. They were bored. I thought you were brave that day. Generous too. You did that for me. Played along. I remember lying on the bare rock, the four of us tanning with nothing much on at all. It was peaceful. Not naive or innocent. We were all much too old for that. But that morning we shared a kindness of sorts. Something unspoken that acknow-ledged each other's trial. We'd kept life's pressures off our little island — as if we all put ourselves on hold, and for once exhaled.

Andy had touched Colin's hand then. Lightly.

There can be peace among complete strangers. Did you feel that? Did you think of it this way? Did you ever recall that day again?

On other nights, Andy's thoughts were in a different realm altogether.

I knew I'd made the wrong choice the first time I was in a courtroom completely alone. I just stood there after the other counsel had left for lunch. I was gathering up my papers and briefs, stuffing them into my bag, and I had this *moment*, you know, this thought that I was, well, not so much unhappy as that I was in the wrong place. You ever have that feeling? Like you're supposed to be somewhere else at that moment? The real you, the one who figured out the right path to take several major life decisions ago was right then enjoying some kind of mean-ingful success, meanwhile you — the wrong you — was living out a humdrum moment?

I should have been thrilled to be finally sitting in court, acting on a client's behalf — all on my own. But I felt, well, numb. That ever happen to you? But I stuck it out, as you do. *Came this far*, and all that. Then I fell apart. Lost my way. So, now antiques. I don't know how I'm going to make a living at it. I had to do something, wouldn't you say?

Outside the shed the nights were cold and dark. There were often snowstorms. On those nights he'd stayed inside, losing himself in books on furniture. It was on one of the worst nights — a blizzard whited out any shadowy view of the lake outside his window — that he began to think seriously of what exactly to do with Colin's body. Sitting in front of his fire, he methodically considered the various methods of disposal available to him.

Soon, he set upon one non-negotiable: he would not do anything to Colin that would mutilate him in any way. Such an act was humanly and morally repugnant to him. Simply driving into the wilderness and dumping him somewhere occurred to him. But, no, that was not right either. Bears. Wolves. Osprey. He would have to bury him. His friend deserved some dignity.

But where, how? He wanted Colin close to him. Their recent, one-sided talks, he needed them; they were lifting some kind of deep burden. Were he to remain close, Andy might still be able to visit his gravesite privately, feel his presence, and continue their talks.

There were practical matters to be considered. The terrain close by his cottage was rocky. Digging a proper grave would, he imagined, be difficult. The days would soon be getting warmer. Climbing above the freezing mark. Colin's body would, he guessed, decompose rapidly.,

Then, indeed, he felt a change in the air — the day rose to plus three. Andy piled snow over the tarp. He was beside himself with anguish. He must think. He needed a plan today. Not to act was to risk having a decaying body on his hands. Then it occurred to him in a snap. He'd put him under a new septic tank. He called the contractor with whom he'd spoken in the fall, and ordered the work to begin. The timing would have to be precise, and so he pressed the man for his to be the first job of the season — offering to pay more as incentive to begin the moment it was possible to dig. The man agreed easily.

Andy finished his beer and picked up the plate. His hamburger had been filling. Then, suddenly, everything notched into place. What had he just done? Good god. While he had not told Trudy where Colin was, she did know he was dead. Where there is death, there is a body. They would want to know. *They* were the police. The media. The law. Mr. Aspinall. Fiona.

And Trudy had it all on tape. Everything.

He ran.

In his new toilet he vomited hamburger violently, the hot at his eyes and throat. He couldn't see properly. Splashing water onto his face, he was crying, crying out Colin's name. Fleetingly, he considered killing himself. How would he do it? Could, should he? He felt too disorganized. No, he must stop her. Get back the tapes. How long ago had she left? Not much more than an hour. He would chase her. Find where she lived. Somehow get the tapes. Then it was just her word versus his.

Scrambling out to his truck, he stopped over the patch of ground under which lay the septic tank, and far beneath that, Colin. He squatted, placing his hand on the scrap of grass and dirt. He grasped a fistful of earth. He released it in the pocket of his jacket, then hit the road for Toronto.

◆ ◆ ◆

Officer Nadeau phoned Mr. Aspinall's office the minute he'd finished with Trudy's call. He left Stuart Aspinall a message, but this time stressed it was urgent. Mr. Aspinall called back in less than five minutes.

I have some difficult news sir, Jim began. I've just spoken with Trudy. It appears that, it seems as if, Andy Kronk has told her that Colin is dead. Yes, I'm quite positive. She's on her way back to Toronto right now. She wants to meet with me. Yes, well, according to Kronk, he was killed in some sort of accident, and your daughter Fiona was involved. Yes. Yes. The whole confession is on tape. Trudy recorded the entire conversation. I will. Yes. Yes. I know it, it's off Bathurst Street. She should be getting home in the next hour or so. I'll leave right now.

Jim shaved, the razor nicking his chin in the rush. He pushed a small piece of toilet paper into it and it turned bright red immediately. He held a wad of Kleenex at the cut for a minute before the bleeding stopped. He spread out his suit on the bed. He hurried out the door of his apartment and jogged up the street to where his car was parked on the side of the road.

He encountered rush hour traffic. When he arrived at Trudy's house, he couldn't find a parking spot and had to circle the block several times before one came free. He wished he were in a squad car — that this was official work. He'd need to talk to the chief soon, given the developments. Make sure this one shouldn't be flipped over, make it above-board.

Mr. Aspinall's voice had been firm and unshaken, given that he'd just learned that his son was dead and that his daughter might have had something to do with it. The instructions given to Jim were to go to Trudy's house, take possession of the tapes, and to meet him in a public parking garage off Bathurst Street where he would hand them over. Mr. Aspinall had told him to be firm about getting the tapes. He was to tell her they were now evidence in a serious investigation, and that he would see to it that if it were possible a copy or transcript would be made for her. If, finally, she was not willing to relinquish the tapes, he was to take them from her forcibly. If he were able to complete this final task, he would be rewarded handsomely. He told Mr. Aspinall that he would not let him down. He meant it.

Jim knocked on Trudy's door and she opened it immediately. It had taken him so long to get clear across the city that it appeared to him she'd been home for some time already. Her bag was lying on the living room floor, and the tapes and her papers were spread out across the couch.

Patrick is . . . she stopped herself. My ex-husband was just here. We were going to listen to the tapes together, with you here. I wanted to have someone else with me. I hope you don't mind? But he thought he'd better go over to see a friend of his to find out if this guy can make a quick copy. We figured you'd want a copy pretty fast. She smiled, then put her hand up to her heart. I'm sorry I'm babbling, this is all just so . . .

This is now a homicide investigation, Trudy. There'll be no copies made of the tapes. They are evidence. Jim walked over to where they lay on the couch and began to pick them up.

Wait! she said.

I'm sorry, but I'm going to have to take them all. Any notes you made as well. It will all be returned to you in due course.

But this is my primary research material. I'm a writer, a journalist, I . . . Jim had swept up the five tapes and three pads of yellow paper.

Is this all of it?

Yes, but you can't do this. I'm calling my lawyer.

Go right ahead. But then Jim stopped and softened his voice. Listen, Trudy, you've been very helpful. I'm sure I might be able to see that a copy is, let's just say, accidentally made of the tapes. We'll call it the copy you were about to make yourself. You and I will pretend that you did in fact make a copy before I arrived. But for now this all has to go with me. I'll be in touch soon. Jim smiled an expression of forced sympathy. Trudy stood aside helplessly as he walked past her and out to the street.

Back in his car, Jim was about to put it in gear when he saw two men walking toward Trudy's front pathway. Jim hesitated. One must be her ex-husband. Who was the other? One of the men got there first and went straight up into the house. The second man appeared unsure about where he was going. Then he took a piece of paper out of his pocket, checked it, then headed on in. Jim knew he should have left by now. He was to meet Mr. Aspinall at the Bathurst Street garage. But he was concerned. Although he'd only seen a photograph of him, and it was taken more than ten years ago, Jim was fairly certain that the second man entering Trudy's house was Andy Kronk. Jim gathered up the tapes, put them in a white plastic shopping bag that he found on the floor, stashed them under the driver's side seat, locked the car, then headed back in to the house.

◆ ◆ ◆

Andy had pushed his truck at a breakneck pace down the highway. He'd been insane. He had told a stranger enough information to either get Fiona arrested for manslaughter — if he was believed — or himself arrested for murder if he wasn't. It occurred to him while he was driving that Fiona had had several months of clear-headed distance to decide upon and rehearse her story. Just how she would react if such-and-such piece of evidence was to come to light, or alternatively, if a different set of circumstances arose. She'd be able to play whatever role the situation dictated. She'd had all the time in the world. He'd been so stupidly preoccupied with Colin's death, with their shared past, with mourning, and the burial itself, he had not even begun to imagine life going on beyond it. He had to get the tapes. He could hear Stuart Aspinall's voice booming in his head, that this was his fault entirely, that he never could be trusted to keep a secret.

Once he entered Toronto proper, he pulled over at a gas station and looked in a phone book. Trudy was listed right there in black and white. He hadn't been sure what he'd do otherwise. Gratefully, he scratched down the address and set off. He knew, more or less, where the street was. Indeed, he found it without difficulty, stopping for a brief moment to double-check his piece of paper with the address scratched on it. He marched up to the door and stood for a moment listening to a conversation that Trudy was having with a man.

I'm telling you, he was just here, she was saying. He insisted.

You didn't ask for a lawyer? Or even if he could have waited, you know, until I came back then . . .

Oh my god, Andy! said Trudy when she finally saw him standing at the door down the hallway from where they were having the conversation. The other man, whose back had been to Andy, spun around.

I had to come, he said. I just . . .

Andy, you don't look well, said Trudy. Do you need a doctor?

Hi. My name is Patrick, said the other man. I'm Trudy's ex-husband. You're Andy then?

I'm here for the tapes you made, Trudy. I said some things I shouldn't have. I just have to listen to them and erase some of the stuff I said. Then you can have it back. I think that's fair, given . . .

Andy, you really don't look well, she said.

Maybe you'd like to sit down? asked Patrick.

The tapes, he insisted. That's all I'm here for. I don't mean to be rude, but I need them.

Well, you're too late Andy, she said. The police have already been here. I had to tell them. Given what you told me. It would have put me in jeopardy not to. Andy, they took the tapes. They're evidence now.

You told the police? Already?

They knew about you, Andy. They suspected something was up. We can't talk now. You better go.

Without warning, two girls walked out of a bedroom and

into the hallway between him at one end, and Patrick and Trudy at the other.

Mommy, Anita has put my hair into two French braids, said one of the girls. Aren't I pretty, Dad? Do you think I'm pretty? she said. Then the other one skipped around her friend toward him.

Andy's sense of space lurched, and he felt as if the girl was going to collide into him. He acted without thinking. He grabbed the little brown girl by the arm, and, accidentally, by her neck. The other girl was startled and instinctively ran at her parents, Trudy gathering her in her arms. Why was he not letting go of the girl? Something would need to happen to make him let go.

Give me the fucking tapes, he said. To his mind, this was the key that would allow him to free his grip. He felt terrible that this girl should be innocently caught in the middle of this. This would resolve things; she'd be safe soon enough.

Stay still, Anita, said Patrick. Trudy shrieked.

His hand stretched most of the way around Anita's neck. A stream of clear snot ran from the girl's nose and tears began to roll down her cheeks. He could feel her fright, her tiny body quivering. She wet her pants. Patrick had raised his two hands up, his palms facing outward and spoke.

Come on, man. Let's not do anything we are going to regret. Just let her come . . .

Then another man's voice, lower, confident, controlled, spoke from behind Andy.

My name is Officer Nyland. I will take out my gun and point it at you if you don't let the girl go on three . . . One . . . two . . . release the girl now . . . three. Andy relaxed his grip. He stood still. He felt himself grabbed forcibly at the upper arm. Let's go then, Andy, said the cop's voice.

Without looking back, Jim walked Andy over to his car and opened the passenger side door.

Undercover, said Jim. It's supposed to be a shit box. Get in.

On the way to the garage, Jim wondered how Mr. Aspinall would react when he saw Andy Kronk in the seat next to him. It couldn't be helped. He had to save the girl. Besides, he was sure Aspinall would want a few words with Kronk.

The only words they exchanged on the ride were just after Jim started the car.

Where are we going?

You'll find out when we get there. I like to concentrate when I drive. Talking distracts me. Get it? He did, and did not say another word.

The parking garage was publicly owned and had two floors. Harsh fluorescent lights lit up the numbered rows that were scattered with parked cars. Jim pulled into a spot and left the car running. They waited about twenty minutes before a long black limousine pulled up behind them.

Stay here, Jim said to Andy, and he reached under the seat for the bag of tapes.

The tinted window rolled down a crack.

Who is in the car with you? asked Mr. Aspinall.

It's Andy Kronk. He showed up at Trudy's house. He was going to hurt someone. So I sort of unofficially arrested him and threw him in my car.

Get in.

Inside the limo, all Jim could smell was new leather. He sank into the seat feeling as if his knees were higher up than they ought to be. Mr. Aspinall was alone and sat across from him.

Are those the tapes?

Yes, here. Jim handed them to Mr. Aspinall. Her notes too.

Good work.

Thank you.

Now please go back to your car. Tell Andy Kronk to get out and to approach the limo slowly. Then open the door for him and guide him in here. He and I are going to take a drive together and I'm going to have a few words with him. I want you to get back in your car and stay put. I will send someone to you in about an hour. They will have an envelope with your payment as promised. I think that concludes our business, Officer Nadeau. We won't be in contact with one another again. He reached out and shook Jim's hand.

Jim ushered Andy Kronk out of the front seat of his car and over to the limo, opening the door for him. He closed it after Kronk had climbed inside. The limo pulled away.

Jim turned on the radio. He couldn't get clear reception in the garage. Only the cbc came through clearly and so he was forced to listen to it. They were talking to a man about Middle East peace, and just what might be possible for a sustainable solution to the problems there. This was what Jim was doing when he noticed a man with an envelope walking toward his car. He wound down the window. The man held out the manila envelope. Jim was about to speak, some basic greeting, his brain sending the message to mouth a word. But the signal never made it. Instead, a bullet passed through his skull. The voices on the cbc continued to talk as another man appeared. They lifted the body into the trunk, and drove Jim's car up a ramp into the back of a large cargo van a few streets away. From there, the car, the van, the men, and the body disappeared. Everything was precisely executed.

♦ ♦ ♦

We should tell Veronica, said Patrick plainly. They were at his apartment. Again. For the third night this week a simple dinner, some familiar and comforting companionship, had transgressed and escalated. Now they lay in the dark.

Tell her what? asked Trudy. She sat up and had the distinct, but odd sensation, that she should leave her life, just give it up, and move in with Patrick. If only he weren't her ex-husband, if only she had someone in her life to leave.

This, said Patrick tapping his two index fingers on her kneecap in an even rhythm.

Are we sure? said Trudy.

Are you sure?

Well, are you? She'd not meant this last question to sound so much like a retort. But it was, and it unintentionally came out of her sounding this way. Level-headedness had a funny way of jarring against her deepest yearnings at critical moments.

She watched as Patrick got up out of the bed and walked over to the window. His apartment was a third floor walk-up, and across the street was a park that had a brightly lit pathway running through it in a wide S-shape. The lamplight put Patrick's naked body in silhouette. He was still long, thin, and fit from drumming.

They'd been moving toward this conversation in fits and starts ever since Andy Kronk showed up at her door demanding the tapes. Patrick had stayed over that night. He hadn't been scared; rather, he consoled the girls and lessened the seriousness of the situation. He spoke with Indira, and when Dilip came around, he walked him through the situation too. With the four of them together in the backyard, it was, suddenly, as if nothing had changed. The gate between their fences swung open and shut all evening as one or another of them came and went.

Finally, Dilip's car pulled out of the driveway. Indira left them to put Anita to bed, and Veronica had already fallen asleep in front of the TV. After Patrick had carried her to her bed, he returned to the backyard and joined Trudy. They sipped on white wine together. Then, alone, in the quiet, Trudy completely broke down. He held her and kissed the top of her head. This was not something he'd done since they'd separated. She didn't know how much she'd missed it.

Time passed strangely after that. Initially, there was the shock of it, the freshness of the violence that had entered her house, violated her family and those closest to her, which needed to wear off. It did, and it didn't. Anita had nightmares. This compounded with the pain of the girl's impending separation from her mother. It was summertime now and the girls were not at school. This lack of routine also made the days feel longer or shorter than they ought to have been.

And there was the matter itself that needed to be resolved. When would Officer Nyland call? Weeks and weeks passed. She and Patrick talked over and over about what she should do. How she should proceed with her book, if at all. She was sitting on a bombshell. Colin Aspinall was, in all likelihood, dead. This was big news. It was also under investigation. What could she say, and to whom? Could she, should she, continue with her book, and, if so, how could she do it without the tapes? Humphrey told her to wait for the tapes. Writing without evidence is at best speculation, at worst fiction, he'd said.

Call the cop, said Patrick. Call Nyland. Enough time has passed that you deserve an update, he continued as they entered the third week of waiting. But she dialed the number only to find it out-of-service with no forwarding number. They waited another week. She looked Jim Nyland up in the phone book in the hopes of matching his number to an address. She called a communications office at the RCMP in the hopes of locating Officer Nyland. At each turn, she found nothing. It was as if he did not exist, and never had. Finally, in desperation, she phoned Andy Kronk. Perhaps he was out on bail, or was not yet arrested. Perhaps she could plead with him to tell her some information about Officer Nyland. Which station had he been taken to, for instance? Andy's phone simply rang and rang.

She and Patrick drove to Broad Lake. It was a risky thing to do; they both knew it. She would stay in the car with it running and he would go to the door and ask the questions. He had a tape recorder in his pocket. But he never got to press record. The cottage was empty. Andy's belongings were still visible, almost as if nothing had changed in the time since she'd been there. She stayed in the car. Patrick broke in through a side window and did not emerge for several minutes.

Doesn't look as if he's been here since that day, said Patrick through the open car window. I checked the fridge. The power is still on, but the food has gone bad. There was a *Globe and Mail* open on the kitchen table. Dated May 13. That was the weekend you were here, wasn't it?

She called Humphrey on her cellphone and filled him in.

Sometimes the price is too high, Humphrey finally said. I believe you, but lost tapes and unfound dead bodies . . . Will anyone else? You've wandered into something bigger than you, Trudy. I know these people. I'll help you get out of it, get you going on a new project. Come see me; it's for the best.

It had been her story, her problem, but gradually Patrick became embroiled. As they had explored various leads and suppositions, they spent more and more time together. Under the auspices of getting to the bottom of this whole mess, they ate dinner together, went on research trips to test theories, and called one another several times a day with updates. The harder they worked, the less they found. They had begun sleeping together.

Anita is going in two weeks, said Trudy. Patrick had not moved, the back of his body the shape of a man as if drawn in light. If we fail at this . . . If it doesn't work, she'll be more confused. We'd be . . .

I get it, he said. I get it. He turned and got back into bed with her. Together, they breathed slow, shallow breaths, their faces only inches apart. With just enough light to see his expression, she watched him smile and hold it. There was dismay, but also genuine delight at the void their future had become. This would not be answered tonight.

Doesn't Colin Aspinall's body have to turn up sooner or later? she whispered.

Do you think Aspinall is behind this? asked Patrick. Maybe Davida was right from the beginning.

All I know is that I want to be with my family. We need time for all this.

This? he asked. By *this*, do you mean that this is the third night this week Veronica's stayed at Anita's?

I just want Veronica and you close by me. Is there anything wrong with that?

He shook his head no.

Veronica understands somewhere deep down, she said. Besides, Anita is leaving. This is the end of their friendship. They should spend it together. It's about to get hard for those two girls. They will grow up, and do it without each other. Then she shifted the topic back. No one is going to believe me without the tapes. Humphrey is right.

There's a body out there somewhere, said Patrick wearily. Just write the book, Trudy. I haven't missed your over-analyzing.

What have you missed?

Everything else, he said. What do you miss?

I miss Trudeau, she said lightly. They laughed a little, and he fell asleep, she watching the rise and fall of his chest, thinking of the day her daughter was born, how hard she'd hurt in so many ways. She would let this whole Aspinall affair go unwritten; she wasn't the writer for this story. She was no hard-edged journalist. Her agent had been right from the beginning. But it didn't matter now. It had led her somewhere unexpected, somewhere familiar, and better. Moments of her childhood flashed before her eyes, the covers of books she'd read, a holiday by the sea out East, her father's gorgeous music floating about her as she began to dream fluidly and evenly about moments that mattered to her, people she loved, places and times she'd enjoyed. Were she awake, she'd have called this for what it was: happiness.

◆ ◆ ◆

Fiona dropped her foot on the accelerator and the Audi's engine roared. She was about to pull past a truck full of cattle, their tails, tongues, and noses poking out of air holes. She caught a whiff of them. If they only knew what awaits them, she thought.

She'd left the city early to help her father direct the movers. She needed to see the exit from Huntington with her own eyes — to be sure it was real. She wanted to be there, even though she'd failed to save it. The developers had decided to demolish it. But it was mostly nostalgia that prompted her to phone her father and proclaim a truce.

Good, I'm glad you've moved on, he'd said. Come then. I need help. Moral support, at least. So she'd agreed.

She hated to be mad at her father. It constituted entirely too much effort, and, admittedly, ultimately, he would always win. But there was something else too. She had come to an impasse about Colin.

What had Andy done with Colin's body? It was a ghastly thought, but it was one that recurred daily now. Would the truth not be revealed? This was her mounting fear.

She slowed to snatch glances at the bovine faces beside her. What are you all looking at? Fucking cows, she screamed, surprising herself.

She was going to Huntington not to see her father on moving day, but to confess.

Her fate felt no better than one of those cows. She was trapped. She needed help. She had to get her story straight. If the private investigators she'd hired were right, then the biographer had visited Andy. Would he have talked? Yes, yes, shit, yes she felt sure he would have. Not out of spite or malice toward her, but out of loyalty to Colin. Of course. She'd been so stupid. How could she not have imagined this before today? She needed her father now more than ever.

Huntington had a strange air about it as she drove down the driveway. The outside potted topiary and statues, the birdbath and glasshouse were all gone. As she entered, Fiona looked up at the ceiling in Huntington's foyer. She'd always loved the wood, the plasterwork, its fleur-de-lys and cornices that wound and ran along the main staircase. About her, draped sheets and bubble wrap, boxes and crates disappeared down the hallways on either side. She heard her father walking toward her. He was whistling in a way that might have been described — back when the house was built — as gay.

Are we alone? she asked as he drew closer.

Just us and thirty illiterate movers with criminal records, he said. So, if you use long words and complex sentences, then I'd say, essentially, yes.

I need to tell you the details about Colin. He's not back in New York, Dad. Do you know exactly what happened?

I do not, he said.

Dad? she said, looking up at the ceiling for strength, her eyes stinging and about to produce tears. Dad, it's awful. When I was with . . .

Let me stop you Fiona. Mr. Aspinall had raised his hand and his eyebrows in a gesture that was both halting and diffusing. Before you go on, he said slowly, ask yourself, would I, would I be compelled, say, as a father, or, as an upstanding citizen, or both, to take some kind of action once you've given me this information? He sucked in air through his nostrils. Would this action further complicate our lives? Would it increase misery? Would it necessitate drastic change? Would it hurt your now publicly flowering relationship with Christopher Llewellyn? Would it make the newspapers, would you need legal representation? He'd emphasized the word *relationship*, hanging on to it in his mouth like a lozenge.

He was not going to help her. Not in the way she wanted. She'd wanted, she realized immediately, to confess and be made to feel better by her daddy. She wanted to be unburdened. She wanted her father to come to her rescue. Instead, he was going to punish her by making her fix it by herself. It was to be another in a long line of lessons in what he would do, were he in her shoes. She was being made to behave exactly as he would.

Yes, she said. She was losing control. She felt her eyes fill with tears. You'd have to do all those things, she added feebly, and sank down onto the bottom stair. Colin's head was again falling away from her, her body swinging the pan, the dead weight of it at him so much harder than she meant. And the sound, the feel and force of it as it made contact, was the dull, faintly agreeable sweet pock of a mallet hitting a croquet ball as far as one could down the lawn.

Had she killed him? Had she wanted to remove the asterisks from the Aspinall name? Did she resent Colin's stand? Did she want all the money? No, she told herself, convinced herself — she loved her brother. It was an accident. That was all.

An accident that she'd rather cleverly made Andy's problem. Yet, she reasoned, this sort of thing was, more or less, historically his job. Why had she doubted herself these past weeks? Get a grip, she thought. While she had a greater accountability than the average person, even she could not be responsible for accidents. And this, she suspected, was her father's point. He was speaking to her again. She looked up.

Fiona, you mustn't tell me information if you can't predict what I will do with it.

Never ask a question to which you don't know the answer, she said, echoing his axiom repeated so often over the years. He smiled.

My advice is this: push through whatever you are *feeling* until you find a rational path. Then come back to me with what you *can* tell me. Then I can assist you, as you know I will.

Fiona looked right up and into her father's eyes. She didn't know what to say. Without thinking, involuntarily, she said, I love you, Dad.

I love you too, he said and smiled.

Just then the first of the moving trucks pulled up outside Huntington, its tires crunching loudly on the gravel.

◆ ◆ ◆

Andy slowed his truck, and parked at the end of the last oak tree. The early August evening was bright and warm. He took it in for a moment before realizing how right Fiona had been. Huntington House had been reduced to a shell. The sight of it was a shock. On the phone, Fiona had told him that the fixtures and fittings had been stripped out and sold before the demolition crews started work. But as he walked toward the old place, he saw that the windows and doors had been removed along with the decorative scrolls and sconces in the eaves. The facade was a frown with teeth missing.

Fiona explained how her plan to buy back Huntington had fallen apart. Someone in one of her London investor's offices once worked for her father. They were out after work at a pub, she began, and my guy was pissed, and just blabbed the whole scheme to his mates. He didn't much care about it being kept a secret — some small real estate deal in Canada. His friend found himself on the phone with a former co-worker in Toronto the next week and mentioned the deal to him. It unravelled for me in less than a day after that.

What did your father say to you?

Nothing much. I think he rather liked my pluck. He sold the estate later that week to a developer for millions more than I was going to pay in any case. That'll teach me to be sentimental. And lord knows what actually gets exchanged out of sight in his deals.

Fiona had called Andy, ostensibly, to ask if he wanted to go see it one last time. They agreed to meet at the house after the work crews had finished their day. So it was about five when Andy pulled up. He walked slowly toward the house. From the gap that used to support a large carved oak door, Fiona appeared, her father behind her.

We just found out they are going to get a start on it this evening, she said as they approached him.

Hello, Andy. Nice to see you, said Mr. Aspinall. He was wearing a blue suit with a burgundy tie. His leather-soled shoes were polished to a shine. They shook hands.

The last time he'd seen Mr. Aspinall had been in the limo. Mr. Aspinall had driven him to the airport and put him on a plane to Cuba. He'd spent six weeks at a private, small hotel there. Lounging by the pool. Waiting for word on what he should do next. When the call came, it was from Fiona. You can come home, was all she said. Everything has been taken care of. Go back to your lake. It's all fine. As if nothing ever happened. He left Havana as quickly as he'd arrived.

Andy returned from his forced vacation oddly refreshed and clear-headed. His place was as he'd left it but with a window broken, nothing stolen. He got to work on his furniture refinishing — spending hours in the same shed where Colin had rested under the tarp. The summer days were green and radiant. On some he felt fragile, waiting for the whole episode to come to light, but mostly he trusted in the absolute power of Mr. Stuart Aspinall, of Fiona too. He must. So he sanded and stained Upper Canadian furniture, and went on long drives to attend garage sales and auctions all over Ontario. He'd have enough to open a small store by the fall if he put his mind to it. That was his goal. During the long quiet nights, on top of the sheets, too hot to sleep, he talked it over with Colin — sensed his friend approved. His new life was coming together after all.

About one hundred metres back from Huntington House, he stood with Fiona and Mr. Aspinall and watched as a young man in a yellow hard hat detonated a charge. A loud crack passed them by, and the house shook on its foundation. An excavator then drove its bucket into the side of the east wall of Huntington. The wall buckled and a hole appeared after the dust settled. A few more similar manoeuvres and the wall and part of the roof fell.

It is a shame, said Mr. Aspinall, that Colin has chosen not to be here with us today. But we all must respect what is his determined desire for privacy and anonymity.

Just then Andy pictured, hanging on a nail in the shed up at Broad Lake, his work shirt. In its pocket were his gloves. He had not moved it since coming in that day and stripping down to nothing. He'd finally washed everything else at the Laundromat before Trudy came, but the work shirt remained where he'd first left it. In the shower, he'd scrubbed at himself with a thin wedge of soap and a nail brush. He'd scoured his hands, the heat of the water, the rubbing turning them redder and redder. He had not cried in the shower. That came later, when the darkness pressed down on him, as he had lain awake avoiding both sleep and dreams. He'd cried, swearing wildly, apologizing to Colin aloud, alone, wailing, the sound of the dirt falling against the plastic tarp thick in his ears, unrelenting, never enough dirt to complete the task, the burial never quite ending.

The front facade fell inward on itself along with the second floor. A cloud of white dust rose into the sky. The sun was now visible, setting over the lake.

You can see the lake from here now, said Fiona. It's a clearer view than I'd have imagined.

This is a new country, said Mr. Aspinall. We thrive on renewal. We are unequivocally accepting and tolerant. At times, these attributes are not entirely negative.

What about the tapes? asked Andy.

There are no tapes, said Mr. Aspinall swiftly.

And Trudy Clarke? Andy pushed. This was the only window he would ever have for information. What if she writes her book anyway?

Without the tapes she has no facts on which to base any accusations, said Mr. Aspinall. She's never met Colin. . . . The book will never be written.

She's pretty tenacious, said Andy.

You are either tenacious or you are not, said Mr. Aspinall.

She is not tenacious. Her agent assures me of this. It will be seen to, one way or another.

Andy, please, said Fiona interrupting. Please don't worry.

Andy, began Mr. Aspinall, raising his hand, from here on, it's not complicated. You're a lawyer. Apply Occam's razor: choose the theory that makes the least number of assumptions. If he's not here, then he must have gone somewhere else. That is what will be thought. Provided that he remains wherever he is now.

Another boom and suddenly there was no structure left. On the ground before them lay the remnants of Huntington.

I once read it described as, *as close to a castle as Canada has*, said Mr. Aspinall. Then he simply said, Good evening, and turned and walked over to his limousine, his driver waiting inside.

Now, thought Andy, it would be a subdivision. Identical houses standing with double-car garages — and televisions, one each in every living room and bedroom. The people that would move here would never associate the name of their subdivision, Huntington Heights, or Huntington Downs, or Huntington Estates, with the Aspinall family. They knew nothing of elite Canadian families; the rich would remain invisible to them.

Andy watched as Mr. Aspinall's car pulled away from a driveway that led nowhere now — the gravel crunching under its tires.

Fiona was engaged to Christopher Llewellyn. She'd told Andy all about her plans on the phone. They'd be moving to Pennsylvania in the New Year, where there would be a splashy wedding followed by a run at Congress. Kimberly is finally getting a divorce, she'd said with a laugh. You can fly down together for the pre-party, come as her date.

He turned now to look at Fiona. She wore a slim-fitting, delicately floral-patterned dress that fell to just above her knee.

Her hair was down. Around her throat was the thin necklace. On her wrist, the matching bracelet. She was stilled.

What did you do with him? she asked. Andy looked away. That information, he instinctively knew, was all that he owned. And it was his one assurance that the story they'd invented for him would stand up to scrutiny. It was the only way he'd remain a free man. It was also his bond to Colin.

So Andy Kronk said nothing. Instead, he watched as a workman leaned against a shovel and waved, sending a convoy of four dump trucks rumbling past them, backing into Huntington's debris. The men were ready to haul it off and quit for the day. The crackle of a walkie-talkie cut the air. Dry brick dust plumed. Ruins were being pushed into mounds by bulldozers as the sun weakened abruptly, the way it does up here in the north.

NOTES AND ACKNOWLEDGEMENTS

The Hardy quotation is the final stanza from his 1867 poem, "Neutral Tones."

"Biography lends to death a new terror" is a quip of Oscar Wilde's.

The author would like to acknowledge the financial support of the Ontario Arts Council and the Canada Council for the Arts.

Initial sections of this book were written at Milton Park in the southern highlands of New South Wales, Australia, and at the Morgan's cottage on Stoney Lake in the Kawarthas. Thanks go to my mother Jocelyn Murphy, and to Ron Murphy; and to Marty and Rhys Morgan.

Thanks to my agent, Dean Cooke, and early readers Eva Blank and Richard Ward, and especially to my editor, Michael Holmes, at ECW Press.

Finally, thanks to my children Thomas and Ivy who both arrived during the writing of this, and, as always, my love and gratitude to my first reader, Wendy Morgan.

BackLit
INSIGHTS FOR
READERS

DISCUSSION QUESTIONS

1. What are the ways that love manifests itself in the story? Is *Entitlement*, at its core, a love triangle?

2. Does Fiona Aspinall change in the novel? If so, how, and who influences her most?

3. Colin resisted his father's control, but it didn't make him feel free. Given his longstanding unhappiness, why do you think Colin persisted in refusing to fall into line as an Aspinall? In what ways do you think he is like his father?

4. Trudy Clark holds the only hope the public has for access to the real truth behind the Aspinalls, but she fails at her task. What do you think the author is saying about investigative journalism, or even about truth itself?

5. When Andy Kronk made a deal with Mr. Aspinall, do you think he betrayed Colin? Did he have a choice?

6. Did this book make you think about class differently? Had

you thought much about the class structure in Canada before?

7. Is *Entitlement* a left-wing or a right-wing book? What do you think is the core message of the novel?

8. What is the role of America and England in the novel?

RELATED READING

Huntington House plays a prominent role in *Entitlement*. Some readers might see it as a character in its own right. As a symbol of the mighty Aspinall fortune, even it, in the end, could not stand up to the will of its owner — the final pages finishing the story *and* dismantling the metaphor.

There is a long history in English-language literature of large houses playing this role of symbol, character, and setting. Here's the author's list of a few well-known novels that employ stately houses as more than just a backdrop.

1. *Brideshead Revisited* (1945), Evelyn Waugh

2. *The Last September* (1929), Elizabeth Bowen

3. *Howards End* (1910), E.M. Forster

4. *Atonement* (2001), Ian McEwan

5. *The Remains of the Day* (1989), Kazuo Ishiguro

INTERVIEW WITH
JONATHAN BENNETT

by Kathryn Kuitenbrouwer

Interview abridged from one originally featured in Bookninja *magazine on September 22, 2008.*

◆ ◆ ◆

KATHRYN: Jonathan, your first novel, *After Battersea Park,* is set both in Australia and Toronto; your second book, a collection of stories called *Verandah People*, is set entirely in Australia. And now *Entitlement*, a novel not just set largely in Toronto, but set among the jet set, the wealthy. I can't think of another topic more avoided in Canadian Letters. How did it happen that you found yourself delving here?

JONATHAN: I conceived of the novel in Australia. I was back on a trip about five years ago and was, very generously, sent for a few days away to a beautiful country inn in the southern highlands. It was off season. My wife and I found ourselves the sole guests in this fully staffed inn, that turns out was the former country estate of a well-known Sydney mercantile family.

It was very odd. Uncomfortably so, in many ways. And in other ways, after a time, well, I found myself thinking, if absolutely pressed, maybe one could adapt?

In any case, I've always loved "big house" novels — especially the early- and mid-twentieth century English ones, like *Brideshead Revisited* or *Howards End.* There's such a history of house as character. I'm a setting guy. I'm also, thematically, interested in class. So, here I am, walking these grounds as if to the manor born, enjoying staggeringly long dinners only to then be obliged to put a few glasses of fine Australian Muscat and Tokay's out of their sticky misery, and were that not enough to cope with, or maybe because of all this, suddenly I felt a novel coming on. But this presented a problem.

Sometime during the late writing and publishing of *Verandah People,* I made myself a promise that I'd move my writing over to where I now call home — Canada. I just couldn't keep setting books in Australia. I'm not there any more, haven't lived there since 1991, and I did not want to risk rewriting the same book, or be stuck eternally somewhere in the fading antipodean past. I like the present, presently at least.

So, the problem was, as you so neatly put it in your question, we don't really do class-themed novels featuring the wealthy in Canada. And that's what, I realized, I wanted to do. Well, why not find out why, was ultimately what I decided.

KATHRYN: While I read *Entitlement,* I got to thinking about my own lack of entitlement that I think may have something to do with a typical Canadian post-war upbringing (Who do you think you are, putting on airs?), a middle class disgust for anything showy. I wonder if, as much as the rich may shun the poor, the middle class shun the rich. Are average Canadians afraid of success? And the obvious corollary to this question: how did you research this novel?

JONATHAN: The patriarchal figure in my novel, Mr. Aspinall, has thoughts on this. He opines, strongly, that the middle class in Canada, through an historical disinclination for conflict, aggression, or showiness, largely ignore the wealthy thereby permitting them a kind of invisibility. He rather likes it, and exploits it. To address one thing you said, I don't think he would suggest (but I wouldn't want to put words in his mouth) that the wealthy shun the poor — on the contrary he'd point to his foundation and philanthropic work. He does, though, point out the hypocrisies present in Canadian culture (on say immigration or aboriginal land rights), but instead of pointing the finger at those in charge or those with power, he points it right back at those who vote and are in charge of running the democracy, i.e., largely speaking, the middle class.

How did I research this? Well, some of it was just observation. The openness of class distinctions present in Australian and Canadian culture differs. I understood the one, so the other seemed askew and interesting to me. Class is very present in Canada, it's just a topic that's seen to be a bit gauche or something. So it simmers away unstirred by the middle class (if Mr. Aspinall is right, the rich quietly benefiting from the cover, the poor having no voice.) Why, I came to wonder, was it collectively decided that class, as a framework of understanding, was not germane to any meaningful investigation of national self with our literature?

Entitlement is malignant. The novel, through various characters and their perspectives, politics and positions, shows union members, lawyers, media, and old money as all entitled in various ways. It makes this point, I hope.

KATHRYN: The love story, such as it is, between the

protagonist, Andy Kronk, and Aspinall's son, Colin, is most poignant, and it is around this hub the story largely revolves. The tension derived less from the rich/poor paradigm than the normal/abnormal one is a new space, too. The wealthy Colin is a Wildean creature destined to extreme behaviours; Andy is the quintessential Canadian dream — a solid middle-class kid with hockey skills. Is not Andy's entitlement portrayed as benign — the entitlement ultimately to be oneself, especially in the face of choice?

JONATHAN: Maybe. A reading might also be that Andy is a puppet of the Aspinalls and lets himself be bought and used for one purpose or another because he's initially ambitious, but then gets in too deep and doesn't know how to break free. He makes a kind of Faustian pact with Mr. Aspinall after all. Whatever the reading, I don't personally see Andy's plight as benign. It's a story that finds bankrupt motives and nuanced outcomes on all sides.

As for their relationship, I have explored the quiet brutality of male relationships before. This one, now set in Canada, finds the same pain and power at play. This book is more overtly homoerotic than some previous work, but I don't see it as a homosexual novel. It's really a love triangle between brother and sister (Colin and Fiona Aspinall) and friend (Andy). I don't think there's an appropriate coupling anywhere in Huntington House.

KATHRYN: Jonathan, could you speak directly to the comment you made about entitlement being malignant? How so? Why? And must it be? Also, in light of that comment, would you say that Colin and his sister, Fiona, and by association Andy, are then formed by entitlement? What I'm wondering, I suppose, is how does this malignancy play itself out?

JONATHAN: The novel, I hope, portrays entitlement thematically, and not in a didactic or pedantic way that gets in the way of the story proper. The book's got a plot. Having said that, I'd hope readers take from the story that the idea of entitlement is dangerous and harmful. In the Americanised world in which we all live, it seems, increasingly, there is no possibility of failure: only working towards success; no opening to admit mediocrity as a final state of affairs: only a brazen belief in "next time." These are not hollow words. These were once aspirations or motivations, but they have metastasized — to push the analogy too far — into full-fledged rights.

It's a serious state of dissolution. And it's on shop floors and in boardrooms, in waiting rooms and classrooms. Everyone has the right to more, better, faster. Their claim is infallible and the logic for it is based on their own existence. This is harmful because it weakens the collective good and furthermore, as a state, it lacks compassion, empathy, and kindness. How, as a society, can we deliver perfection to the never-satisfied? Even in death those who love us are now seemingly entitled to be pain free. We've pathologized mourning and have outsourced to grief counselors any healthy need to not cope, and just be fucked up for a while.

We expect this sort of disillusionment from the offspring of the wealthy, such as Fiona and Colin. At least there, there is noblesse oblige — he says cheekily. But the entitlement exists elsewhere in the story, in Andy's unionist father who steals from his employer and justifies it by equating it with the brass getting Air Miles, and in Andy himself when he takes advantage of a young women (in fact, two) because he's handsome and sure. I hope the book pokes its barbed theme into all the characters.

KATHRYN: Jonathan, I have heard it said by a few people, you included, I think, that this book is stylistically a departure from your earlier writing, which has been characterized as lyrical. Of course, you have recently published a collection of poetry, *Here is my street, this tree I planted*. Is this a form/function decision? Also, I'm curious about the limitations you set yourself around punctuation. It is markedly more difficult to write fiction without dialogue punctuation, for instance; what is the payout to you in terms of craft for this decision?

JONATHAN: I've spoken before about my penchant for the lyrical line. It's the long-standing David Malouf influence I endure. But, now I've written two novels, a collection of stories, and a book of poems, I've come to see the laden lyrical line as burdensome for the reader of a novel. It gets in the way of the story, is too showy. I used every bit of everything I had to keep this novel within its own form, not over-tighten, and not clot it with poetic lines and images. (That said, yep, I left some in.) These days, when I feel these urges come on, I write a poem. I've gained a respect for the novel form. I began, ten years ago, wanting to all but destroy it. Now, I submit to it, because there is a time and place for everything. And, while I know Canadian Poetry will never fully let me be an insider because I write more fiction than I do poetry and they hate part-timers, I simply enjoy writing poems and I'll just keep doing it anyway.

You asked about the stylistic decision to write dialogue without quotation marks. My brother in Australia is into cars. One day I was in the passenger seat and we were bombing along Sydney's twisty streets, and I noticed sometimes he was shifting gears without engaging the clutch. When I asked him about this, he said if you get the revs exactly right, it's unnecessary. I don't know if this is true, but I like what it means. Kathryn, you know, for a book that has a whole section which is a formal taped interview, dropping the quotation marks seemed to de-clutter the page, at times destabilized the line between direct speech, indirect speech, interior monologue, and thought — and all of that worked for my purposes. I like the free play and the uncertainty — as long as it doesn't pull the reader out.

KATHRYN: *Entitlement* seems to me a tragedy not of Andy

Kronk, but of Colin Aspinall. It is Colin whose station is reduced, after all. He cannot be fulfilled in any way, and once he finally tries for some middle road, he is cruelly stopped. Andy's ability to maneuver freely is limited by the Aspinall family's entitlement, but his limitations leave him much as his father lived, with a little hope, and large emotional burden. Is this not the parameter most Canadians live within? Surely, all our lives cannot be viewed as tragic?

JONATHAN: Well, I suspect you're being purposefully provocative but, to get at the beginning of your question, yes that reading of which one, Andy or Colin, is the tragic figure is indeed there. Might not be the only or right one, though. I'm not sure it's my job to answer the latter half of the question. So I'll parry. Is it inevitable that it be writ large in the way you suggest? If you strip away the misguided entitlement, must you be left with tragedy? Might not you simply be left with the reality most Canadians live within?

KATHRYN: Purposefully provocative? Me? Jonathan, will you speak a little about your writing process with this book? It is a diversion from your previous work, certainly in terms of voice; how did you go about constructing this novel?

JONATHAN: I wrote my first novel the hard way — through a very free and open-ended process of discovery. Then I spent enormous energy re-writing and editing into something I liked. With this one, I actually constructed the shape of it ahead of time: a novel idea, that, using an outline. Turns out it makes the writing process more manageable. It took me longer, but we had two children during the writing, which slowed me down, as you might expect, or even hope. Still, I did do some small but important structural editing with Michael Holmes, my editor at ECW Press. What I learned about writing and novels through this book I don't yet know. It will take a year or two after publication when I'll begin to see exactly what I did right, and wrong. The aftermath. I think that's the most instructive part of processes for me. Because really, how could I begin another one without completely digesting what I'd done previously? So, for now, I'll write some more poems as I let this book go off and "be" for a while.

ABOUT THE AUTHOR

Photo: Christina Roberston Photography

JONATHAN BENNETT is the author of two novels, a collection of short stories and two books of poetry. He is a winner of the K.M. Hunter Artists' Award in Literature. His work has appeared widely in journals and magazines including *The Walrus*, *Descant*, *Globe and Mail*, *Antipodes*, and the *Literary Review of Canada*. Born in Vancouver, raised in Sydney, Australia, Bennett lives near Peterborough in the village of Keene, Ontario.